PIECES OF US

Hannah Downing

OMNIFIC PUBLISHING

DALLAS

Omnific Publishing
P.O. Box 793871, Dallas, TX 75379
www.omnificpublishing.com

First Omnific eBook edition, April 2011
First Omnific trade paperback edition, April 2011

The characters and events in this book are fictitious.
Any similarity to real persons, living or dead,
is coincidental and not intended by the author.

Library of Congress Cataloguing-in-Publication Data

Downing, Hannah.
   Pieces of Us / Hannah Downing – 1st ed.
   ISBN 978-1-936305-68-1
   1. First Love — Fiction. 2. Finding Yourself — Fiction.
   3. Connecticut — Fiction. 4. Divorce — Fiction. I. Title

10 9 8 7 6 5 4 3 2 1

Cover Design and Interior Book Design by Coreen Montagna

Printed in the United States of America

This book is dedicated to my mother, Leslea Downing, for filling my childhood with books and sharing her love of reading and writing with me.

And to JLA—Time heals all wounds. Forever and always xxx

"I'm selfish, impatient and a little insecure. I make mistakes, I am out of control and at times hard to handle. But if you can't handle me at my worst, then you sure as hell don't deserve me at my best." — Marilyn Monroe

Chapter One

The Journey

"Charlotte," Cameron whispered in my ear. "Wake up."

I opened my eyes groggily and looked around the room. Embarrassed, I rolled away from him.

"Sorry, I didn't mean to fall asleep. Is the movie over?"

He chuckled, resting his hand on my shoulder and turning me back toward him. "Yes, it finished a while ago."

"Did the zombies kill everyone?" I asked, sitting up and trying to cover a yawn with the back of my hand.

"No, that big tattooed guy we thought had died came and saved the kids. Happy ending… Well, not for the zombies," he added, reaching out to smooth my hair.

I raised my hand to touch the beehive on top of my head and groaned. In my daydreams about waking up with Cameron, of which there were many, it was never this embarrassing.

Cameron and I had been dating for about a month, and I still felt kind of nervous around him. Dating in high school had been different. It was all official dates: going to dinner or a movie, and then home. Being with Cameron was a real adult relationship; we went on official dates, but we also just spent time together. We hadn't gotten to the spending-the-night stage yet, though, so I was mortified to have bed hair in front of him already.

I ran my fingers through my hair, brushing out the knots as best I could before giving him a shy smile.

"You're cute when you're asleep," he said, smiling back at me.

I pushed him playfully and stood up to stretch my legs. His couch was comfortable, but my muscles were tight from being in one position for so long. I glanced at the clock on the wall and saw it was close to midnight.

"I better be getting home."

I'd begun to dread the end of our nights together. It felt like I was leaving a part of myself behind, and I hoped one day we'd move in together and never have to say goodbye again. He frowned and grabbed my hands, pulling me down to his lap.

"You could stay," he cooed into my ear.

My head fell back to his shoulder, and I sighed loudly. He had no idea how much I wished I could, but my father was the sheriff of our town, and he'd made it quite clear that no eighteen-year-old daughter of his would be "catting" around with boys at all hours of the night. My parents had given me a curfew, and I was expected to keep it.

"You know I can't," I whined.

"Call your parents and say you're staying with Lucy. They won't mind that. Besides, I don't like the idea of you driving this late at night."

I thought about his suggestion. My parents *would* be fine with me staying at my best friend's house—and I was awfully comfortable in Cameron's arms. A wicked grin spread over my face, and I pulled my cell phone out of my pocket.

"Just give me a second?"

He smiled and nodded, releasing me so I could get up to make the call. I dialed quickly while I walked down the hall and into the kitchen for some privacy. I knew my dad would be the one to answer. He had to be on call at all hours for work.

"Sheriff Barnes," he answered, using the authoritarian voice he reserved for official business and when he was angry with me.

"Hi, Dad, it's me," I said, suddenly feeling very nervous.

"It's almost curfew, Charlotte. Are you on your way home?"

"Actually, I was wondering if you'd mind if I stayed at Lucy's tonight."

There was a pause and my heart rate sped up. My dad wasn't a stupid man, and he was an experienced police officer. He could tell when people were lying. I tried to keep my breathing even and stay as calm as possible so he wouldn't suspect anything.

"I thought you were out with Cameron tonight," he finally said.

"Oh, I was earlier…but I'm with Lucy now, and she's been dumped by her boyfriend and really just needs some girl time."

I felt bad lying to my father. I'd never done it before. Sure, I'd omitted the truth on occasion, but never an outright lie until now. I hoped the mention of "dumping" and "girl time" would be enough to stop him from asking follow-up questions and just agree.

He mumbled something I couldn't make out, and I heard my mother talking in the background.

"Char?" my Mom asked. My father had handed her the phone.

"Hey, Mom," I said, trying again to sound normal. My "girl time" excuse wouldn't work as effectively on her. I started to wonder if I should just go home and forget about spending the night with Cameron.

"Is she okay?"

"She'll be fine. She just needs a night of girly movies and ice cream… You know the drill."

"Well, give her a big hug from me and tell her not to worry. There are plenty more fish in the sea," Mom said encouragingly.

"I will, Mom. I better get back to her. I'll see you tomorrow."

"Goodnight," she said before disconnecting the call.

I breathed a sigh of relief and made a mental note to tell Lucy she had to pretend she'd just broken up with someone if she saw my mom around town. I put my phone in my pocket and went back to the living room, but the light was switched off and the room was empty.

I made my way upstairs and saw that Cameron's bedroom door was slightly ajar and a ribbon of light spilled out into the hallway. I suddenly began to feel nervous, having never spent the night with a guy before. Plus, Cameron's parents would see my car in the driveway when they came home. Would they be angry that I was staying the night?

When Cameron's family came to Fairfield a few months ago, they all moved in together while getting settled. Cameron was driving back and forth to Hartford for college classes and kept saying he felt ready to get a place of his own. I wasn't in any rush for him to move out of his parents' house for fear he'd decide to live in Hartford to be closer to school, but now I could see the benefit of him having his own place.

Trying not to think about the trouble I could get in, I slipped into Cameron's room and closed the door as quietly as I could. When I turned around, Cameron was sitting on the bed, wearing pajama bottoms and a T-shirt, and it suddenly dawned on me that I didn't have anything to wear.

"How'd it go with your parents?"

"Good. They think I'm with Lucy. What about your parents? Did you call them to ask if I could stay?" I asked, hooking my thumb over my shoulder toward their bedroom door.

"Ah, don't worry about them." He smiled. "They'll be cool. Here, I thought you might like something to change in to." He pointed to his desk chair and some clothes folded neatly on the seat.

I gave him a grateful smile before collecting the clothes. "Thanks. I'll just go change… Don't fall asleep," I said, giving him a shy smile.

"Oh, don't worry. There's no way I'll be asleep when you get back."

I headed down the hall to the bathroom and changed as quickly as I could. I brushed my fingers through my hair again and rinsed my mouth out with water.

The image of Cameron lying on his bed made me move at a speed I didn't think possible, and after what must have been only two minutes, I made my way back to his bedroom, stepped inside, and closed the door behind me. I looked over at the double bed and saw that Cameron was indeed sleeping soundly—at an awkward angle, but looking peaceful.

I smiled, laughing softly to myself, and turned off the light. I tried to climb under the covers as gently as I could, so as not to disturb the sleeping man beside me. He groaned and rolled toward me but didn't appear to wake up.

I lay in the darkness with my eyes open, worried I wouldn't be able to get to sleep. Cameron shifted beside me, and his arm fell across my chest, pulling me to him. I was surprised at how comforting it was to have his arm around me. It was more intimate than a normal hug.

His breathing was slow and steady, and it flowed over my throat as his head lay on my shoulder. I snuggled down into his embrace and twisted my leg between his, trying to be as connected with him as possible.

With Cameron wrapped all around me, I was warm and comfortable, and it wasn't long before I fell asleep too. My last words were whispered softly into his ear. "I'll love you forever."

⤳⧉⋇⧉⤶

After more than a year of dating, Cameron and I had settled into a comfortable familiarity. But that's not to say he didn't get my pulse racing on occasion.

"*Stop it!*" I squealed as Cameron's fingers tickled my ribs and stomach. "Seriously—I can't breathe!"

"Say it!" Cameron chuckled without stopping his torture.

I wiggled and kicked and tried my best to get out of his grasp, but he was kneeling over me on the couch, and he was too strong for me to push off—especially when I was weakened from laughing.

"I'll never say it!" I yelled between shrieks of laughter.

"Your choice," he replied, tickling me harder and faster than before. "I can keep this up all night!"

Cameron and I had moved in together the week before, and as a housewarming gift, his brother Ryan had bought us a game console. I challenged Cameron to an alien-killing duel, and he agreed on the condition that if he were to win, I had to admit he was the "King of All Games." He won the game, but as competitive as I was, now I didn't want to pay up. So we were in a stalemate that had evolved into a tickle war, which I was losing.

"Please... stop..." I begged, tears forming in my eyes from laughing so hard.

"Only when you say it," Cameron taunted with a huge grin. He was enjoying this a little too much.

The phone started to ring, and I silently thanked whoever was calling for disrupting our "game."

"Damn, saved by the bell. This isn't over!" Cameron joked, climbing off me to answer the phone.

I sat up and straightened my clothes before wiping the tears from my eyes. As much as I'd been begging him to stop, I wasn't upset. His playful nature was one of the things I loved most about Cameron.

After he'd been gone for a while, I got up to get myself a glass of water. I walked past the study on my way to the kitchen and heard him mumbling into the phone.

"...do the doctors know what happened?"

I froze. Doctors? I stuck my head into the study and was shocked when I saw Cameron. He was sitting in the desk chair. His elbows rested on his knees, and he looked down at the floor.

"Cam?"

He looked up at me, and I saw tears welling in his eyes. Something was very wrong.

I rushed into the room and knelt on the floor next to him, grabbing his hand that wasn't holding the phone.

"Yes. We'll come over tomorrow and help you out... Are you sure there's nothing we can do tonight? ... Okay, see you tomorrow... I love you, Mom."

He put the phone on the desk and sighed loudly, leaning back in the chair and covering his face with his hands.

"Is everything all right?" I asked tentatively.

"My grandmother died about an hour ago," he choked out.

Suddenly I felt like crying too. I'd met Cameron's grandmother once when she'd come to visit the family, and I thought she was lovely. I was sorry I wouldn't get to know her better.

"I'm so sorry." I leaned forward and kissed the only part of him within kissing reach: his knee.

Cameron's hand came down and stroked my head lovingly, his fingers twisting in my hair. "Mom said Dad is really upset. He's locked himself in his study and is listening to old records."

"I can't imagine how hard it would be to lose your mother. I'm sure he's coping the best way he knows how," I said. "What happened?"

"The doctors don't know anything yet except that it was sudden and completely unexpected. We should know more tomorrow." With that he stood up and moved back to the living room. I followed, wanting to make this easier for him.

I walked over to where he'd seated himself on the couch and gave him a weak smile. "Can I get you something? Coffee—or scotch, maybe?"

"Just sit with me?" he asked, reaching out his hand.

I sat next to him and grasped his hand tightly in mine, offering him the comfort of my touch.

We sat in silence for most of the evening—Cameron staring off into space and me watching him for any signs that I could do something to help.

"She was a great woman, you know," he finally said, his voice cracking.

"Yes, she was."

He turned to look at me, and his face softened.

"You must be tired. It's late." He ran his hand distractedly through my hair.

"I'm fine," I said, but a traitorous yawn gave me away.

"I'll be fine here. Go to bed," he encouraged.

"I'll stay," I said stubbornly, laying my head on his lap and stretching out over the length of the couch.

I wanted to be there for him while he was mourning. I knew I couldn't take his pain away, but I wasn't going to leave him alone.

Cameron didn't say anything, but his fingers stroked through my hair gently until I fell asleep.

⟡

Shoes, dresses, flowers, music, tuxedos, limo, seating arrangements, and center pieces—not quite one year after the loss of Cameron's grandmother, every detail of my wedding raced around in my head. I now understood why wedding planners were so popular. Getting married was extremely stressful.

I shouldn't have tried to plan the wedding all on my own. Cameron's little sister Bonnie had been great, helping me where she could, but she was still in high school, so all the final decisions landed on me, and this was taking its toll.

Since I was a little girl I'd dreamed of my wedding one day, with a huge princess dress and my own Prince Charming. Now that mythical "one day" had become tomorrow, and I was suddenly terrified and overwhelmed.

I desperately wanted our wedding to go off without a hitch. What if the minister was drunk and slurred his words? What if my limousine broke down and I had to take a taxi—or walk—to the church? What if everyone came down with food poisoning at the reception? What if Cameron got cold feet and wasn't there?

I froze. Suddenly all other fears were gone and a black hole of panic remained. What if Cameron changed his mind? Wasn't it common for men to balk at the idea of commitment and spending their whole lives with one person?

My heart pounded in my chest, and I sat down on the couch, knocking over the seating arrangement chart I'd balanced on the cushion. I kept repeating *Cameron loves me* in my head, over and over, trying to reassure myself. But I couldn't shake the nagging feeling he might not show up.

I tried to be reasonable and logical, reminding myself that he hadn't shown any hesitation about our wedding. He seemed just as excited as I was. I remembered that when he said he couldn't wait until we vowed to spend our lives together, his voice hadn't wavered. He'd seemed so sure. Was he *too* confident? Was he so convinced this was right for us that he was overlooking serious issues?

How many children did we want? Would we move to a bigger city once he graduated from college? Would we share a bank account? Weren't married couples supposed to know these things?

My phone beeped, signaling a text message, and I shook myself out of the downward spiral. I flipped open my phone.

This time tomorrow you'll be mine for all eternity.

His words did little to alleviate my fears. I put the phone down and paced the room, letting my thoughts wander.

My phone beeped again.

Everything okay?

I frowned. No, everything wasn't okay, and as much as I wanted to reply that it was, I knew I should be honest with him.

Just a little nervous, I guess.

I pressed the send button and waited for his response, which came less than a minute later.

There's no need to be nervous.
I love you. I'm going to love you forever.

I read the message over and over, trying to believe the words. I wasn't questioning his feelings for me. I knew he loved me. It was the last word I couldn't quite believe. *Forever.* You hear about it all the time — people growing apart and falling out of love. How could we be sure we wouldn't become another divorce statistic? I had to ask.

How can you be sure?

He didn't reply right away, and I wondered if I'd upset him. I thought about calling him to make sure everything was all right, but I decided to give him some space.

I got up and made myself a cup of tea, hoping it would help settle my nerves. When I came back to the couch, there was a message waiting on my phone.

I have hundreds of reasons why I'm sure.
I'll tell you. Keep your phone close today.

I wasn't sure exactly what he meant, but I did as he'd asked and made sure my phone was in my pocket as I went about my last-minute errands for the wedding.

About an hour after his last message, my phone beeped again, and I checked it eagerly.

1. You are the kindest person I know.

The phone beeped again almost right away, and I looked at the next message.

2. I always smile when I think about you.

Three more beeps sounded in a row, and I clicked on them all in order.

3. You will make a wonderful mother one day.
4. Your pouty face is the cutest thing I've ever seen.
5. I could never love anyone more than I love you.

Tears began to form in my eyes as I read his reassuring words. Cameron always knew exactly what I needed to feel better. I waited for the next beep, but nothing came so after a few moments of silence — and re-reading the messages — I returned to my chores.

I received messages at random intervals throughout the day, and each one was just as special as the last.

13. I love waking up next to you every morning.

28. I'm only whole when I'm with you.

79. You are my angel.

81. You are my first and last thought of the day…
and will be for the rest of my life.

As each message came in, my fears and concerns started to recede, leaving me with a sense of calm. It was as if each message chipped a tiny part of my wall away, and when the final message came through, I was ready to rush down to the church and marry him on the spot.

100. My heart has belonged to you since the first moment we met.

I took a deep breath and closed my eyes, letting my head fall forward slightly to pull my nerves into check. I felt much more secure after the one hundred text messages Cameron had sent yesterday. I was no longer nervous about being married, just about the day going perfectly. I wanted this, wanted Cameron, for the rest of my life, and I didn't doubt that or him at all anymore. But standing up there in front of all those people was not something I was looking forward to.

"Are you ready?" Bonnie whispered, turning to look over her shoulder at me.

I opened my eyes to see my about-to-be sister-in-law. She looked beautiful, and I felt a swell of gratitude for her friendship and help planning the wedding. She was young — just about to finish high school — but she had an enthusiasm for party planning I envied, and her organizational skills were unparalleled. I quickly swept my eyes over her champagne-colored dress and nodded with a smile.

The double doors ahead of us opened, and I could hear the rumble of dozens of voices talking at once. In just a moment all of those people would be staring at me. I began to shake with nerves, but then I thought of Cameron and how much he loved me. I knew he was standing on the other side of those doors waiting for me, and I felt immediately grounded.

I watched my friends Sarah and Lucy walk through the doors in front of us, and Bonnie and I moved forward a few steps. I looked on as my closest friends walked away from me slowly, and as I watched their receding forms, my earlier anxiety was forgotten and my heart rejoiced. It was almost time for me.

Bonnie quickly smiled at me before she joined Sarah and Lucy. I counted to ten and the music suddenly changed to a familiar tune. I heard the voices in the room ahead of me fall silent.

"This is us," my dad whispered in my ear before he looped his arm through mine. I looked up and smiled when I saw the happy look on his face. His deep brown eyes, just like mine, were sparkling at me. His dark hair, combed back so formally today, was graying slightly at the sides. I brushed a few strands off his forehead. He guided me through the doors and along the carpet my friends had just walked down.

The mass of faces in front of me blurred together. I focused on Cameron standing at the end of the aisle, waiting for me. My Cameron. His face glowed as he watched me walk, and he gave me a little wink—a private moment between us while surrounded by everyone we knew.

"I'm so happy for you," Dad whispered as we neared the end of our walk, his hand squeezing mine gently.

"I love you, Daddy," I whispered, unsure why I'd used the childish name for him. But at that moment, it felt right.

"Love you, Charlotte," he whispered back as he kissed my cheek, releasing my hand to sit next to my mother in the front row.

Cameron held his hand out, and I took it quickly, feeling calm once we were touching. I looked into the eyes of the man I loved and knew my life with him was going to be wonderful. He smiled, and I saw the love in his eyes—love for me, for us, and for our future together.

"Dearly beloved," the minister began, "we are gathered here today to witness the union of Cameron Samuel Harper and Charlotte Grace Barnes…"

⋅⋅⊰⋅⋅⋅⊱⋅⋅

I coughed and sneezed three times in rapid succession. There was dust flying around everywhere, and I wondered what I'd been thinking when I had the bright idea to get started on my spring cleaning. I'd seen on an episode of Oprah how refreshing it could be to de-clutter your home, and I thought I'd give it a try. I just hadn't realized how much work—and dust—would be involved after just seven months of marriage.

Resigning myself to finishing the job, I reached back into the hallway closet and pulled out another box. I sat cross-legged in front of it and peered inside: comic books and baseball cards, an old worn-out cap, and some super hero action figures—all the kinds of things you'd expect a young boy to have. Why did Cameron bring these childhood mementos with him when he moved out of his parents' house? I sighed and made a stack next to me. I'd ask him when he came home if he wanted to keep them.

I kept digging through the box and found an old photo album. The cover was crinkled at the corners where it must have been dropped a few times. I flipped it open and saw pictures of Cameron's whole family from about a decade before. Cameron looked to be in his early teens—awkward and long-limbed with spiky, gelled hair. I giggled at the photo, looking forward to laughing over it with him later.

Cameron's parents looked much younger. It was surprising how much people aged in just ten years. I smiled as I flipped through the pages and saw the Harper family on various vacations and special occasions. It was interesting to see how they changed at each event, as if I was watching them mature on fast forward. I turned the last page and saw a photo of Cameron and me, not long after we'd first started dating. We were sitting cuddled together on his parents' couch, legs entwined and fast asleep. I remembered the day. We'd all gone out his father's boat. It was my first experience at sea, and Cameron had taught me how to tie a reef knot. We'd all come home with a pink tinge to our skin, feeling completely worn out. Cameron and I had snuck in a nap before dinner—I just wasn't aware it had been captured on film.

"I'm home," Cameron called from the front door.

"In here!" I yelled, standing up and brushing some of the dust from my clothes.

Cameron appeared in the doorway and looked around at all the work I'd done. The bookcases had been rearranged, the rug on the floor had been shaken out and was fluffy again, and there was a pile of things by the door that I wanted to give to charity.

"What have you been up to?" he asked, walking over to kiss the top of my head.

"Spring cleaning," I said proudly.

"It looks great. You must be exhausted." He placed his hand gently on my shoulder. "And you have dirt on your face."

He laughed and ran his thumb over my forehead a few times, attempting to remove the smudges. I wiggled out of his grasp and rubbed the back of my hand over my forehead a few times before deciding more drastic measures were needed.

"I'm going to run upstairs and take a shower," I said, leaning forward to kiss his lips briefly.

In the bathroom, I removed my dirty clothes and dropped them into the already-full hamper, vowing to do the laundry tomorrow. I got into the shower and let the water run over my head, plastering my hair down flat. I relished the feel of the heat seeping into my aching muscles. I hadn't realized how sore I was until I stopped working. I moved my neck from one side to the other, allowing the warm water to bead down over my skin.

After just enjoying the feel of the water, I got to work shampooing my hair and lathering myself with body wash. Once I was as clean as I could possibly get, I allowed myself to stand under the water for a few more minutes, feeling the ache in my muscles melt away.

Once I stepped out, I toweled off and pulled on the soft, fluffy robe that had been hanging on the back of the bathroom door. As I went to the living room I could hear soft jazz music, Cameron's favorite, coming down the hallway.

"Nice shower?"

"Mmm…the best." I accepted the glass of wine he handed me and took a sip.

"Thanks for doing all this," he said, nodding his head around to indicate the cleaning.

"It was kind of fun, actually. It felt good to de-clutter."

He took the wine glass from my hands and placed it delicately on the coffee table before slipping his arms around my waist and pulling me close. He gently swayed to the music.

"What are you doing?"

"Dancing with my wife," he replied with a shy smile.

"The last time we danced was—"

"Our wedding. Too long ago," he finished for me. He twirled me away from his body and pulled me close again, his lips finding mine.

In that moment I didn't think anything could make my life more perfect. I was completely in love with a man who adored me, and we had our whole lives to be blissfully happy. I was the luckiest girl in the world. I had my happily ever after at twenty-two.

Chapter Two
The End

I love you. I had such a wonderful time last night. xxx

I read the text message from Lucy on Cam's phone over and over, each time hoping the words would change. My brain just couldn't comprehend the message—sent from my best friend to my husband. I put his phone down on the counter and walked through the house in a daze. In the living room, I stood in front of the Christmas tree, which mocked me with its illusions of joy, love, and family. This would be only our third Christmas together—was my marriage already over?

I felt numb as I bent down and gathered the presents I'd bought for my husband and carried them out of the room. I placed them next to the front door, neatly stacking them so their shiny red and green bows wouldn't be crushed. I stood there staring, trying to form a coherent thought. But the only thing in my head was the fact that my best friend was in love with my husband. I heard the shower turn off, and I automatically went to the bedroom and opened Cameron's closet door.

"Babe, can you grab me something to wear?" he called.

I stepped into the walk-in closet, looked at his clothes hanging neatly in front of me, and selected a pair of dark-wash jeans and a navy blue T-shirt from one of the shelves. Pulling open his top drawer, I grabbed a pair of black boxer-briefs and stood by the bathroom door for our morning ritual.

I knew I should be yelling and screaming at him, yet I couldn't bring myself to do anything but stand and wait for him to leave the bathroom. My heart thudded in my chest, my hands shook slightly, and I heard a weird static in my ears—as if my brain had tuned out.

Right on cue, the door opened slightly, and his hand stuck out. I placed the clothes in his grasp. He pulled them in and closed the door loudly.

I selected his clothes every morning. He said he liked that I dressed him, and if he'd dressed himself, he'd look like a vagrant. I didn't mind this little quirk, and normally I enjoyed the task. But today I realized I'd been selecting the clothes Lucy had seen him in—and maybe even removed from his body.

The bathroom door opened fully, and he walked out, looking every bit as handsome as I knew he would. His dark hair was still wet and gleamed under the bright bathroom light. He gave me a smile as he kissed me lightly on the cheek.

"Thanks," he said on his way out of the room and down the hall.

I couldn't move. He was acting so normally, and yet my whole life had changed. I felt like I was standing on the edge of a cliff where a strong wind threatened to blow me over the edge, and there was nothing I could do to stop it.

"Charlotte, did you move the coffee? I can't find it anywhere," he called from the kitchen.

Bile rose in my throat, and I swallowed hard before taking a few deep breaths, wanting to stay in control. I walked slowly down the hallway, like an inmate to her execution. I caught a glimpse of him out of the corner of my eye, but I stayed focused on the cupboard behind him, afraid that if I saw his face, it would all become too real.

Tears welled in my eyes, and my heart continued to pound. I needed to talk to him—needed him to tell me Lucy was some crazy stalker and he wasn't cheating on me. But I couldn't get any words out. If I opened my mouth, I might vomit.

I looked down at the beautiful diamond ring on my left hand and choked back a strangled sob. We'd only been married for two years. Was he already bored with me? I pulled the ring off and placed it on the kitchen counter, then proceeded to remove my earrings, necklace, and watch—all gifts from Cameron. I set them carefully next to the wedding ring.

Tears streamed down my cheeks, and I could see Cameron staring at me in confusion.

"Charlotte?"

I picked up his cell phone from the counter and handed it to him, the offending message still on the screen. His face paled as he read it, and he looked up at me nervously. The loud static in my ears was back, and I was starting to feel extremely hot.

"*Fuck!*" he yelled, throwing the phone against the wall. It clattered to the floor undamaged, unlike my heart.

We stood staring at each other for a moment, neither of us saying a word. Then his eyes broke from mine and slowly moved down to my jewelry, abandoned on the counter.

"Charlotte," he said softly, moving toward me with his arms outstretched, as if to pull me into a hug.

"No," I whispered, stepping backward and out of his grasp.

His face fell, and he stood still, staring at the floor.

"Do you love her?" I choked out between sobs. I felt the warm tears flowing over my cheeks as I watched him think about his answer.

He was silent for a moment, and his shoulders sagged.

"I feel something for her," he said sadly.

I sank to the floor, sobbing uncontrollably. The numbness that had been clouding my heart suddenly lifted, and the pain of what was happening hit me all at once. There wasn't a single part of my body that didn't hurt. I watched as my tears dripped onto the polished wood floor. Cameron's shadow moved toward me, but I held my hand up to stop him before he could touch me.

"Do you love me?" I whispered, looking up at him.

"Yes, very much!" he insisted, dropping to his knees in front of me. "I'm so confused. I know what this looks like, but I want *you,* Char. I love you—"

"I think you should go," I whispered, cutting him off. As much as I wanted to hear something that would explain away his infidelity, I couldn't listen to him right now.

"What?" He leaned closer to hear me.

I glanced up and looked at his eyes for the first time since I'd learned he was cheating on me. He must have seen something reflected back because despair washed over his face.

"I want you to leave," I replied a little louder.

"Charlotte, please don't do this. Can't we just talk about it? I swear, it's not what you think."

I glared at him.

"It's Christmas Eve," he protested as I shook my head, not wanting to hear his excuses.

"Everyone is coming here for lunch tomorrow," he added desperately. "I might deserve to be punished, but our families don't. Please don't ruin everyone's Christmas."

I wanted to scream that *he* was the one who'd ruined everyone's Christmas, not to mention my life, but I couldn't stand to destroy this special day for the people I loved. Cameron's family had been nothing but wonderful and supportive of me and our marriage.

Nodding slowly, I stood up without looking at him. I knew it would be hard to keep up the illusion of our happy marriage with our families, but I thought I could do it for one day. I remembered the stack of presents by the front door and carefully carried them back to the living room, rearranging Cameron's gifts under the Christmas tree and fussing absentmindedly with the bows, making sure they looked perfect.

I felt his presence in the room behind me, and the blood in my veins chilled, a feeling I'd never expected to experience around my husband. I stood and turned to face him.

"I'm going to stay with my dad tonight, but I'll be back in the morning to start cooking lunch," I said quietly.

"Charlotte, please stay so I can explain," Cameron protested as I walked past, ignoring him, and went to the bedroom.

I quickly looked around the room and suppressed the tears I felt coming when I saw our wedding photo on the bookshelf. I closed my eyes to block the picture from my mind, but my memory jumped into overdrive, and all I could see, hear, and smell were the events of my wedding day playing out on the inside of my eyelids, and there was no way to escape them.

With a loud sigh, I yanked the closet door open and started pulling out random clothes, not even paying attention to what I was packing. No matter how hard I tried to concentrate, my brain was stuck on pause. It just kept replaying our wedding, which was now intermingled with the past few minutes, over and over in my head.

Once I had my overnight bag full, I walked back out to the kitchen and grabbed my purse and car keys off the counter. Cameron was nowhere to be seen, and I was glad I didn't have to face him as I left.

My luck didn't hold, however, as I stepped into the garage and saw Cameron leaning on the hood of my car, his arms folded over his chest, a determined look on his face.

"Don't go," he said softly.

I could see the pain in his eyes, but I couldn't feel anything besides the agony in my heart. I couldn't think of anything other than the fact that he'd cheated on me. There wasn't room in my heart for forgiveness—or explanations—at the moment.

I put my overnight bag in the trunk, slamming it closed a little harder than was necessary. I saw Cameron flinch slightly as the sound echoed around the garage.

"Please, just give me space tonight. I'll be back in the morning. We can talk after everyone leaves tomorrow." I climbed into the driver's seat of my car and closed the door without waiting to hear his response.

I opened the garage door and reversed quickly down the drive. Cameron watched me as I drove off down the street.

I'd never know how I managed to hold myself together on the drive to my dad's house, but I did. I pulled into his driveway and collected my bag from the trunk. I knocked at the front door, but after a few minutes of no response I pulled my key out and let myself in.

My dad had insisted that I keep a key to his house. He wanted me to feel like I always had a sanctuary, somewhere safe I could go. Right now I couldn't have been more grateful to him.

I walked up the stairs to my childhood bedroom and looked around. It was exactly as I'd left it: a single bed in the corner and an ancient computer on the old wooden desk under the window with stacks of teen novels around the monitor. The last time I'd slept in this room was the night before my wedding. I quickly put that thought out of my mind and lay down on the bed.

Then the tears came. I cried for what felt like hours. Warm, salty water soaked my pillow, but I couldn't move from the fetal position I'd automatically assumed. The pain in my chest was more intense than anything I'd felt before. I tried to take some deep breaths to calm myself, but I could only manage short, shallow gasps. I cried until no more tears would come, and despite the sunlight shining though the window, I fell into a restless sleep.

⁂

I opened my eyes groggily, a hazy glare coming through the window. Realizing where I was, my heart broke all over again as I remembered why

I was in this room. When my eyes started to prickle with tears, I shook my head and tried to force myself to calm down.

Knowing I'd have to put on a brave face all day for my family, I forced myself to get out of bed and showered quickly. After dressing in some of the clothes from the overnight bag, which matched better than I expected, I went downstairs to get ready to go face my husband.

Dad was sitting at the kitchen table, drinking a cup of coffee and eating a slice of toast.

"Merry Christmas, kid."

"Merry Christmas," I said without any enthusiasm. I poured myself a cup of coffee and sat opposite him at the table.

We sat in comfortable silence as we drank, and I felt immense gratitude toward my father for not prying into my life. He must have known something was wrong or I wouldn't have been there, but he didn't question me.

"Is lunch still on today?" he asked cautiously, breaking the silence.

"Yes…I'm heading home now to start cooking." I was surprised by how unemotional my voice was. It was like I was numb. Maybe one day of this wouldn't be as hard as I thought.

I drained the last of my coffee and rinsed the mug in the sink. I kissed the top of Dad's head gently as I walked past.

"You okay, Char?"

I turned back to face him with a half-smile. "No. See you at twelve for lunch."

I walked out of the house and got into my car to return to the home I had shared with Cameron for the past two years. I circled the block several times before I finally built up the strength to pull into the driveway. I didn't open the garage. I just left my car in the drive—in case.

I opened the front door and slipped inside as quietly as I could. The familiar smell of the house immediately put me at ease, but then sent a sharp pain through me because I realized I wouldn't be my home for long. For a moment I thought I could get to work in the kitchen and not be noticed by Cameron until the others arrived. I knew I was being cowardly and weak, but I really didn't know what to say or how to act. My brain was telling me to be angry, to demand an explanation and then scream and yell. But my heart didn't want any answers. It couldn't take it. If I heard his justifications it would break me even more.

As I looked over the living room, I spotted Cameron slumped on the couch, sleeping. He was still wearing the now-wrinkled clothes I'd picked out for him the morning before. His hair stuck up in all directions, and I could tell he'd been running his hands through it repeatedly, his usual stress reaction. He had dark circles under his eyes, and a glass sat on the coffee table in front of him, still half full of amber liquid.

That shocked me. I'd never known Cameron to drink away his problems, but I guess I didn't know him as well as I thought I did. The alcohol was just one more thing to add to the list of new facts I'd learned about my husband in the past twenty-four hours.

Despite his slumber, he didn't look peaceful at all. He looked troubled and restless. I turned the lock in the front door as quietly as I could, but the noise still woke him. He jolted in his seat, his eyes fixing on me and relief washing over his face.

"I wasn't sure you'd come back," he said in a husky voice as he sat up and rubbed his hands over his stubbly chin.

"I said I would," I replied curtly, turning to the kitchen.

I washed my hands and pulled the turkey from the fridge. With it safely on the counter, I bent down to find a baking tray in the cabinet. When I stood up, Cameron was behind me.

"I'm sorry," he said softly.

I could hear the emotion in his voice, and I honestly believed he *was* sorry. But it didn't change the facts, and if I was going to make it through the day I couldn't have this conversation.

"Not now," I said, my voice harsh. "Why don't you go take a shower before everyone gets here?"

Without saying a word, he took my hand. I felt something cold and hard touch my palm as he squeezed gently and then released me. I looked down and saw my engagement ring and wedding band sitting in my hand.

"Please wear them today," he whispered.

I nodded and slipped them quickly onto my finger, holding my hand out to look at them. I remembered doing the exact same thing not long after we were married, admiring how the rings would look there for the rest of my life. Suddenly the metal felt hot on my skin, as if it was burning me, and I shook my hand slightly to rid myself of the odd sensation.

I looked up, and Cameron nodded silently before walking down the hall to our bedroom. After a moment I heard the water in the shower and let out a sigh. I could do this. I just had to hold myself together until our families left after lunch. I could do this.

I prepared the turkey slowly, adding the stuffing I'd made a few days earlier and basting the skin. When I was satisfied with how it looked, I started peeling potatoes. Despite my hands being busy, my mind remained focused on the man down the hall. What was he thinking right now? Was he thinking about me or Lucy?

The shower shut off, and I tensed, suddenly wondering if he'd be waiting for me to hand him clothes. Should I go and pick some out for him? I decided I'd keep peeling my potatoes and leave him to pick out his own clothes. I didn't owe him any favors.

After I'd put the turkey in the oven and peeled a dozen potatoes, Cameron still hadn't emerged and my curiosity got the better of me. I pushed the bedroom door open to find Cameron standing in a towel in front of the closet with tears in his eyes. For the first time in twenty-four hours, I felt a bit of sadness for him.

I pushed past him into the closet. Keeping focused on my task, and not on the fact that he was standing so near that I could feel his warm breath on the back of my neck, I pulled out a pair of beige linen pants and a black v-neck sweater and handed them to him.

"Thank you," he said, and before I could react, his arms were around me.

He pushed me gently into the wall and pressed his body against mine as he hugged me. My body automatically responded. His scent surrounded me and the warmth of his body felt familiar and safe. But while my body enjoyed the sensation of being close to my husband, my heart pulled away.

He'd started to pepper gentle kisses through my hair and onto my forehead before I gathered the strength to push him away. "Don't, Cam!" I pleaded, my voice sounding more emotional than I wanted it to.

"Charlotte—"

I'd just had a demonstration of how my body was ready to betray me, and I needed to stay strong. My heart and my head were going to steer me through this, not my physical urges.

"I have to get back to the kitchen," I said hastily, slipping out of his grasp and almost running down the hall.

I leaned on the kitchen counter, trying to calm my heart rate and slow the flood of tears threatening to flow down my cheeks. I didn't know why I went to the bedroom in the first place, but it had been a huge mistake.

Cameron was like a magnet, and even though my heart was shattered into a million pieces, those broken shards were still drawn to him. Being around him now was like stabbing myself with a dull blade—painful and self-sabotaging.

"Merry Christmas!" a muffled voice called through the front door. I looked up and saw Cameron's older brother, Ryan, staring through the door's glass panel, smiling.

I took a deep breath, drew my shoulders back, and let him into the house. I held the door open as he walked through, arms laden with presents. He was followed by his wife, Sarah, carrying a plate of food. Ryan, the eldest Harper child, looked most like his parents. With his father's broad jaw and tall build, and his mother's Spanish genes, he was the traditional "tall, dark, and handsome." Sarah was a classic beauty: long, red curls, bright blue eyes that were always smiling, and a peaches-and-cream complexion that almost glowed. The light smattering of freckles over her cheeks added a down-to-earth quality.

"Sarah, you didn't need to bring anything," I said, my normal self coming back a little.

"I know, but I wanted to. It's just cookies for after dinner." She placed the plate on the table and turned to give me a hug.

I sank into her arms, not realizing how much I needed to be hugged and comforted by someone who wasn't Cameron.

"It smells great in here," another happy voice said from the doorway. I looked over my shoulder to see Cameron's sister, Bonnie, walking in. She was dressed in a glitter-covered shirt and Santa hat.

"Merry Christmas," I said, smiling at her.

"There's my baby sister," Cameron called as he appeared in the room.

Bonnie ran over, and as Cameron hugged her his eyes locked on me over her shoulder. I turned away and walked through the archway into the kitchen to check on the turkey and vegetables. When I pulled the oven door open, I was accosted with a wave of heat delicious smells. For a just a moment, I could pretend this was any normal Christmas Day.

"Merry Christmas, sweetheart," I heard from behind me. I turned to see Cameron's mother, Ellen, smiling at me, her soft features showing nothing but love and joy.

Soft lines had formed in the corners of her eyes from years of laughter, and I hoped I would age as gracefully as she had. Her once dark hair was now peppered with gray, but despite her talk about needing to dye it, she was beautiful just the way she was.

"Merry Christmas, Mom," I replied, standing up with a genuine smile on my face. Cameron's parents had insisted I call them Mom and Dad after we were married, and I had to admit it was nice to feel like a real part of their family.

My own mother had run off with my father's best friend just a few months ago, which had shaken me to my core. It disgusted me that she'd been having an affair for years with a man I'd always considered more of an uncle than a family friend. When my father confronted them, she didn't even show remorse. She just packed her belongings and left my father behind. Since then I'd done my best to look after my father, but it was taking its toll on me. The fact that Cameron could do the same thing was incomprehensible, and yet he had.

Ellen surrounded me with a hug. "You look just as tired as Cam does. Is everything okay?"

I didn't know what to say, so I just smiled. "We're fine," I replied with as much conviction as I could muster.

Her head tilted as she took in my tone and expression, but I was saved when my father arrived, and I excused myself to greet him.

A few minutes later we were exchanging gifts. An array of sweaters, movies, and electronic devices were unwrapped and gushed over. Then Cameron's father, David, gave a toast for the blessing that everyone in our family was happy and healthy. As he neared the end of his speech, Cameron caught my eye briefly before I turned away.

Before I knew it, we were all seated around the dining table. Dad sat directly opposite me, and I smiled at him. All through lunch he gave me curious looks, and when he thought I wasn't looking, he glared at Cameron.

David was seated at the head of the table, where he expertly sliced the turkey and passed some to me. Of course Cameron sat next to me, but I leaned as far away from him as possible without being obvious. Cameron, however, was leaning into me as much as he could, and he kept pulling his chair closer to mine.

I tried to ignore him and eat. The food tasted good, but it gave me no enjoyment. I looked at the smiling faces around the table and reminded myself why I was maintaining this charade. I sighed and took another bite of turkey just as Cameron began stroking the back of my other hand lovingly. A surge of anger shot through my body, and my fork froze mid-way to my mouth as I turned to look at him. He was talking with Ryan about the amount of studying he'd been doing for his degree and not even looking at me. The gesture was so casual, as if he didn't think twice about touching me.

"Excuse me, Cam?" I said softly, so as not to alarm Ryan.

He smiled at me and leaned in close, his fingers still touching my hand. I clutched my fork tightly, trying to hold my anger inside.

"Get your hand off me or I will stab you in the thigh with this fork," I whispered.

He froze, the smile dropping from his face before he reluctantly pulled his hand away. I went back to eating my food and realized part of me was saddened by the loss of his touch, but only a very small part. Cameron gave me a look before turning back to Ryan and resuming his conversation.

"So how's Lucy? I haven't seen her in ages!" Bonnie asked, leaning around her mother to look at me.

I felt Cameron's body go rigid beside me. I thought of several ways I could handle this situation. I looked down at my plate and pushed the last of the food around. I decided to take the high road.

"She's fine."

"So, David, how's work? Are you getting many new patients through your clinic?" my dad asked loudly, directing the attention away from me. David was a chiropractor, and Cameron was currently in the process of obtaining his dentistry degree with the hopes of one day having a family clinic with his father.

Cameron's hand slipped onto my knee under the table, and he squeezed it gently. Before I could tell him to remove his fingers from my leg, he patted my knee one last time and moved his hand back to his own lap.

⤙❧ ♧❦❀❦♧ ☙⤚

I watched David's car pull out of the driveway, and as soon as it was out of sight, the smile dropped from my face. Cameron and I stood in silence for a moment in the front yard, and I could feel him staring at me, but I didn't have anything to say to him. My brain was still trying to process all I'd learned in the past twenty-four hours.

I looked over at Cameron and saw his hands jammed in his pockets and his foot tapping nervously. We both knew what was coming: the talk.

My breathing quickened, and I felt panic in my chest. I couldn't bring myself to talk to him. I wasn't strong enough for that yet. So instead of saying anything, I just shuffled my left foot nervously and watched the little chunks of dirt moving around under my shoe.

"Charlotte…" Cameron started, but when I looked up and met his eyes, he stopped talking.

"I'm going to clean up," I said, walking past him.

His hand jerked slightly, as if to reach out to me, but he held it back and let me pass. Part of me longed for his touch of his warm skin, but my brain knew it was best that he keep his distance. I started stacking plates to carry into the kitchen, where I placed the dirty dishes in the sink and ran the water. One by one, I rinsed the plates and stacked them on the counter.

"Want some help?" Cameron asked from the doorway.

Without waiting for me to answer, he moved next to me and began placing the rinsed plates into the dishwasher. It had been our nightly ritual almost the entire time we'd lived together: I would rinse and pass the dishes to him, and he would load the dishwasher. We'd always been a team, equals, a complete unit—or so I thought. We weren't a team anymore, and we never would be again.

For the first time, it truly became clear to me that Cameron and I weren't going to have a future together. This home we shared wasn't *ours* anymore, and suddenly I didn't want to be in it. I could have told Cameron to leave, but I knew I'd never be able to get over him, get over the pain, if I was surrounded by objects that had been *ours*. I needed to get as far away from him and this house as I could.

"It's not what you think," Cameron whispered, trying to initiate the conversation I was doing my best to avoid.

I sighed and held another plate under the water. "I know I promised you we'd talk tonight, but I really don't have anything to say." I felt the tears I'd suppressed earlier start to form in my eyes.

"I'm moving out," I added when he didn't reply.

"What are you feeling, Charlotte?" He reached across me to turn off the faucet so I was unable to hide behind the chore. "Not what you're thinking, but what's in your heart?"

My husband knew me so well. He could see the war going on inside my body—the struggle between what my head wanted and what my heart begged for. He also likely knew my heart wanted him.

"I don't know." I was being honest. At that point, I mostly felt numb, though I was sure anger and hurt would come in larger doses soon. Right now I didn't want to yell, and I didn't want to fight. I just wanted to leave and be alone. I felt more exhausted than I ever had, and it was an effort just to keep myself from collapsing.

"Would you stay if I asked you to?" He was leaning against the counter and staring intently at me, trying to maintain eye contact.

"No, I can't be around you right now," I choked out, emotion clouding my voice as the comforting numbness began to recede. Amazingly, the two warring parts of myself agreed on this point. My head didn't want to be anywhere around him ever again, and although my heart craved his touch, it was in too much pain to stand being near him now.

Cameron's hands — the hands that I loved, but had caressed another woman — moved up, and he scrubbed them roughly over his face.

"When will you leave?" he asked, his voice shaking.

"Now." I turned the faucet back on and rinsed the last few plates before stacking them neatly in front of him. I wiped down the counter and swept the floor. Cameron leaned against the counter the whole time, silently watching me.

"I never meant to hurt you, Charlotte. I honestly love you, and if you'd just let me explain, I think—"

"Don't!" I almost yelled as I finally started to cry. "I can't talk about this now."

"We *have* to talk about this. I'm not going to let you just walk away from me...from *us*," he yelled back, waving his arms emphatically. "If you would just *stop* and listen to me for two minutes—"

"There's no *us* left to talk about," I replied, cutting him off. I was trying to stay calm, but my traitorous voice was shaking.

"Char!" he called, moving toward me.

He held his arms out, and I stumbled backward. I saw the hurt in his face when I wouldn't allow him to comfort me, but I couldn't believe he thought it was appropriate. Surely he could understand that his were the last arms I wanted around me right now.

"Char, please just listen to what I have to say," he pleaded.

"I'm just going to get some more clothes."

"No! You *have* to listen!" he protested, his voice rising.

"No, I don't," I shot back.

"I didn't—"

"Stop it!" I yelled, cutting him off.

"No, you will hear me!" he demanded, grabbing my arm and trying to hold me in place. "Lucy and I—"

"*Shut up!*" I screamed, wrenching my arm from his grasp and stepping away from him.

He opened his mouth and looked as if he was going to protest again, but then he nodded sadly and went into the living room. I walked quickly to the bedroom, grabbed some clean underwear and a change of clothes, and shoved them roughly into my handbag. I took a quick glance around the room, but since Cameron had slept on the couch, it looked exactly as it had when I left the day before.

When I woke up yesterday morning, my life was in order and I was happy and in love. How things changed in just one short day.

I went back through the living room on my way out and found Cameron sitting in the same position he'd been in when I'd arrived this morning: slumped on the couch with a glass of amber liquid in his hand.

"Merry Christmas, Cam," I said softly as I went to the front door.

His eyes snapped up to mine, and he gave me a hopeful smile. "Merry Christmas, baby." He held his glass up to me in salute.

I wanted to smile at him. I wanted to hug him goodbye and promise that I'd see him soon. But as I looked at his face, my eyes focused on his lips, and all I could think about was those lips pressed against the lips of my supposed friend and bridesmaid at our wedding. I turned away quickly and pulled the door closed so he couldn't see my pain anymore.

◦⟨♡✳♡⟩◦

"Are you coming to breakfast?" Cameron asked softly.

I rolled over in bed, holding my cell phone tightly to my ear, relishing the husky sound of his voice. I was hurt and angry, but his voice had a calming effect on me.

"I don't think so," I replied with a long, sad sigh.

"I want you to. Everyone would want you there."

Every year on the morning after Christmas, the entire Harper family had breakfast together. The tradition—a big meal, followed by a relaxing day of games and movies—started when the family was young and had carried over into Cameron's adulthood. I always loved those breakfasts. There wasn't the pressure of making everything perfect like on Christmas Day, but there was still excitement in the air.

"Tell them I'm not feeling well." It was the truth, after all.

"I'll just call and say we both can't make it. They'll ask fewer questions that way," he sulked.

"No, you should go. Your family needs to find out that we… aren't together anymore," I stuttered, holding back tears. I heard Cameron grunt at the finality of my words.

I was overcome by a surge of anger. What right did he have to be hurt? *His* actions had ruined us. I was the one who'd had my life ripped out from under me and was now dealing with the consequences of *his* decisions. If he wanted Lucy so much, he should be happy I was out of the way. He was now free to be with her.

"Okay, I'll go. I'll miss you, though. It won't feel right without you there."

"Well, maybe you should have thought about that before…" I stopped, not able to end the sentence. I didn't mean to lash out like that, but I hated his martyrdom and spoke before I'd thought it through. I wasn't sure why, but I wanted to stay calm. I didn't know if it was for me or for him, or for the life we'd had, but I didn't want to break down within earshot of him.

Cameron remained silent, and I decided not to speak either. The silence, punctuated only by the steady rhythm of his breathing, lasted several minutes. When he finally spoke again, I wished he'd stayed silent.

"I truly am sorry, baby," he whispered.

His apologies were meaningless. If he hadn't wanted to hurt me, he wouldn't have had an affair with my best friend.

"I'm going to go. Give Ellen a hug from me."

I hung up without waiting to hear his response. As much as losing my husband had destroyed me, losing his family — my family — was almost as bad.

He didn't try to call back.

I put my phone down and in the silence and loneliness of my childhood room, I cried. I cried for the loss of my mother and the woman I thought she was. I cried for my father and the pain he lived with after losing the love of his life and his best friend all in one moment. I cried for Ellen and how she would feel when she heard this news. I cried for David and the disappointment I knew he'd feel about his son's actions. I cried for Ryan and the brotherly hugs I'd never have again. I cried for Sarah and the friendship we shared as the outsiders welcomed into the Harper family. I cried for Bonnie and how I'd never get to see her fall in love or graduate college. And finally, I cried for myself. I cried for the loss of my lover, the loss of my best friend, and the loss of my soul mate. I cried for the life Cameron and I should have shared. I cried for the children we'd never have and the home I'd never live in again. I cried for hours. I cried until there were no more tears.

Once my eyes were dry and my sobbing had slowed to deep breathing, I thought realistically about where my life was headed. Cameron had stolen my previous life from me, and I now had to build a new one from scratch.

At 10:30, I dragged myself out of bed with a new determination and decided it was time to be proactive. I walked downstairs and was relieved to see my dad wasn't home. I hadn't actually had the "breakup" conversation with him yet, and I didn't feel like doing it today.

I rummaged around in the garage for a few minutes before finally throwing my hands up in defeat. I was sure Dad had some packing boxes, but they were nowhere to be found. Instead I grabbed a box of large garbage bags and drove to the house I used to share with Cameron.

I sat in the driveway and looked at the house, remembering the day we'd moved in. While Ryan and my dad carried in most of the heavier furniture, I'd stood in the front yard and looked at the house in wonder. I remembered Cameron's arms slipping around my waist from behind and his kiss on the side of my neck. I'd been sure that was the start of our happily ever after. Now when I looked at the house I saw broken promises and the life I'd cherished chopped into tiny pieces and scattered around the yard.

With a long sigh, I got out and let myself in. Cameron had indeed gone to his family breakfast and wasn't here to try to stop me from packing. I scanned the living room for anything that belonged to me, but there wasn't much. I lived with my parents right up until Cameron and I moved in together, and we'd bought everything for this house. Nothing was mine or his — it was all *ours*.

I went straight to the bedroom and found the sheets pulled back and still messy from his sleep the night before. The bedroom smelled like his cologne, and I took a deep breath, allowing the scent to permeate my senses. When I felt my throat tighten with unshed tears, I snapped myself out of it and walked quickly to the stereo, picking the loudest heavy metal album in our collection and turning it up to full volume to drown out my feelings.

I pulled open the closet and started throwing my clothes into a large pile on the bed. Once I emptied my side of the closet, I pulled everything out of my dresser drawers and moved on to the bathroom. I collected my makeup, shampoo, and body wash, dumping them unceremoniously on top of the clothes. I then moved to the bookcase and removed the photos of my family, the candles, and the books I'd accumulated during our marriage and dropped them all on the bed.

Even though I'd just done it, seeing all of Cameron's things still in place while everything I owned was in a pile was like a slap in the face, a mockery of my self-worth, and I longed for this day to be over.

I was stunned at how easy it had been to remove my presence, as if I'd never been here in the first place. I suddenly felt the urge to be gone from the house as quickly as possible, so I shoved my belongings into the garbage bags, not caring what went where.

Once the bed was empty, I took one last look around and said a silent goodbye. I turned off the stereo and the instant quiet was eerie, making me feel even more alone. I carried the bags out to my trunk. Everything I owned fit into four garbage bags, and the pain in my chest increased as I realized how little of a life I had away from Cameron. Everything I was had become tied to him.

I walked back in to do a final walkthrough. I was leaving everything behind. I didn't want our plasma television, I didn't want the new leather sofa, and I didn't want anything from him. He'd already stolen my happiness, and without that, *without him*, all the material possessions in the world meant nothing to me. I walked over to the dining table and slowly slipped my wedding and engagement rings off my finger, placing them in the center of the dark wood. I adjusted them so they were perfectly lined up, and without looking back, I walked out of the house.

◦⊰ ♡ ❖ ♡ ⊱◦

"Come on, Charlotte. You haven't come over in ages!" Ann whined into the phone.

Ann and I were barely more than acquaintances, but she was the only friend in my life who was completely separate from Cameron — now that Lucy was gone. So I was relying on her more than I ever had.

"I know. I'm sorry. I haven't really been up to it," I said.

The last few weeks had been rough on me. I moved back in with my dad and developed a safe rhythm of keeping busy. I continued my work as a babysitter for several of the police families in my dad's precinct, and when I found myself around the house, I read and spent time on the computer, not allowing myself any time to dwell on my life as a twenty-three-year-old about to get a divorce. Cameron tried calling me over and over, but I never answered and hadn't seen him since Christmas Day. He left voicemail messages begging me to talk to him, apologizing, and asking if I was all right, but I didn't want to hear his excuses and hollow apologies, and I certainly didn't want him to see how crushed I was.

I had created the perfect "happy mask" that I slipped on as soon as I crawled out of bed in the morning and never took off during the day. Nights were a different matter, though. I cried every night, and the only way I could eventually fall asleep was with the television on as background noise. The white noise helped stave off the Cameron dreams and allowed me some peaceful sleep.

After the shock of discovery had worn off, I realized I wasn't even surprised by Cameron's actions. My mother had done it, so it stood to reason that the same thing could happen to anyone, including me. "You need to get your mind off that douchebag, soon-to-be ex-husband of yours and start living your life again," Ann insisted.

I knew she was right. I really wanted to forget all about Cameron and move on. I knew I was young enough to start over and pretend — if I wanted to — that I'd never been married at all.

"Okay, I'll come over and watch a movie, but I'm not staying late," I agreed half-heartedly.

"Great, can you grab some orange juice on your way over? I want to make cocktails!"

❧⟨♥⟩☙

An hour later, I was at the grocery store on my way to Ann's house. I strolled through the aisles, enjoying the mundane activity. In the past few weeks, I hadn't done any of my normal tasks. I'm embarrassed to say I'd gone back to letting my dad take care of me, so being in the grocery store was a novelty. I could almost pretend I was just like all these other people, not the broken husk of a person I felt like.

As I approached the refrigerated section, I glanced down one of the aisles and saw Cameron. I froze. Part of me wanted to say hello, and part of me wanted to run. The decision was made for me, however, when Lucy came around the corner carrying a box of cereal and placed it in the cart in front of Cameron. Then I watched in horror as she leaned in and kissed him on the lips. It was so casual, like she'd done it a million times before and expected to do it a million more. My heart was in a vice, right there in the cereal aisle, and I stood frozen, trying to catch my breath.

I was torn out of my trance when Cameron glanced over his shoulder and saw me staring at them. A huge smile spread over his face, then vanished as he looked quickly at Lucy, then back to me.

"Shit!" he said, loudly enough for me to hear from the other end of the aisle.

I turned and walked away as fast as I could, pushing past some people waiting at the checkouts and racing out the doors.

"Charlotte! Charlotte, wait!" I heard from behind me. "I'm sorry you saw that."

I couldn't wait. I couldn't talk to him and watch his lips moving—lips I'd just seen kissing another woman. I approached my car and dug furiously through my bag for my keys.

"Fuck!" I threw my bag onto the hood of the car and rifled through it frantically. I couldn't find my keys anywhere, and there was nowhere for me to hide from him as he approached.

"I've been calling. How…how are you?" Cameron asked as he ran up to the car, breathing heavily from chasing me.

"I haven't answered your calls because there's nothing to say, and I would appreciate if you'd stop calling," I replied curtly as I pulled every item out of my bag and placed it on the hood of the car. The keys weren't there. I sighed in frustration.

Not being able to find my keys was the last straw, and I allowed myself to feel the anger that had been bubbling inside me for the past four weeks.

"So are you with her now?" I spat, making eye contact with him for the first time.

"No, not really," he replied, looking at the ground.

"What does that mean?" I hastily pushed everything back into my bag and leaned against the car. I felt something hard in my pocket against the metal of the door and remembered shoving my keys in there when I walked into the store. I pulled them out and heaved a sigh of relief.

"It means that no matter what's going on between Lucy and me, you're the one I want," he said meekly, shoving his hands in his pants pockets.

"You were picking out cereal together, Cam. *Cereal.* She's obviously spending the night."

I folded my arms across my chest and waited for him to reply. He didn't. He just stared at me apologetically, and I felt the fury rise again like bile in my throat. I allowed the rage to boil for a moment before I noticed people staring at us from their cars. I gritted my teeth and forced my anger back down.

"Cam, I don't want to see you again. Ever."

I heard the coldness in my voice and was shocked at how even and calm I sounded. I unlocked my car and sat down inside.

He yelled, "Fine!" just as I slammed the door and started the car.

I knew he didn't really mean "fine." The pain on his face and the desperation in his voice led me to believe he meant the exact opposite, but I wasn't going to challenge him.

As I drove off I saw Lucy walk out of the store with an angry look on her face, and I accelerated to get away from them faster. Before I left the parking lot, I glanced into my rear-view mirror and saw Cameron watching me drive away. His shoulders were slumped, and his hands were buried in his hair, but I wasn't turning back. I was beyond hurt now. I was done.

Chapter Three
All Around Me

"How does it feel to be home?" Owen asked, stroking my thigh softly. I sighed and looked out the car window, focusing on the trees and fluffy white clouds flying by, not the buildings and houses. They were certainly familiar, but also painful. I associated everything in Fairfield, Connecticut, with *him*.

After the confrontation in the grocery store, I'd packed up and left town in a hurry. I hadn't seen or spoken with Cameron since. I'd moved to Boston and tried to start my life over. I changed my name back to Charlotte Barnes, and within twelve months of leaving Fairfield, the divorce was final. My father had liaised between us for the divorce proceedings so there was no face-to-face contact needed. I was eternally grateful to my dad for understanding my need for space.

About a year after the divorce came through, I met Owen. He was a police officer who'd pulled me over for speeding. He always joked that when I handed him my driver's license, he'd memorized my address so he could call me later.

Owen was everything Cam had turned out not to be: loyal, trustworthy, and dependable. I turned down his advances time and time again, but despite my apparent disinterest, Owen pursued me relentlessly. After the debacle that had been my marriage, I wasn't in a hurry to trust a man. I wasn't sure my heart could take being broken again. But one night, about three months after we met, I found Owen standing outside my apartment in the rain, waiting for me to come home and holding a bouquet of flowers. Taking pity on him, I finally agreed to the date. A part of me hoped it would go really badly so he'd finally leave me alone, but I was surprised by how much I enjoyed being with him. The pain of my divorce lessened when I was around him, and I discovered I was still able to laugh and have fun for the first time in two years.

We spent more and more time together, and as the months passed, I found myself not only trusting Owen, but feeling connected to him. I could talk to him like I hadn't been able to talk to anybody, even my ex-husband, and it was a refreshing change. What started as a pity date evolved into a true partnership—one that I quickly knew I couldn't live without. We traveled to Italy on vacation for our first anniversary, and not long after that we moved in together. On my twenty-seventh birthday, after we'd been dating almost a year and a half, Owen asked me to marry him. As the words left his mouth, *his* face flashed through my mind, but I pushed it aside, refusing to allow the past to haunt me any longer.

Even if my feelings about my previous marriage weren't completely resolved, I wanted to be happy again, and I knew I could find that with Owen. I had no doubt he loved me, and I loved feeling like I was his whole world. I wouldn't pass up spending the rest of my life with the man I loved and the first person in years I'd been able to trust. I'd accepted Owen's marriage proposal and never looked back—until today.

As we drove past the "Welcome to Fairfield" sign, my stomach rose into my throat; I wasn't sure if I was ready to be back. My dad had been asking me to move home for years, and he finally got his wish when Owen accepted a job as a police officer in Hartford, Connecticut.

Owen had actually brought up the idea of moving back before he had employment. He'd been adamant that there were issues in Fairfield that needed to be resolved before we could move forward with our life together. I was against the move. I thought I'd moved past the person I was when I lived there, and I was happy with the life we were building in Boston.

Then Owen came to me and said he felt like I was holding some part of myself back from him. He didn't want me to have any doubts. I knew I had baggage from my ex-husband and my mother—issues we had discussed at length—but I hadn't realized how deeply they were affecting Owen and our relationship. Realizing my very future depended on it, I agreed, reluctantly, to go.

We'd contacted my father, who was overjoyed to hear of our decision but wasn't able to offer Owen any work. I was secretly relieved, thinking the lack of a job would convince Owen we should stay in Boston. But my father had connections with the Hartford Police Chief and managed to secure Owen a position.

Since he'd be working there, I thought we could live in Hartford, which was still closer to my dad than Boston, but Owen insisted that we live in my home town, despite the hour-long commute he'd have to and from work every day.

Owen's job started in a month, but I was moving early to spend some time with my father, to find us a house to live in, and—with Owen's encouragement—to start putting my former life to rest once and for all. We both knew this meant I might have to face Cameron at some point, but I wasn't going to think about that until the time came.

To distract myself from the familiar sights outside the car, I looked over at my fiancé and smiled. His thick blond hair was squashed flat on the back of his head from pressing it into the headrest, and I giggled as I reached over and ran my fingers through it, trying to remove the bed-head before we saw my dad. He looked over at me, his blue eyes sparkling. Owen's eyes were one of the things I loved most. They always showed so much emotion.

I directed us to my dad's house and tried to relax as we pulled into the drive. I'd taken him the long way around town under the guise of showing him the sights, but my real intention had been to avoid driving down the street where I'd lived before—with *him.*

Dad's smiling face appeared in the doorway, and he bounded down the porch stairs into the front yard. I'd just removed my seat belt and stood up, stretching my legs from the long drive, when he enveloped me in a hug.

"It's so good to see you, Charlotte!"

"You too, Dad," I replied, smiling and squeezing him back. "It's been too long."

I hadn't been back since I'd left town, so the only times we'd seen each other over the past five years were during his annual trips to Boston.

"Michael," Owen said, holding out his hand.

"Good to see you again," Dad replied, shaking Owen's hand firmly.

Owen and my father had connected instantly. I wasn't sure if it was because they were both in law enforcement or if they had some unspoken male bond because they both loved me, but whatever the reason, it warmed my heart that they got along so well.

"I hope you don't mind, but I thought I'd invite a few of the boys over and give Owen here a big Fairfield Police Department-style welcome. I also invited a few of the Hartford boys you'll be working with," Dad added, turning to address Owen.

"It's fine, Dad," I assured him. I needed the distraction.

Dad and Owen carried my suitcases upstairs to my old bedroom while I stood at the foot of the stairs and closed my eyes. The smell of my dad's house was familiar and comforting, and a small smile crept over my lips. Maybe I *could* do this.

I heard loud footsteps coming down the stairs and opened my eyes when Owen's arms slipped around my waist.

"How're you doing?" he whispered, softly kissing my neck.

"I'm good." I was sure many men would feel defensive or jealous about being in the same town as their fiancée's ex-husband, but Owen's only concern was how *I* was handling it. And it had been his idea. I felt very lucky to be loved by someone so supportive.

"How long until everyone arrives?" I asked Dad as he joined us downstairs.

"You've got a few hours. I told everyone to come mid-afternoon."

I turned to Owen and cocked my head to the side. "I could use a nap. How about you?" We'd left Boston before sunrise, hoping to make good time on the road before rush hour traffic. I was exhausted.

"Sounds great," he replied with a smile.

"We'll be back down before everyone arrives," I called over my shoulder, taking Owen's hand and leading up him up the stairs to my old bedroom.

We collapsed on the bed and fell quickly asleep. When I opened my eyes, I could already hear muffled laughter coming from downstairs, and I supposed Dad's friends had arrived. I looked out the window and noticed the sun low in the sky. We must have slept for quite a while.

Owen stirred next to me, and I rolled to face him.

"Hey," he said, his voice gruff from sleep.

"Hey," I echoed, smiling.

"How did you sleep?" He smoothed my hair with gentle strokes.

"Pretty well, actually."

I stretched my arms over my head and enjoyed the sensation of my muscles pulling against each other. After being stuck in the car for several hours and then the nap, I was quite stiff.

"Mmm…me too," Owen said, yawning.

"We should probably head downstairs and be social."

"I know you're right, but I'm just so comfortable," Owen said, chuckling and snuggling up to wrap his arms around me.

I enjoyed the comfort of his embrace for a few moments, but when a particularly loud bark of laughter broke through from downstairs, I pulled away and climbed off the bed, straightening my clothes and running my fingers through my hair.

Owen pouted but also stood up. "Let's get this over with. The sooner we go down, the sooner we can come back to bed."

"I think you'll have fun with the guys. They're all just like you," I joked, poking him in the side as we descended the stairs.

Owen gave me a skeptical look but then sighed and nodded.

"Char, Owen?" Dad called from the kitchen.

"Yeah?" I asked loudly, steering Owen through the house.

"Come on out back," my dad said, smiling when we entered the room. "We're going to turn on the grill, and we have a cooler full of beer."

"Sounds good," Owen called as he moved through the kitchen, his fingers laced through mine, pulling me along behind him.

"Oh my God! Charlotte?"

"Hey, Charlotte."

I looked around at the familiar faces and smiled. It *was* good to be home. I watched as Owen introduced himself to the men in my father's backyard and shook each of their hands. Then I sat next him and snuggled into his side as we listened to them tell him all about the Fairfield Police Department and the cases they'd worked on. They even suggested a few houses in town that were available.

After what seemed like forever, the barbeque was lit and the meat sizzled temptingly. The smell made me realize how hungry I actually was. Based on childhood experience with my father's grilling, I knew the meat wouldn't be ready for a while. My grumbling stomach wasn't going to wait that long, so I decided to find something to tide me over. I went inside and poked around the kitchen. Just as I suspected, there was very little in the way of nutritious food to be found, so I made a mental note to go to the grocery store in the morning and stock up on some necessities. It made me feel a little guilty for leaving town only six months after my mother had abandoned my father, but I needed to get my life back on track, and I wouldn't have been able to do that here.

There was a loud knock at the front door, and I smiled at Dad as he made his way through the kitchen to get it. He returned a moment later with a concerned and guilty look on his face.

"Ah…Char, I'm sorry," he began. "I meant to tell you…"

"What is it?" I walked around the kitchen table to where he was standing.

As I moved closer to my father, his latest guest came into view. I started to feel very hot and grabbed the back of the nearest kitchen chair to keep myself standing.

"Charlotte?" Ryan said, looking just as shocked as I felt.

I looked at him, unable to tear my eyes away. His face had aged. There were smile lines around his eyes, and he seemed bulkier than I remembered, but he was the same Ryan from my other life.

"Hi…Hi, Ryan," I stuttered softly, jumping when the back door slammed loudly.

Arms slipped around my waist from behind, and I registered confusion, realization, and then sadness as the emotions crossed Ryan's face.

"You okay, baby? You look like you've seen a ghost," Owen said, holding out his hand to shake Ryan's. "I'm Owen."

Ryan opened his mouth to speak but was cut off when one of the guys came in. "Hey, Harper, good to see you," he said, opening the fridge and helping himself to a beer.

Owen stiffened behind me, recognizing my old surname, and squeezed me tighter. We all stood in uncomfortable silence for a moment before Dad grabbed my hand and pulled me into the living room.

"Charlotte, I'm sorry. I didn't even think. Ryan joined the force two years ago and is a deputy of mine. I just invited everyone at the station and didn't think until later that maybe I shouldn't have included him. I was going to tell you, but it completely slipped my mind. Is it okay that he's here? Are you all right? I can ask him to leave."

I took a deep breath and looked over my shoulder into the kitchen. I could see them standing there silently — Ryan with his back to me and Owen with his arms folded over his chest. From behind, Ryan reminded me of Cameron. Their builds were different — Ryan had always been taller and broader than his brother — but the way he was standing, with one knee slightly bent and his body resting on the door frame, was identical.

"It's fine, Dad. It would be rude to ask him to leave when everyone else from the station is here. It's not a problem, really," I assured him. I was feeling a little dizzy, but I wasn't going to let Dad know that.

"Okay, if you're sure." He squeezed my arm gently before walking back into the kitchen. "Come on, Ryan, why don't you help me with the grill?"

Ryan looked over his shoulder at me, and I gave him a slight nod. He nodded back before following Dad outside. I heard loud cheers from the guys out there, and I guessed Ryan was pretty popular at work. I wasn't surprised. I remembered him as a fun-loving and very loyal man.

Owen walked over and laced his fingers through mine before he sat down on the couch, pulling me into his lap.

"Are you okay?" he asked softly. "I can understand that you might be upset, seeing him."

It dawned on me that Owen must have thought Ryan was my ex-husband.

"That wasn't him. That's his brother, Ryan."

Owen relaxed a little and cradled me against his chest, rocking slightly.

"We can stay inside if you'd like. Maybe go upstairs and unpack a little?"

His suggestion was tempting. Part of me wanted to run up the stairs with Owen and hide from everyone and everything, but I knew I couldn't hide forever. If I was ever going to move on with my life and give my heart to Owen completely, I'd have to deal with how I felt about Cameron.

The warmth of Owen's arms around me was so comforting, and his scent so familiar, that I hummed with contentment. I would do this for him.

"No, I'm fine, really. Let's go outside," I said, standing and holding my hand out.

"Okay, let's do this," he said with a chuckle, swinging his arm over my shoulder and walking with me through the kitchen.

Everyone was laughing at a story Ryan was telling, and we were able to sit down without anyone commenting on our absence.

"…and then he fell in the lake!" Ryan roared, and the group burst again into laughter.

I saw Ryan look over at me and take a long drink of his beer. I couldn't maintain eye contact with him because his deep brown eyes reminded me too much of the ones I'd thought I knew so well.

The rest of the day was much the same: humorous stories from the men, me avoiding eye contact with Ryan, and Ryan chugging his beer much faster than anyone else. After several of my dad's friends headed home and the sun was setting, I started to clean up some plates.

"Owen, come and have a look at my fishing equipment. A group of us are going out on the harbor tomorrow. You should join us," Dad said happily, clapping Owen on the back as he walked out to the shed in the rear of the yard, followed by the remaining guests.

I took the stack of plates into the house and turned on the water in the sink. As it filled and I added soap, I heard the door open and prayed silently that it was one of Dad's friends and not Ryan coming into the room.

"How are you, Charlotte?" Ryan asked. His eyes were glassy, and I frowned when he opened the fridge and helped himself to another beer. I didn't remember Ryan ever being a drinker, but so far today I'd seen him down at least six bottles.

"I'm good, Ry, really good." I turned off the water and leaned back on the sink.

"You look good…happy," he said hesitantly.

I nodded and folded my arms protectively over my chest. "How are you?"

A big smile spread over his face, and he looked just like the young, playful Ryan I remembered.

"Sarah's pregnant with our first."

All the tension I was feeling disappeared, and I pulled the man I'd always considered a brother into my arms and hugged him as hard as I could. "Congratulations!"

He gave me the killer Harper smile in return, and I stepped back a little, feeling as if I'd been hit in the chest. I turned my back for a moment and closed my eyes so I could regain my composure.

I pictured Owen and reminded myself that I was fine, that I was loved. Slowly, when my breathing returned to normal and I began to feel a little more in control, I turned back to see Ryan staring at me, a look of concern on his face.

"Charlotte, what really happened back then?" he asked, sitting in one of the dining chairs and kicking out the one opposite him for me.

"He didn't tell you?" I asked as I sat down.

"He gave us excuses—his side of it. I want to know what happened *from you.*"

The look in his eyes was so intense and sincere that even though I *never* talked about it, never even thought about it if I could avoid doing so, I found myself telling him everything.

I explained how I'd found the text message on Christmas Eve and how much pain I'd been in during that last family Christmas. I described how hard it had been for me to move everything I owned out of our home while *he* was at his parent's house. I talked about seeing him and Lucy together at the grocery store and our last words in the parking lot. I recounted packing up and moving to Boston in only a few days, and then how I'd met Owen and slowly put my life back together.

I watched a darkness descend on Ryan's face as he heard about the way I left, and his expression didn't clear as I talked about Owen. If anything, it became even darker.

"Do you love Owen?" Ryan asked — the first words he'd spoken since I started talking.

"Very much," I said with a smile.

I didn't know how to express to Ryan that Owen had fixed me, had made me whole again and brought me back to life. I didn't think someone who'd never had his heart broken in that way could really understand what it was like to piece yourself back together after being shattered. Ryan would never understand the internal battle I'd waged about whether I could allow myself to feel loved again or just keep myself safe behind my emotionless wall.

"But you still love Cam," Ryan stated firmly, not leaving any room for the alternative.

I cringed at the sound of his name. I tried to say it — and think it — as little as possible. I hesitated for a moment. I'd gone over this in my head many times, and I could honestly say I didn't *think* I was still in love with him. I cared about him as a part of my history, but that was all I allowed myself to feel for him now.

"No, my feelings for Cam…for *him* are in the past. It's ancient history," I said firmly, but my hands were shaking, and I wasn't sure if he believed me.

"Okay."

I was grateful he wasn't going to push the issue.

We sat in silence for a moment, both of us staring into space until Ryan let out a loud laugh and banged his fist on the table, making me jump.

"What is it?" I asked, eyes wide.

"Bonnie's going to kill you!" he practically shouted.

"Why?"

"She's been furious at you for five years because you wouldn't talk to her after you split from Cam, and then you left without saying goodbye. She tried to call you, but you never returned her messages. When she finds out you're back in town she's going to rip your head off—literally."

"You didn't tell her?"

"I didn't know until I saw you here," he admitted.

"What did you think the barbeque was for?"

"I didn't really think about it," he said with a shrug. "Your dad's had us all over before, and I just assumed it was a work get-together type thing. I swear I didn't know you'd be here. Trust me, if my family knew you were back, Bonnie would've demanded to come with me tonight to see you."

"How is she?"

"You wouldn't recognize her. She graduated college and is working as a personal assistant in an accounting firm now. Oh, and she has a boy-friend—an accountant. They're pretty serious, I think. She brought him home to meet my parents last weekend," he finished with a frown.

"You don't like him?"

"He seems like an okay guy, but he's screwing my baby sister, so I automatically don't like him."

"How are David and Ellen?"

"They're great. Dad is looking at early retirement, so all Mom can talk about is a big trip to Europe they're planning for next spring."

"I went to Italy last year with Owen. It was beautiful. I'm sure they'll love it."

Suddenly Ryan stood up, came to my side of the table, and knelt in front of me.

"Are you happy, Char? Really happy? You can tell me the truth," he pleaded, his words slurring slightly from his intoxication.

"I'm happy," I insisted before leaning forward to give him a hug. "I missed you."

"I missed you too." He was silent for a moment after we broke the hug, staring at me as he returned to his seat. "Cam's not happy—" he began, but he was cut off by a group his coworkers entering the room on their way out.

"See ya, Harper. Bye, Charlotte," they called.

"It was good to see you again," I said with a smile and a wave, but I was shaking from what Ryan had started to tell me.

Just then arms slipped around me from behind, and I instantly felt calmer as warm lips pressed against my cheek.

"I love you," Owen whispered in my ear.

I smiled and leaned back into him, enjoying the warmth. "Thanks, I needed that."

"I thought you might. Are you okay?"

"I'm much better now that you're here," I sighed with a smile.

I turned in his arms to face him and rose on my toes so I could press my lips to his. We kissed for several seconds before Ryan cleared his throat to remind us he was standing right there.

"I'll get you a drink," Owen whispered as he quickly kissed me again and went over to the fridge.

I turned back around to find Ryan giving me a knowing look. I went outside to find my dad. Before I made it out the back door, I heard Ryan asking Owen to get him yet another beer.

I stepped outside, switched on the patio light, and saw Dad cleaning the grill. He smiled when he saw me.

"Hi, kiddo. It's so good to have you home."

"It's good to be home." The possibility of facing Cameron still terrified me, but the comfort of being in such a familiar place was hard to resist.

The back door opened, and Owen and Ryan came outside, carrying beers for everyone. After we managed to coax Dad away from the grill, the four of us sat around the backyard table, drinking our beers and listening to Dad regale us with stories about criminals he'd caught and ones who had gotten away.

Ryan offered to provide the lowdown on some of the Hartford boys, which seemed to please Owen. I smiled at him as a thank you for being nice, and he winked back at me. I couldn't work out if this newfound acceptance of my fiancé was him being nice or him being intoxicated, but I appreciated it either way.

Just as I'd convinced myself to lean toward the first option, Ryan stood up and almost fell down, managing to knock his chair over in the process.

"Whoa!" he chuckled, gripping the table to stay on his feet.

Dad jumped out of his seat and held Ryan upright as Owen picked up the chair. After they'd managed to get him to sit down again, Dad said, "I think I should call Sarah to come pick you up," and headed for the house.

I moved around the table and sat on Owen's lap. We chatted with an increasingly disoriented Ryan until my dad came back out.

"She'll be here in a minute," Dad announced, helping Ryan stand and swinging his arm around his waist. "Owen, I'm gonna need your help, I think." Dad grunted with the effort of trying to steer Ryan's large frame.

Owen jogged up to the other side and helped support Ryan's weight as we walked back into the house.

"*Stop!*" Ryan yelled. We looked at each other nervously, and I wondered if I was doomed to spend the night cleaning vomit off the kitchen floor.

"I want to give my baby sister a hug goodbye!"

Owen looked confused, and I could have sworn I saw Dad looking around, thinking Bonnie Harper had appeared in his house without warning. But I knew better — Ryan was talking about me.

I walked around Owen and stood in front of Ryan, who encapsulated me in his arms. "I'm so happy to see you, Charlotte," he slurred against my collar.

"I'm happy to see you too." I patted him on the back before pulling out of his grasp as I heard tires on gravel in the front yard.

"Sarah's here," I whispered to him.

I watched Owen and Dad help Ryan to the front door and then went upstairs to get ready for bed. Part of me had wanted to say hello to Sarah, but one Harper was all I could manage for today. I walked slowly up the stairs and went into my bedroom. I hadn't fallen apart. Maybe Owen was right when he told me I could face my past.

I unzipped my suitcase and pulled my pajamas out, laying them on the bed before taking some of the clothes over to the closet to hang up. I hated ironing, and if I hung some things tonight, I might avoid it completely.

As I walked to the closet, I passed the window and glanced outside to see Owen shaking hands with someone in the shadows. I felt my blood turn icy cold as the realization hit me. *He* was outside.

I watched in horror as my fiancé's hand slipped inside the hand of my ex-husband, grasping it tightly. I wasn't sure if Owen realized who he was shaking hands with, but he still had a pleasant smile on his face.

I couldn't see Cameron's face, but I didn't need to. I'd know him anywhere. He was thinner than the last time I saw him, and his hair was a little shorter than I remembered. Inexplicably, a part of me wanted to sprint down the stairs and run into his arms. Another part wanted to scream at him out the window. I resisted both urges and just stood frozen, watching them.

The thumping of my heart was so loud in my ears that I couldn't hear any noises drifting upstairs, so I had no idea what was being said. My dad looked angry and kept gesturing to Cameron. Suddenly the expression on Owen's face turned hard and then slightly sad, and I guessed he'd worked out that the man in front of him, who he'd just shaken hands with, was my ex-husband.

Cameron had his head down and was now quickly helping Ryan into the car. He said something to Owen, then climbed into the driver's seat and sped away. I watched the taillights disappear around the corner, and when I looked down into the yard again, I saw Owen staring up at me sadly.

I tried to smile and waved for him to come up to our room, and he nodded slowly before disappearing inside. I hung the clothes up quickly, trying to calm myself after seeing Cam and mentally preparing myself for the conversation to come. I took a few deep breaths and tried to put *him* out of my mind as I put my pajamas on. I was over him and didn't want him to affect me.

"So that was him," Owen said from behind me.

Taking one last deep breath, I spun around. "Yes," was all I managed to get out before my breath caught in my throat.

"Your dad doesn't like him much," he added as he started pulling his own clothes out of his overnight bag.

"No. He didn't treat me very well."

"Michael kept demanding to know why he was here and saying he'd told him he wasn't welcome. Cameron said Sarah was tired and asked him to come instead and he was just trying to do Ryan a favor."

"I hope he didn't say anything rude to you," I said. "As far as I know, he didn't know I was coming back, so it was a surprise when he found out who you were." I tried to imagine what Cameron could have said to Owen.

"He seemed nice enough. Very polite. I didn't give him any details about who I was, so I think he assumed I worked with your dad." He shrugged, but I could hear the strain in his voice.

I sighed and sat down on the bed. "Owen, come here." I tapped the mattress next to me.

He gave a weak smile and came to sit next to me. He put his arm around my shoulders and pulled me to lie against his chest.

"Are you okay with all of this?" I prayed he was. I couldn't lose Owen. He was the only reason I hadn't imploded.

"Yes. We both knew you'd run into his family when we came back here, and I think it's important for you to face this issue before we get married. All I need to know is that when you talk to him, you aren't going to run off and leave me. I couldn't bear it," he whispered, kissing my head softly.

I looked at him, my mouth hanging slightly open. "You *want* me to talk to Cameron." It wasn't a question, because I knew he did. Part of me wanted Owen to act possessive and demand that I never speak to Cameron again, but that wasn't him. He only wanted what was best for me.

"I think you should get it all out. You must have things you need to say to him, and until you clear it all up, you'll never have a complete understanding of the situation. You told me you never really talked to him after you found out he was cheating. I think you might need some closure so you can let it go and move on. As much as I hate the thought of you and him alone together, I know it will be best for *us* in the long run…and I trust you." He ran his hands through the long strands of my hair that had come free of my clip.

I stared at him, feeling completely astonished. I'd never met a more selfless person. "How did you get to be so wonderful?" I asked, kissing him softly.

"Just lucky, I guess." He chuckled as we broke apart. "But I'm saying all this as much for myself as you. I want you to feel free when we get married. I don't want your past to be hanging over us forever."

I turned to face him and grabbed his right hand, stroking it softly and kissing each of his fingertips. "I'm not going anywhere with *anyone*. I love you, Owen," I said, continuing to stroke his hand.

He smiled contentedly and pressed his lips to mine. "Love you more," he whispered as he broke away.

I felt his whole body relax as he lay back against the pillows and pulled me tighter to his chest. I ran my fingers absentmindedly over his hand until I realized I was lying here declaring my love to my fiancé in the same bed where I'd lost my virginity to Cameron. I was stroking the hand that Cameron had just shook. I tried desperately to stop thinking of my ex-husband and the way the moonlight had reflected off his hair tonight.

But no matter how much I wanted him out of my life and out of my heart, Cameron was all around me.

Chapter Four
The Beginning of Confusion

I woke to a rustling sound and opened one eye to look around. It was still dark, and I sat up slightly, wondering what the noise could be.

"Oh, shit. Sorry, baby, I didn't mean to wake you." Owen sat on the edge of the bed and smoothed my hair with his hand.

"What are you doing?" I asked groggily.

"Looking for my boots," he whispered before kissing the top of my head and going back to his search.

"Why do you need boots at…" I looked at the alarm clock on the bedside table. "Four-thirty in the morning?"

"I told your dad I'd go fishing with him today."

"Have fun," I grumbled, pulling the covers up over my head to block out Owen's chuckling.

When I next opened my eyes, it was to the sound of chirping birds. I threw the covers off my head and squinted at the sunlight pouring in the window. The clock on my nightstand said it was 8:22. I closed my eyes and took a deep breath, noting that the air in Fairfield felt fresher and easier to breathe.

It was weird to wake up in my childhood bedroom, and I giggled as I thought about how I used to lie here, the biggest stress in my life being what I would wear to school. The comparison to how complicated my life felt now was astonishing. I stretched and looked around. The room really did look exactly as I remembered it, except for the suitcases Owen and I had brought from Boston.

I forced myself to get out of bed. I slipped on my robe, tying the belt as I walked downstairs into the kitchen. I tried to imagine Owen on a boat with my dad and laughed. When Owen and I were in Italy, he'd gotten seasick on the gondolas in Venice, so I couldn't see him faring any better in my dad's dinghy.

I suddenly remembered my dad had taken Cameron out fishing as a way to welcome him to our family. It hadn't gone well. Cameron fell overboard, and my dad yelled at him for scaring all the fish away. To add insult to injury, Dad made him ride home in the back of the truck because he smelled like pond water. My dad had never really accepted Cameron, probably because of my decision to forgo college and stay in Fairfield to be with him.

I quickly started a pot of coffee and opened the fridge for the milk, noticing how empty the shelves were. There was milk, beer, bread…and nothing else. Yet another reminder that I needed to get some groceries.

While I sat and sipped my coffee, I did everything I could *not* to think of Cameron, but it was impossible. He'd looked good, from what I could see of him from behind and in the dark. I recalled the moonlight reflecting off his hair and the silhouette of his shoulders. I remembered the way his muscles moved as he supported his brother and recalled how those same muscles looked without the shirt. Even after five years I could see his body clearly in my mind, and I closed my eyes, mentally tracing my fingers over his shoulders and down his chest, through the light smattering of hair. I sighed and shook my head. No good was going to come from that train of thought.

I poured the rest of my coffee down the sink and went upstairs to shower. I decided to go to the grocery store sooner rather than later so I could relax and unpack a little in the afternoon before Dad and Owen came home.

⊸❖⊰

As I pulled into the parking lot of the grocery store, the clouds, which had been gathering all morning, opened up and the rain began. *Perfect timing.* Looking across the lot, I had a flashback of me telling Cameron I never wanted to see him again. I regretted those being the last words I might ever say to him, but it was the truth. Even five years later I didn't want to face him.

I got out of the car and jogged across the parking lot to get out of the rain as quickly as possible. As I stepped into the brightly lit store, I found it exactly as I remembered. I wheeled a cart quickly down the first aisle and started looking for food my dad would not only like to eat, but could cook for himself.

Fifteen minutes later my cart was half full, and I was feeling quite proud of the selection of meals I'd chosen. I went to turn into the next aisle, but as soon as I saw the rows of cereal boxes, I stopped dead in my tracks and turned around quickly. Images of Cameron and Lucy flooded my mind, and I took a few deep breaths. Dad could eat toast for the next few days. I turned down the cosmetics row instead.

There was only one other lady in this aisle, and she had her back turned, examining some facial cream bottle, so I felt secure enough to stop for a moment, leaning against the cart for support. I hadn't expected the cereal aisle to affect me so much, but I could still feel my heart hammering in my chest.

"I'm fine," I said softly to myself. I could feel eyes on my back and looked carefully over my shoulder. I felt like I'd been kicked in the stomach when I saw that face cream lady was, in fact, my ex mother-in-law, who was now waving and making her way toward me at an alarming pace.

"Charlotte? Is that you?"

"Hello, Ellen," I said awkwardly, looking around for a quick escape and finding none.

"What are you doing just standing over here?"

"Oh…you know, just looking at this," I said as casually as I could, reaching onto the shelf and picking up the first box my hand touched. I stared at the item I chose, trying to keep a normal expression on my face. "Uh…spermicidal jelly." Mortified, I dropped it into my cart.

"Oh…well, that's very nice, dear," Ellen said uncomfortably, clearing her throat.

As we stood in silence for a moment, I tried to think of something to say to her. "I'm sorry I left without saying goodbye," I said softly, looking down into my cart.

Ellen's hand grasped mine tightly. "I understand. We all understood." She gave my hand a squeeze before letting out an "Oh!" of surprise and pulling away.

She stared at my finger, and I automatically moved my right hand over my left to cover my engagement ring.

"You're engaged?"

"Yeah." I stopped awkwardly. I didn't know what to say.

Ellen cleared her throat again and gave me a weak smile. "So tell me, are you here visiting your father?"

"No. Actually we've moved back to town. My fiancé just got a job in Hartford, and we drove from Boston yesterday."

"You were in Boston?"

I felt terrible that the woman I once thought of as a mother figure didn't know where I'd been for the past five years of my life. I suddenly found myself questioning my decision to cut the Harpers off completely. Would it have been so hard to call or send an email just to let them know I was okay?

"Yes. It's a lovely city," I said, not knowing how to express my guilt.

"Well, I'd love to hear all about it—and about the rest of your life. Would you come to dinner next Saturday?" she asked, a genuine smile on her face.

I envisioned a big Harper family dinner, and my heart rate sped up. I wasn't ready to face them all as if nothing had happened.

"Um…"

"Of course you're welcome to bring your fiancé," she added kindly, if not a little uncomfortably.

"Oh, well… Sure, I guess that would be okay. Can I ask a favor, though?"

Ellen smiled. "You want me to make my double-fudge brownies?"

I laughed. "Well, yes, actually, I would love that. But I was going to ask if it could be a small dinner…only you and David?"

She nodded solemnly. "Of course. I understand," she said, squeezing my hand again. "Just me and David, I promise."

"Thank you," I said gratefully, giving her a half-smile. It was hard for me not to see Cameron when I looked at her, but I tried my best.

"Well, I have to get going—lots to do today."

"It was good to see you."

"You too, sweetheart," she replied, giving me a quick hug. "See you next Saturday about seven. You remember how to get to the house?"

"Yes, I remember." As if I could forget. I'd spent almost as much time in her home as my own while I was married to Cameron. I mentally walked through the rooms and could almost smell one of Ellen's cherry pies baking in the kitchen.

"Goodbye, Charlotte," she said, giving me one last look.

My simple trip to the grocery store had turned out to be quite stressful. Of course I knew I'd be bumping into people from my past life, and I'd even suspected I'd see the Harpers around town, but I never expected to be confronted with them all within the first few days.

I finished up the last of the shopping as quickly as I could so I could return to the safety of my dad's house. I was piling my items on the conveyor belt at the checkout when I heard an excited voice.

"As I live and breathe — Charlotte Harper. I didn't expect to see you back in town," the cashier drawled.

I flinched at my married name and instantly recognized Amanda Foster, a girl I went to high school with.

"Hello, Amanda. It's Charlotte *Barnes,* actually."

"Oh, of course. How rude of me. Habit, you understand," she said with a shrug. She blew a bubble with her chewing gum as she started swiping my items over the scanner.

The ten years since high school had not been kind to Amanda. She'd gained at least thirty pounds, and her once-auburn hair was now showing signs of gray.

"How've you been?" I asked, hoping I could keep her talking about herself so she wouldn't have a chance to ask anything about me.

I only half listened as she droned on about having married Ethan Davis, our high school quarterback and my senior prom date, and how they had four children. Not soon enough, she had all of my items scanned, and I paid her.

"Bye," I called over my shoulder as I carried the bags out as quickly as I could.

Before I could turn to see where I was going, I smacked into someone and fell to the floor, my bags spilling everywhere.

"Shit," I whispered under my breath, frantically picking up my fallen groceries and shoving them roughly into the brown paper bags.

"I'm so sorry, miss. Let me help you," a deep voice said from above me, stopping me cold. It was Cameron. I'd know his voice anywhere.

Fuck, fuck, fuck, fuck, fuck! I tried to think of an escape plan.

I kept my head down and allowed my hair to hang over my face as I finished collecting my items. The only thought in my mind was to get away from him as quickly as possible, so I didn't want to look up or speak—I knew he would recognize me. I prayed he wouldn't bend down to help.

Once I had the last of my items, I sprinted out the door without acknowledging him at all. I was grateful that the rain had slowed, but I still had to maneuver around some of the larger puddles. I dumped all the bags in the backseat and ran around to the driver's door. I could hear deep laughter coming toward me, and my hand froze at the door handle. Cameron was behind me.

"Miss, you um…forgot your spermicidal jelly," he said, chuckling.

Fuck, fuck, fuck, fuck, fuck, fuck, fuck! I had two choices. I could jump into my car, ignore him completely, and have him think I was just some rude bitch, or I could turn and face him. I chose option one and wrenched the door open, ready to speed off down the street.

"Hey, miss," he said more firmly.

Then everything came to a standstill.

Cameron's hand clamped around my wrist, and his fingers rubbed the back of my hand. I sucked in a deep breath and closed my eyes as he spun me around to face him. He was silent for a moment, but he didn't let go.

"Char—Charlotte?"

I kept my eyes closed and tried to teleport myself anywhere else on the planet, but the chilly air and warm hand holding me in place did not change. With a sigh, I slowly opened my eyes, but I looked at the ground, not wanting to see his face.

"Hello, Cameron," I whispered, my voice cracking and barely leaving my throat as I stared determinedly at my shoes.

"Oh, this is yours," he said awkwardly, holding the jelly out to me.

"Thanks." I grabbed the very edge of the box, keeping my fingers as far from his as possible. Touching him was not something I was willing to do.

I could feel tears starting to burn in the corners of my eyes, and I wanted to get away from him, but he was still holding my arm. I pulled against his grasp, and he let go, as if he hadn't realized he was still holding on.

"Charlotte…"

"There's nothing to say, Cam. I've moved on," I said as strongly as I could, but my hands were shaking and my voice wasn't as steady as I would have liked.

He looked at me sadly and nodded. My curiosity finally got the better of me, and I looked up to see him properly for the first time. I had to bite my lip to swallow back the sigh.

He was my Cameron.

Sure, he was older—he had small lines around his eyes, and he'd lost weight in his face—but it was him, and part of me cried out to hold him. I wanted to soothe the dark circles from under his eyes and run my fingers across the stubble that covered his chin. My body was betraying me again, as easily as it had five years ago, so I stepped back, pressing myself against the side of my car.

"Are you happy?" he asked, looking at me with his soulful, dark eyes.

I froze and gasped for air. Eye contact with Cameron was paralyzing, and I didn't know how to break out of his hold. He just stared straight into my eyes.

I wasn't going to let him suck me in. I was already emotionally vulnerable, so I had to be extra strong. I gave my head a quick shake to clear my thoughts and folded my arms over my chest.

He noticed my change in demeanor and straightened his posture. "I… I'm sorry,"

I looked at him incredulously. Did he really think a simple apology would mean anything to me now? "I don't need your apologies, Cameron. I meant what I said in this parking lot five years ago. I don't want you in my life."

I was quite proud of myself. Inside I felt like jelly, but I didn't think I gave any indication of that to Cameron. I turned to get into my car, and he grabbed my arm again.

"Please, Charlotte, will you just talk to me?"

"About what? There's nothing to say!" I yelled, giving him the full force of my anger. I pulled my arm out of his grasp and tried to get into the car again.

Cameron slammed the door closed just as I was about to get in and stood in front of it. I could feel the fury building inside me, and before I even registered what I was doing, my hand shot up and slapped him hard across the face. He let out an "oof" as it made contact, and he looked at me in shock.

My hands covered my mouth as I realized what I'd done, and I took a few steps back. I wanted to apologize, tell him I didn't intend to hit him, but I couldn't find the words. No matter how horrified I was, I also felt quite justified.

"I deserved that." He rubbed his bright red cheek. "Is it out of your system now, or would you like to take another shot?"

The rage surged through me again. He was joking around as if we were play-fighting. He obviously didn't take me or our situation seriously at all.

"Let me get into my car," I stated firmly.

He stared at me for a moment, testing my resolve, and finally stepped away. I pulled the door open and sat down. Before I could pull it closed, however, Cameron stood in the way and leaned down.

"Where are you staying?"

I just glared at him.

"I would just like a way to contact you. I think we need to talk… sort this all out."

His eyes were sparkling, and I could feel my anger ebbing away. *Danger!* my brain shrieked. I could tell he wasn't going to move or let me leave without giving him some information, so I sighed and twisted in my seat so I was facing him.

"My *fiancé* and I are staying with Dad until we find a place of our own," I said angrily.

His face went pale, and he leaned back as if I'd slapped him again. His eyes traveled down my arm and froze on the ring on my left hand.

"I believe you met him last night. Owen,"

He nodded slowly, and I could see tears forming in his eyes. Any elation I felt at causing him pain for the first time, instead of him crushing me over and over again, quickly disappeared. As angry as I was and as much as I wanted him to leave me alone, it still hurt me to hurt him.

"Goodbye, Cam." I pulled the door closed and started the car.

For the second time in my life, I drove out of that parking lot, watching Cameron in my rear-view mirror. My hands shook on the wheel, and the thought of going home to an empty house was not appealing. I could imagine myself sitting and crying all day, not to mention that Cameron now knew I was staying there, and he could show up without warning.

I stopped quickly at Dad's to drop off the groceries and grab a blanket, and then I got back in the car and drove out of Fairfield. I'd often enjoyed driving through the forest when I was a teenager, and I took the turnoff to Southport, the next town over. I drove the usual fifteen-minute drive in ten and pulled up in the parking lot at Southport Harbor.

Grabbing the blanket off the passenger seat, I opened the door and took a deep breath of the fresh air, feeling instantly calmer. Walking slowly down to the harbor's edge, I soaked in the view. It was just as beautiful as I remembered.

I kept walking until I found a spot of soft grass where I could sit. I wrapped the blanket around my shoulders and pulled it under me as I looked out at the waves. So many of my memories of Fairfield were tied up in Cameron, but this was one place I could come and have memories where he wasn't featured.

Cameron and I had come here together, of course, but I'd had many childhood friends in Southport and spent plenty of time here with without him. I lay back on the grass and looked up at the sky. I felt completely at ease here and made a mental note to bring Owen to my special place.

Cameron's words kept running through my head, and the sound of the water, relaxing as it was, did nothing to drown them out. Was he right? Did we need to talk? Did I even want to sort things out with him? And if I did, where would that leave us? I was with Owen now, and I was happy. But Owen had told me he *wanted* me to talk with Cameron. Would he be upset to learn I'd had that chance and run away? I needed Owen and couldn't bear the thought of hurting him. Despite my urge to run, I knew Owen was probably right. I'd have to talk with Cameron eventually.

I breathed in the salty air and watched the sun move across the sky and behind the clouds. I don't know how long I lay there thinking, but when the clouds started to turn pink I decided to head home. I took one last look at the water lapping at the rocks and stood up, brushing the grass from the blanket and giving it a quick shake before heading back to my car.

The drive back to town went quickly, and before I knew it, I was turning into my dad's driveway. His car was there so I knew they were home from their fishing trip.

"I'm home!" I called as I came in the front door.

Owen appeared from the kitchen with a big smile on his face and pulled me into his arms, kissing me and spinning me around in the air.

"I missed you today," he whispered, placing me back on the floor and leading me into the kitchen with one arm around my waist.

"We have dinner, Char. Fresh fish," Dad said, beaming as he prepared the filets in the sink.

"That's great!" I smiled as I pulled away from Owen and opened the fridge, taking out some of the vegetables I'd bought to make a salad.

"What did you do today?" Owen asked.

"I went grocery shopping and then out to Southport to sit at the harbor."

"The harbor used to be your favorite place to think," Dad said with a smile.

Owen gave me a curious look, and I cursed silently. Now Owen was going to wonder why I went there today.

"Yeah, I just went there to ground myself and see if it had changed." It wasn't a lie. I couldn't help it if some thinking had occurred while I was there.

"How was the fishing?" I asked, changing the subject.

"Great!" Owen said, hugging me to his chest.

I loved how he always had his arms around me, as if he couldn't get enough. I snuggled into his embrace. I felt safe there.

"Your boy is a natural fisherman," Dad said with a grin. "Don't let this one go!"

"I won't."

Owen kissed the top of my head and sighed contentedly. "Can I do anything to help?"

"You could peel the carrots," I said with a giggle. "But don't peel your fingers!"

Owen was good at almost everything he tried, except cooking. He'd offered to help me in the past and had come away injured several times.

"I'll do my best," he said, giving me a wink.

I chopped some parsley and garlic, mixed it with butter, and spread it over a freshly halved loaf of bread. I put it in the oven to bake, then started on a lemon pepper dressing for the salad as Dad went to grill the fish. Owen mixed the vegetables together next to me. We didn't talk, but it was a comfortable silence.

Once all the food was ready, we sat at the dining table, ready to dig in.

"Damn!" Dad swore, jumping out of his seat.

"What is it?" I asked, alarmed.

"I forgot the beer!" He chuckled and pulled three bottles from the fridge.

"To coming home," Dad said, holding his bottle in the air.

"To coming home," I echoed.

"To a new life," Owen added with a smile.

We clinked our bottle necks together and took a sip before turning to the food before us.

"So how was your first day back in town?" Dad asked through a mouthful.

"It was a little bizarre, to be honest. Everything is exactly the way it was when I left. It's like traveling back in time."

I remembered my conversation with Ellen and promise to join her and David for dinner next weekend. I knew Owen was going to be uncomfortable with that.

"I bumped into Ellen in the store," I began.

Dad froze, fork halfway to his mouth, and stared at me. Owen looked from Dad to me curiously.

"Who's Ellen?" he asked.

"Ellen is Cameron's mother," I said, reaching across the table to hold his hand.

He just nodded and took another bite of his food.

"How was that?" Dad asked cautiously.

"It was okay, actually. You remember how lovely she always was to me. She treated me like her own daughter. She actually invited me to dinner next weekend." I took a long drink from my beer, watching Owen carefully and cringing when he choked a little on his food.

"That was, um…nice of her?" Dad questioned, shifting in his chair.

"Yes, it was *very* nice of her. She invited me and Owen to come over, so you'll be on your own."

He shook his head at me. "I've been doing fine on my own for years, I think I can manage for one evening."

"You agreed to go?" Owen asked, looking shocked and a little annoyed.

"I'm sorry. She was being so nice, and it seemed rude to say no. You don't have to come if you don't want to. I know it will be really uncomfortable for you."

"Oh, no. I'll be there," he replied firmly, taking another bite of fish.

We ate the rest of the meal in silence, and afterward I helped Dad with the dishes and Owen went upstairs. I knew when I got up there we were going to have a very uncomfortable conversation, and I was dreading it.

"Thanks for helping, but I can finish up," Dad said.

"Okay, goodnight," I said, kissing his cheek. When I walked upstairs, I could see the light on under the bedroom door, and I knocked softly before going inside. I wasn't sure why I'd knocked on my own bedroom door, but I felt like I should let him know I was coming in.

Owen sat on the bed with his legs out in front of him, ankles crossed. He patted the mattress next to him and gave me a half-smile.

"I'm sorry," I blurted as I sat down.

His arm wrapped around my shoulder. "Is this dinner important to you?"

"The dinner isn't important…but Ellen is."

Owen flinched at my words, and I realized how they must have sounded.

"Let me explain. To me, Ellen has nothing to do with Cameron. I mean, I know she's his mother, but she's so much more than that. When I left Fairfield, I felt like I walked away from *my* mother, and it would be nice to have her back. It has nothing to do with Cameron, I swear." I paused for a moment. "I feel guilty, Owen. She didn't deserve to have me walk out on her without a word. I owe her one dinner."

Owen stroked my hair, and he let out a long sigh. "Okay, let's go to dinner."

I reached up and placed my hand on the back of his head, pulling it down so I could kiss his lips.

"Thank you," I whispered against his mouth.

He smiled and kissed me again, pulling me into his lap.

"But I need you to promise me *he* isn't going to be there. I couldn't handle that. I mean, I know you'll have to talk to him at some point, but I'd prefer not to see him again," he said, looking vulnerable.

"Of course. I made Ellen promise it would just be her and her husband. No one else," I assured him.

He nodded. "Okay. Dinner."

I snuggled against his chest and thought about how lucky I was to have him in my life. A pang of guilt hit me, and I knew immediately it was because I hadn't told Owen I saw Cameron. He deserved to know.

"Owen."

"Mmm?"

"I also saw Cam at the grocery store today," I said quickly. I knew he'd heard me because his hand stopped rubbing my back, and he sucked in a quick breath.

"He said he wanted to talk to me, but I yelled at him and told him I didn't want him in my life and then I…" I hesitated for a moment before deciding to tell the whole story. "And then I slapped him."

Owen was silent, and I felt his body shake slightly beneath me. I was horrified that I'd made him cry, but when I sat up I was surprised to find him smiling.

"You—you slapped him?" he asked between gasps. He was laughing in earnest now.

"Yes," I said, looking down and picking at a loose thread on the bedspread.

"He must have really pissed you off!"

"He did!"

Owen's face went serious for a moment, and he looked down at me with concern. "Are you okay? Did he upset you? Hurt you?"

"I'm fine. I told him about you," I added, hoping this would help Owen feel more secure.

He nodded, pulled me back into his arms, and switched off the lamp. His fingers ran through my hair soothingly for a moment, and when his breathing slowed, I knew he'd fallen asleep. For the second night in a row, I fell asleep in the arms of the man I loved, who meant everything to me, while thinking about the man who'd hurt me deeply enough to make me doubt everything.

⁂

I woke up the next morning to the sounds of Owen rustling around again. I opened my eyes and watched him packing clothes in his bag. It was nice to have a moment to observe without him knowing it. He was so masculine. The toned muscles in his back moved lithely as he picked up his boots and sat on the bed to put them on.

"Good morning, beautiful," he said, smiling when he saw me watching him.

"Morning. Do you *have* to leave today? Can't you stay a little longer?"

"It's only for a few days. I'll be back this weekend so we can look at some houses," he said, leaning down to kiss the top of my head.

"I'm going to miss you," I pouted.

Owen chuckled and bent down to put his boots on. I sat up and rubbed his back, trying to stay close until he had to leave.

"Okay, I better get going. I have to work this afternoon."

I got out of bed and followed him downstairs. "Please drive safely, and call me as soon as you get home." I kissed him on the lips and savored his taste.

"I will. I'll call you every night. Just enjoy being home and spending some time with your dad."

"I love you." I squeezed him tightly and tried to hold back tears. I knew it was stupid because he'd be back in a few days, but I'd really grown to depend on him.

"Love you more," he said, heading out the door.

I didn't follow him outside. I didn't want to watch him drive away. I walked slowly back up to my room and crawled into bed, pulling Owen's pillow close and inhaling his sweet scent. I groaned when my phone beeped loudly, but I reached across and grabbed it, smiling when I read the message.

I miss you already xxx

I smiled and held the phone to my chest. Five days. He would be back in five days. I couldn't wait.

Chapter Five
A Waltz Down Memory Lane

"What do you think of this one?" Owen asked, peering over the top of the newspaper.

"Describe it to me," I said through a mouthful of toast and peanut butter.

We sat at the dining table in my Dad's kitchen, eating breakfast and looking over the houses for rent in the newspaper. Owen had arrived about half an hour before. He'd left Boston before dawn so he could spend most of the day with me.

"Three bedrooms, two bathrooms, on Lindley Street, remodeled kitchen, and attached two-car garage."

"Sounds good." I took another bite of toast and brushed the fallen crumbs onto my plate. "I'll call to see if we can see it today with the others." I'd made several appointments for us during the week, but today's paper was adding to the list.

"Agreed," Owen said with a smile. "I need to have a shower, and then we can head out."

I picked up my cell and dialed the number listed in the paper.

Fifteen minutes later the appointment was made and Owen came down the stairs in jeans and a sweatshirt, looking sexy with his hair still a little wet.

"Let's go find our new home," he said, kissing me gently before smacking me on the ass and walking me out the door to the car. I held my hand out for the keys, but he raised an eyebrow at me stubbornly.

"You don't know your way around town. It makes sense for me to drive."

"Well, I'll never *learn* my way around if I don't drive myself. You can direct me." He got in and had started the car before I'd even opened the passenger door.

We drove in silence except for me telling him where to turn as I sulked about not being allowed to drive. Fairfield was such a small town that he practically found the way without my directions.

We pulled up in the driveway of the first house and stared at it.

"This is not where we live," I said bluntly, folding my arms over my chest.

"I agree wholeheartedly," he said, pulling back out of the driveway and driving us toward the next house on our list.

I tried not to be snobby, but when I thought about home, it did not include a rusted bathtub in the middle of the front yard and half the pickets ripped off the fence.

We pulled up to the curb outside the second house.

"What do you think?" Owen asked.

"Looks fine so far. Let's check inside."

Owen turned off the car, and we got out. We walked up the drive holding hands, our earlier disagreement forgotten. We approached the front door and were greeted by a bubbly young man who showed us into the entryway.

"You must be Charlotte and Owen," he said. "Nice to meet you."

He held out his hand to Owen and gave me a warm smile. "The house was built ten years ago and has only had one owner—"

"We don't need the spiel, thanks," Owen interrupted, clapping the guy on the shoulder. "But we'd like to have a look around if that's okay."

"Oh, sure," he said enthusiastically. "I'll be downstairs in the study when you've finished. Please let me know if you'd like an application."

We gave him a nod and walked through to the lovely kitchen with marble countertops and new appliances. Owen let out a whistle and turned to me with his eyebrows raised, clearly impressed.

"Before you get too attached, let's check out the bedrooms," I said with a laugh.

We walked down the hall, and I was immediately taken with the large master bedroom and bath, which had a Jacuzzi, his-and-hers sinks, and a spacious walk-in closet.

"I like it," Owen said.

"It does look good. What was the rent on this one?"

"I don't remember, and I left the ad in the car, but I wouldn't have suggested it if it was out of our price range. We can afford this," he said excitedly, taking my hands and pulling me into the bathroom. "We could soak in that Jacuzzi with champagne, and then move into the bedroom for…you know."

To emphasize his point he pressed his body against mine and ran his hands up my stomach, cupping my breasts and squeezing them through my shirt as he kissed my neck.

I laughed and teased that he had a one-track mind, but I stopped laughing when I was struck by déja vu. The memory flooded my mind so powerfully that I couldn't have stopped it if I tried…

…"What do you think?" I whispered as we walked into the bedroom.

The real estate agent had been shadowing us all over the open house, but we'd finally managed to lose him when an elderly couple came into view the house as well.

"I like it. You?" Cameron asked, his hand finding mine.

"I suppose I could live here," I joked coyly.

When we reached the landing at the top of the stairs, Cameron pulled me into the master bedroom and pressed me against the wall.

"We could be making love in this room every night for the rest of our lives," he whispered huskily in my ear as his hands roamed over my body.

"Mmm." It was hard to think coherently with him touching me so intimately.

His hand slipped between my legs and rubbed my sensitive flesh through my jeans. I moaned again, a little louder this time, and bit his shoulder to keep myself quiet. We heard footsteps on the stairs, and Cameron swore under his breath as he pulled away from me.

"How do you like it?" the real estate agent asked as he entered, followed by the elderly couple.

"We'll take it," Cameron said with a laugh before looking over at me for confirmation.

I nodded with a big, cheesy grin on my face. The elderly couple gave us a happy smile, as if they were looking at a younger version of themselves, and wandered on down the hall.

"I guess I mean we'd like to make an offer," Cameron said more seriously.

"Let me just go out to the car and get some information for you to look over. Then your agent can be in touch," the man said before disappearing.

"I can't believe we're going to own our own home!" I gushed excitedly.

"We already have our own home," he chuckled, nuzzling his nose just below my ear.

"We have a rental. This will be *our* place."

"Our place, huh? And we can do anything we want here?" He pulled his head back to look at me. I could see a glint in his eye, and I knew he was up to something.

"Yes," I said warily.

"Come on, quick!" Cameron grabbed my hand and pulled me into the master bath, locking the door behind us.

"What?"

"I have to have you," he said, breathing in my ear as his hands quickly undid the button fly of my jeans. Then he started on his own pants.

"Cam, we can't. He'll be back any second," I scolded, reaching down to pull my jeans up while he pouted at me.

He sighed. "You're right. I'm sorry. I just got carried away."

"No need to ever apologize for wanting to make love to me. I'll make it up to you when we get home." I trailed kisses down his jawline. "And when we move in, we can christen every room."

"I like the sound of that," he said, chuckling and kissing me again. "Let's get home then."

I fastened my fly before following him back out into the bedroom where the agent was now standing, giving us a very smug look. I could feel heat radiating from my cheeks and knew I must be as red as a tomato. Cameron had a silly smirk on his face, and he smoothed my hair, which must have been looking crazy.

"Here's some additional information for you," the agent said with a smile.

"Thank you." Cameron took the papers and grabbed my hand. "We'll have our agent be in touch with a formal offer."

The agent smirked at me again, and I began to feel uncomfortable with his stare.

"Let's go," Cameron whispered.

We ran down the stairs and out to the car…

I was pulled out of the memory by dizziness that almost knocked me over with its intensity.

"Are you okay? What happened?" Owen asked, panic in his voice.

"I'm fine. I just need some fresh air," I gasped.

He led me out onto the large balcony off the main bedroom. I took a few steady breaths and could feel my heart rate slowing and the panic subsiding. Owen rubbed my back and pressed soft kisses against my forehead.

"It was hot in there. If we decide to live here, we'll have to remember to leave some windows open."

"Do you like it?" I asked, my voice shaking slightly.

"I think it's perfect for us." He smiled and kissed my forehead again.

"I think so too. Let's not look at the other houses. I'm happy with this one."

"You're sure?" Owen asked, looking into my eyes.

"I'm sure," I insisted, giving him a reassuring smile.

I called the other rentals to cancel our appointments while Owen and the property manager talked about our application, going over the details and requirements for living in the house. We took the paperwork and promised to return it early the following week, along with a check for first and last months' rent.

As we drove home, I noticed Owen's excitement about finding a house seemed to have waned.

"What's wrong?" I asked, stroking the back of his neck.

"I'm just thinking about this dinner we're going to tonight," he grumbled.

I let my head fall back on the seat and folded my hands tightly in my lap. "Are you sure you're okay with it?" I asked nervously.

If Owen asked me to cancel the dinner, I would. But I dreaded having to call Ellen and tell her.

"Yes. Well, no. But I'll go for you."

"I love you, Owen Cooper," I whispered, kissing his cheek and stroking my thumb over his chin.

"I love you, Charlotte Barnes."

"Ooh, stop!" I shrieked suddenly. Owen slammed on the brakes, and the car behind us honked.

"What?" he asked, looking around.

"Sorry. I just wanted you to pull over so I could show you something," I said with a guilty look.

Owen's eyes widened, and he burst out laughing. "You never fail to surprise me." He shook his head as he spun the wheel to pull over to the curb. He stopped the car and turned in his seat to look at me.

"Well?"

"Come on!" I said, jumping out of the car and running across the street.

I could hear Owen's footsteps as he ran behind me, but I didn't stop until I'd reached the grass. I spun around just in time to see Owen catch up and look around curiously.

"This," I stated loudly, throwing my arms out, "was my high school."

Owen laughed. "It's nice," he said, obviously not impressed.

"Well, I know it's small, but this is where I spent my teen years. I had my first kiss, learned to love Shakespeare, and danced at my senior prom all right here at this school."

"Who was your prom date?" Owen asked, looking as if he didn't really want to know.

"Ethan Davis, the school quarterback."

"Not Cameron?" Owen asked, a little surprised.

"No, I didn't meet him until the year after graduation."

Owen smirked as he took my hand, and I led him around the school buildings.

"So did Ethan get lucky after prom?"

"Ewww, no! I caught him making out with Amanda Foster in the girls' bathroom."

Owen looked furious for a moment, and then sad. "So you were upset at your prom?" he asked, stroking my cheek tenderly.

"Well, at the time I was sad, but now I'm fine," I laughed, thinking back to that night and realizing what a lucky thing that betrayal had been. Without it, I wouldn't be here with the man I was going to love for the rest of my life.

We wandered further into the complex, and the gym came into view, looking exactly as I remembered it. We peeked inside an open door, finding streamers everywhere and decorations on the walls.

"I wonder what's going on," I said.

"There was a fundraiser dance last night," said a voice from inside.

I looked over to see the same janitor who'd worked at the school when I went there. He looked at me for a moment and smiled.

"You look familiar," he said, squinting.

"I was a student here. Do you mind if we come in?

"Sure, have a look around," he said jovially.

Owen smiled and pulled me into the gym. Once inside, I let go of his hand to look around. The decorations were all blue and silver, the same as they'd been for my prom all those years ago.

"Will you dance with me?" Owen asked, holding out his hand.

I giggled and accepted, feeling a rush of excitement as he twirled me around and held my waist tightly, waltzing me around the gym.

"Close your eyes," he whispered.

I obeyed and smiled when he hummed a slow tune for us to dance to. If I allowed myself to believe it, I felt like I was back at my prom. Only this time, Owen's strong arms around me made me feel content.

"Thank you," I breathed.

I sensed him moving closer before his lips softly touched mine. I leaned into his chest and moaned softly against his mouth.

"Ewwww... There are old people kissing in here," a girl's voice screeched, completely ruining the illusion.

Owen and I stopped dancing and looked over at a group of young girls staring at us, horrified. I could feel Owen's body quivering against mine, and I knew he was trying his best to hold in laughter.

"Sorry," I called as Owen and I made our way out of the gym and into the locker rooms at the back entrance.

Once we were safely in the girls' locker room, Owen looked around with awe.

"What is it?" I asked.

"This is the *girls'* locker room."

"Uh-huh," I replied, not really understanding.

He shook his head slightly and gave me a boyish grin. "Sorry. It's just a teenage fantasy of mine to be in here."

"Ah, and I'm sure in the fantasy there were lots of naked girls."

"Just one," he said huskily.

I squealed and giggled as I ran while he chased me around the room. When he finally caught up to me, he tickled my stomach before picking me up and spinning me around in his arms.

"What are you doing in here?" a stern woman's voice asked.

Owen and I turned around with guilty looks on our faces.

"Sorry, we were just leaving," Owen told her as we hurried out the door and back to the car. We laughed all the way back to Dad's house.

⁓⚬❦⚬⁓

We sat in the car, staring at the Harpers' house. As nervous as I was, I couldn't even imagine how Owen was feeling. I was terrified about being in the same room with my ex-in-laws, but thinking about Ellen and what she'd once meant to me helped steel my resolve. We could do this.

I unfastened my seat belt and reached over to run my fingers softly through Owen's hair. He turned and gave me a small smile, trying to be strong.

"Let's do this," he said, motivating himself as much as me.

I nodded, and we got out of the car. Owen took my hand as we walked to the front door. He knew I needed support, and I loved him for it.

"Are you okay?" he whispered.

I nodded. "You?"

He nodded back as we reached the door. We both took a deep breath, and I pressed the doorbell. I heard the chiming inside and footsteps approaching.

I squeezed Owen's hand as the door opened and a smiling Ellen appeared in the doorway.

"Charlotte!" she exclaimed happily, pulling me into a hug with my arm twisted awkwardly behind me since I was still holding Owen's hand. "And you must be Owen. It's lovely to meet you."

She hung our coats on the rack by the door, and we followed her to the living room.

Just like everything else in town, the house was almost exactly as I remembered it. There were a few new pieces of furniture added here and there, but everything was so familiar that I felt instantly at home, despite the stress of the situation. I had to resist the urge to kick my shoes off and lie down on the couch.

"Your house is lovely," Owen said. I squeezed his hand again, thanking him.

"Thank you. We like it," she said with a smile that didn't reach her eyes.

I was sure to Owen she seemed very pleasant, but I could see she was uncomfortable, and I wondered if this dinner was as hard for her as it was for Owen and me.

In the kitchen we found David stirring something on the stove with his back to us.

"Our guests have arrived," Ellen said as she walked around the counter and peeked into the oven, a delicious smell filling the room.

David turned and smiled warmly at us. My mouth hung open at the sight of him, and I had to consciously think *close mouth* so I wouldn't look like a fool.

I'd never noticed how much like his father Cameron actually was, and for a split second, I'd thought it was Cameron standing there. David's hair was streaked with gray, and his face had a few more lines than I remembered, but his features were almost identical to his son's.

"It's so wonderful to see you, sweetheart," he said as he came to hug me.

"You too, Dad," I replied automatically, freezing us both. "Um, sorry. I mean David."

He pulled back and held my shoulders, looking me over with sad eyes. "You look good, Charlotte…so grown up."

He released me and turned to Owen with his hand outstretched. "And you must be Owen. It's a pleasure to meet you."

"It's nice to meet you too, sir," Owen said, shaking David's hand.

"I hope you're taking good care of our girl here."

"I do my best," Owen said with an awkward smile.

"He does a great job." I slipped one arm around Owen's waist and rubbed his chest softly.

"Ah, well, good," David responded stiffly.

Ellen frantically stirred whatever was on the stove as we all stood in uncomfortable silence.

"Drinks!" she shrieked suddenly, making me jump. "David, would you get everyone a drink?"

"Vodka, lime, and soda, Charlotte?"

I nodded and smiled back. "You remembered!"

He gave a quick nod before turning to Owen. "Would you like a beer or a spirit? We also have wine."

"A beer is perfect, thanks," Owen said as we followed David into the living room.

Owen and I sat together on the loveseat under the window, and he casually threw his arm around my shoulders. David was behind the bar mixing drinks when Ellen appeared with a platter of nuts and cheeses.

"What would you like, dear?" David asked Ellen as she sat on the sofa opposite Owen and me.

"I'll have a glass of chardonnay," she said as she stared at Owen's hand on my shoulder.

"Here we go," David said, handing Owen a bottle of beer and me a short glass garnished with a wedge of lime.

He reached over the bar and collected the other two drinks before sitting next to Ellen. I took a sip and smiled. David mixed it in exactly the proportions I liked.

"So how did you two meet?" Ellen asked sharply. She couldn't seem to hide her disappointment about my new relationship. Tension filled the air, and I cleared my throat before I spoke.

"Owen pulled me over for speeding," I said with a nervous laugh.

"Are you a police officer?" Ellen asked, leaning forward in her seat slightly.

Owen nodded, and David let out a warm chuckle. "I bet Michael loves that!" he said before taking a long sip of his scotch.

"He does," Owen said, laughing along with him.

"So he showed up at my house one day and asked me out. I said no—several times, in fact—and then one night I came home late from work and Owen was standing outside my apartment in the pouring rain with a bunch of flowers. He'd been standing out there for hours, but he just waited for me." I rubbed Owen's thigh softly.

"I knew it would take a grand gesture to get her to notice me," Owen said with a shrug.

I relaxed a little. He seemed to be getting more comfortable.

Ellen and David looked at us with the same expression on each of their faces: a painted-on smile of politeness. It was obvious they weren't happy with the story of our romance. I wondered if they'd hoped Owen would be a horrible person.

I decided that for the comfort of the evening, and because I wanted to support Owen, I had to say something I was hoping could be left unsaid. I leaned forward and placed my drink on the coffee table.

"David, Ellen," I began, taking a deep breath. "I know this is an uncomfortable situation and we're all feeling slightly awkward, but I hope you can respect that I'm happy with Owen. I know it must've been painful for you to learn what happened between me and Cam, but the truth is that he hurt me."

I stopped and looked down at my lap, fidgeting with a loose thread on the hem of my shirt, and Owen rubbed my back soothingly. When I finally looked up again, I noticed David had shifted in his seat and he and Ellen now seemed confused.

"I fell apart, and I had to put myself back together again. Owen helped me do that. I think you can both see he's a wonderful man, and he loves me very much. Owen is in my life, and he's here to stay. We *are* getting married, and I'm very happy with my new life."

I stopped talking and picked up my drink, taking a long sip as I watched my ex-in-laws process my rant. Owen continued to rub soothing circles on my back while we waited for a response.

"Thank you for having the courage to say that, Charlotte," David said. "I think we were all avoiding the elephant in the room, and now I feel like we can talk openly about it. I'll be honest with you. This *is* hard for us, as I'm sure it is for you. You're a daughter to us and always will be, and I can honestly say we're happy you found someone who loves you as much as Owen obviously does. His presence in our home tonight is testament to that. We're so sorry Cam hurt you so badly that you felt broken. We obviously don't know the whole story about what happened back then. And I have to apologize to you, Owen, because what I'm about to say may be inappropriate, but I have to add that we wish things were different."

Ellen wiped a tear from her cheek and nodded solemnly.

"I can appreciate that, but things aren't different. I would love to have you both in my life again — I've missed you so much — but Owen is part of the package. You can't have me without him, and if that's not something you can accept, then we'll leave and not come back. No hard feelings."

I fought back tears. I now realized just how much I'd missed them and wanted them to be part of my life, even in some small way.

Ellen and David looked at each other and seemed to communicate silently. After a moment they turned back to me.

"Owen," Ellen said, turning to face him, "you are welcome here, and we apologize if we've made you feel uncomfortable at all."

Relief washed over me, and I smiled, turning to Owen.

"Thank you," he said. "I can see how important you are to Charlotte, and I wouldn't want her to lose you."

We sat in silence for a few moments, sipping our drinks. I didn't really know what to say after the big share session we'd just had. The silence was more comfortable now because everything was out in the open.

Just then we were saved by a high-pitched *ding* from the kitchen.

"Dinner's ready," Ellen exclaimed, sounding much more like the cheerful Ellen I remembered.

As we moved into the dining room, Ellen disappeared into the kitchen and David went to pour more drinks.

"Will you be okay if I leave you with David for a few minutes? I want to help Ellen serve the food," I whispered in Owen's ear.

"I'll be fine," he said softly. I squeezed his hand before walking into the kitchen.

"What can I do to help?"

"You can come over here at let me look at you," Ellen said, chuckling as she held her arms out.

I moved around the counter and stood in front of her, doing a little spin.

"You look lovely. So grown up!" She looked solemn for a moment before I saw resolve in her eyes. "Can I ask you something personal, dear?"

"Yes," I replied nervously.

"What you said in there—about being broken and Cam leaving you to pick up the pieces—what did you mean by that?"

"What has Cam told you about what happened?"

"Not a lot."

I paused again before deciding to forge ahead. "He cheated on me. With Lucy."

"Lucy Pearson?"

I nodded and tried to hold back the tears I could feel building. "And I left town because a few weeks after I found out about the affair, I saw them kissing in the grocery store, and it was too much for me. I knew I couldn't stay here and see them together all over town."

Ellen nodded, her sad look replaced by one of anger. She hugged me but didn't say anything right away. "I'm very sorry you had to go through that," she said finally. "We knew Cam and Lucy dated after you broke up, but we never realized she was the reason for your separation."

"Why did you think I left?"

"We didn't know. You wouldn't talk to us after you moved out, and Cam had nothing to say either. After we realized you were completely gone, we asked Cam again what had happened, but he still refused to talk about it. He was in such a bad state that we didn't want to push him. I even cornered your father in the hardware store one day, but all he'd say was that you'd built yourself a new life and we all had to move on. It's been hard—losing you and not even knowing why," she said, her voice almost a whisper.

I nodded and wiped my eyes. "I wouldn't have left without a good reason."

She nodded sadly and clasped her hand in mine. "Don't you worry. I'll see that David fires her first thing Monday morning."

"Fires who?"

"Lucy," she replied, squeezing my hand. "She works for David. But not for long."

I opened my mouth to say something, but instead stayed silent as she led me back into the dining room. I sat next to Owen, but Ellen remained in the doorway and folded her arms over her chest.

"David, can you help me in the kitchen for a moment?" she said

"Yes, dear," David said, following her out.

"How're you doing?" Owen asked, stroking my hand.

"I'm fine."

He looked at me skeptically.

"I mean, it's been an emotional night, but I'm holding up."

Ellen and David appeared in the doorway, the strained expressions from the beginning of the evening back on their faces.

"I made your favorite, Charlotte," Ellen said as she placed a large roasted chicken in front of us.

"It looks lovely," I said, taking a big sniff of the warm aroma coming from the tray.

David placed a bread basket and bowl of salad on the table silently and took his seat while Ellen sliced the chicken.

"Please help yourselves," she said with a curt smile.

I took some salad and a roll, and just as I was reaching for the plate of chicken, the sound of keys rattling came from the entryway. Ellen and David looked at each other curiously as we heard the front door open and footsteps come down the hall.

"Hey, Mom! Something smells great in here," Cameron's voice called out.

I froze, staring at Ellen with narrowed eyes. Had she planned this?

Chapter Six
His Silent Words

Everyone at the dinner table sat frozen. Ellen and David stared at me, and Owen looked determinedly at his plate, his hands balled tightly at his sides and his jaw clenched. I glared at Ellen through narrowed eyes. She'd promised me Cameron wouldn't be here tonight.

My whole body was rigid as I analyzed Ellen's expression. Had she planned on Cameron showing up? Would she really invite him knowing Owen would be sitting right here? After I'd specifically asked her not to? I refused to believe Ellen would do something so cruel and disrespectful. The shock on her face *seemed* genuine enough, but I wasn't sure if I trusted my own judgment.

Cameron's footsteps grew closer, and I saw his shadow move past the doorway as he walked into the kitchen.

"Where are you?" he called. He appeared in the doorway a second later. His eyes widened as they took in the scene in front of him, and as realization set in, his features hardened into anger.

"What the hell is *he* doing here?" Cameron yelled, pointing at Owen.

"Cam, calm down," his father warned.

Cameron's eyes flashed, but he backed down. His gaze met mine, and it burned with an emotion I couldn't place. I tore my eyes from his and looked at Owen. I reached over to take his hand and squeezed it, not sure if I was reassuring him or myself. Either way, he squeezed back firmly, and I felt instantly better.

"Cam, dear," Ellen said very calmly, "we have guests right now, and I think you should leave."

Cameron's jaw dropped. "Are you seriously kicking me out?"

"It's not appropriate for you to be here now," Ellen said, anger seeping into her voice.

"I can't fucking believe this!" Cameron exclaimed, throwing his arms up in the air.

"Cameron," David said again, more firmly this time. He stood up, his cutlery clanking loudly against his plate.

The pain on Cameron's face was gut-wrenching, and I felt my heart soften a little, in spite of my anger. Owen's hand in mine kept me grounded, anchored to my seat.

He wasn't getting anywhere with his parents, so Cameron turned his attention to me. "Charlotte, can I speak to you in the living room?" he asked gently, all the anger gone from his voice.

I couldn't help the gush of breath I exhaled at his words. "There's nothing to say, Cameron," I said softly, looking down at my lap, my heart racing.

I heard him sigh with frustration. "There's *a lot* to say!"

Owen pulled his hand from mine and was on his feet, his chair skidding backward.

"You are going to back off!" he said firmly in his "police" voice.

"Just butt out," Cameron sneered back. "This is between me and my wife." His voice held so much hatred that if I hadn't seen his mouth moving, I wouldn't have believed the words came from him.

"She's not your wife anymore! Charlotte is *my* fiancée."

"Okay, boys, let's calm down," David said firmly, holding his hands up.

Cameron folded his arms over his chest and glared at Owen. I could feel the tension building, and it made me very nervous. I wasn't sure what I'd do if a fight broke out.

"Cam, please come with me." Ellen stood stiffly, throwing her napkin on the table and heading out of the room. Cameron looked at me and begged silently with his eyes. I turned away, but watched out of the corner of my eye as he turned and followed his mother.

"Charlotte, Owen, I'm so sorry for this. I promise you Ellen and I had no idea Cameron was going to show up tonight," David said, sitting back down and taking a sip of his drink.

"Do you want to leave?" I asked Owen.

Owen sighed and sat facing me in his seat. "It's important for you to be here."

But looking in his eyes, I could see how stressful this was for him. As angry as I was that Cameron was here, and as much as I wanted to lash out at him — or stay just to prove he couldn't make me leave — Owen was my priority now. I turned to David and gave him a weak smile.

"David — " I began, but he held his hand up to stop me.

"I understand, sweetheart. I really am sorry for this."

We all stood up, and David held his arms out to me just as he had at the beginning of the evening. I melted into his chest as they wrapped around me. He squeezed tightly and kissed my cheek.

"It was so good to see you. Please don't let tonight stop you from keeping in contact," he said before releasing me to shake Owen's hand.

I nodded, found Owen's hand, and held it tightly as we moved toward the door. Ellen appeared at the top of the stairs and looked down at us with red eyes. She came quickly down the stairs to give me a hug.

"You're not leaving, are you?" she asked, sniffling.

"I'm sorry. I hope you understand," I said. "Thank you so much for the invitation.

She nodded as David came over and put a comforting arm around her shoulders.

As I turned to leave, I noticed Cameron walking slowly down the stairs. I met his gaze, and his eyes burned into mine until he took the last step and stopped in the entryway with the rest of us.

My stomach did a weird flip-flop, and it was as if everyone but Cameron and I disappeared as we stared at each other. I didn't know why he could still do that to me, but he could. Then Owen's arm swung around my shoulder possessively, breaking me out of the spell and pulling me toward the door.

I looked back over my shoulder and saw Cameron gripping the banister so tightly his knuckles were white. He looked absolutely heartbroken. I reminded myself that I didn't know Cameron anymore, and maybe I never had.

Owen opened the front door and ushered me outside. I turned back to say goodbye to Ellen and David and gave Cameron one last look. He mouthed something to me before Owen tugged on my hand, pulling me toward the car.

Owen opened the car door, and I sat down. I fastened my seatbelt with my mind still in the living room watching Cameron's lips form those words. I must have read him wrong. He couldn't have said what I thought he did.

Owen pulled out of the driveway, then looked over at me with a smile. "Thank you, but we didn't have to leave," he said, patting my thigh gently.

"Yes, we did. I'm sorry he upset you," I replied, rubbing my thumb over the back of his hand.

"I just didn't like the way he was speaking to you."

"I'm sorry about David and Ellen too."

"It's okay." He shook his head. "I didn't want to like them—I had myself convinced tonight was going to be torturous. But apart from the unexpected guest, it was a nice night once we cleared the air. I think that was important for you."

I nodded, only half-listening to what he was saying. My mind was still on the words Cameron had mouthed and the pained look on his face. Why was I so sympathetic to him? He'd broken my heart and crushed my spirit, yet one sad, puppy-dog look and all my defenses came crashing down.

"Earth to Charlotte," Owen said.

"Huh?"

"I asked if you wanted to pick up some food since we didn't get to eat our dinner," he repeated.

"Oh, um, I'm not really hungry."

"Are you okay?"

"Yes…well, tonight was difficult, but I'm fine."

"Let's go home and talk," he suggested, glancing over at me before returning his eyes to the road.

I thought for a moment and decided going home was a bad idea. The walls were thin, and I didn't want to risk my dad hearing our conversation.

"Actually, I know somewhere where we can go and talk in private," I countered. "I'd love to show it to you."

I knew I'd feel relaxed there, and I hoped the sounds of the water would keep our talk peaceful. I gave Owen directions, and as we got closer, I felt myself calming. The town looked different in the dark than it did during the day. The usual open windows and doorways were all closed up, and although it wasn't really late, the streets were practically empty. Owen stopped the car at the end of the street, and we walked together down to the water.

"This is amazing!" he said as he took in the view.

I flicked my hair out of my eyes as the sea air blew it around my head. The full moon reflected brightly off the water and bounced up onto the shore, giving us enough light to navigate safely over the grass to the benches near the water.

Owen's hand wrapped around mine, and we kicked off our shoes. The grass was cool between my toes, and I took a deep breath of the fresh, salty air.

"Where shall we sit?" I asked.

"I don't know. This is your spot," Owen said, turning to me.

I was glad he appeared calmer now too, but I couldn't help but wonder how he'd feel after we talked. I knew what I had to say might upset him.

We held hands and smiled as we sat cross-legged on a bench, facing each other.

"Your special place is lovely. Thank you for sharing it with me."

"I want to share everything about my life with you," I said, smiling back at him.

Owen squeezed my hand and nodded. I slid off the bench, lying on the grass with my knees bent. Owen joined me, and we looked up at the moon and stars. One thing Fairfield had over Boston was a clear night sky—without all the city lights.

"So…" Owen started.

"So…" I echoed before letting out a long breath and readying myself for the conversation. Owen always encouraged us to have open communication in our relationship, and even though we'd been together almost three years, we'd had very few fights. We usually talked things out before they got to that point. That was a major difference between my relationship with Owen and the one I'd had with Cameron. Cam and I very rarely discussed issues as they came up, so nothing was ever resolved. I knew I could talk to Owen about this, but I was still nervous.

"How did you feel when Cameron showed up tonight? Exactly?" I asked. I thought I should understand how Owen felt before I started to talk.

"Honestly, it worried me. I can see that he still loves you, and even though I trust you and believe that you love me, that makes me nervous."

Hearing Owen say he could tell Cameron still loved me was like having a light bulb switch on. Suddenly I couldn't *not* see what was right in front of me: Cameron's love.

"How did *you* feel when Cameron showed up tonight?" he prompted after I didn't say anything.

"At first I felt angry. I wasn't sure if Ellen had arranged for him to be there, but once I could see how genuinely surprised she and David were, I knew it was a coincidence," I said, turning back to face him again. Taking a deep breath, I elaborated. "I felt so many things — shock, pain, worry…curiosity."

"Can you tell me why you were feeling those things?" Owen asked, gently brushing some hair off my forehead.

I thought for a moment. I had so many thoughts running through my head it was hard to keep them all straight. "I felt shock because I didn't expect him to be there. I was just starting to relax and enjoy the night. I felt pain because he always reminds me of my past with him and what he did to me. It was like a slap in the face, like it had all just happened —"

"I'm sorry, baby," Owen whispered, leaning over to kiss the tip of my nose and run his hand softly through my hair. He still looked tense, but he was comforting me, like he always did.

"I was worried about you. I knew Cameron being there must have been hard for you, and I was concerned you'd be angry with me for not just yelling at him to get out."

"Did you want to yell at him?" Owen asked with a chuckle.

"Part of me did — and scream at him and kick him in the shins."

"That would be the same part that slapped him last week?"

"Yes." I gave him a sheepish smile.

"I love that part of you," he replied, winking and returning my smile. "And the curiosity?"

"The curiosity… Well, that's because I never really spoke to him about what happened." I sighed loudly. "And I suppose there's a part of me that's curious to hear what he has to say."

"Why didn't you ever talk to him? I can't believe you'd just walk away without an explanation."

"I didn't want to hear it," I said, pulling blade after blade of grass. "There was nothing he could have said that would change what he did. I didn't want to hear his explanations or excuses, and I didn't want to be near him, so I just left."

Owen was silent, the light-heartedness of our earlier moment gone. I watched him run his fingers through the grass softly, and after a long silence he looked me directly in the eye.

"Charlotte, are you over Cameron?" he asked, a slight tremor in his voice.

"I am," I said firmly. "I'm just curious about what he has to say."

We lay in silence for a moment, staring into each other's eyes, and I could feel anxiety rising in my throat. For the first time in our relationship, I'd lied to Owen. I'd just told him I was over Cameron, but I knew it wasn't true.

If he'd asked me that question before we came back to Fairfield, I would've given the same answer — but it would've been the truth. However, seeing Cameron at the grocery store, and then again tonight, and feeling myself instinctively react to him had brought back all the emotions I thought I'd buried a long time ago. I was wrong when I thought I'd left it all behind. Now I didn't know how I felt.

Except I did know I was in love with Owen. My feelings for him hadn't changed at all, and that was a relief. It confirmed for me that Owen wasn't second best — my love for him was real.

It's just that I'd thought allowing someone else into my heart meant I'd let go of Cameron and moved on. But now I wasn't sure whether Cameron had ever left it.

"What if he says he loves you and wants you back?" Owen asked.

"Are you worried about that?"

"Very much," he said, a sad look crossing his face.

I curled my leg over his hip and scooted as close to his body as I could. I rested my face next to his so our noses were touching.

"I love you. I probably don't tell you enough, but I love you."

The corners of his mouth turned up, and he nodded. "I do know that, but thank you for saying it," he whispered before softly pressing his lips to mine.

I allowed myself to melt into him, but I couldn't shake the image of Cameron at his parents' house this evening. I pulled away and sat up, hugging my knees to my chest.

"Are you ready to head home?" I asked, hoping he'd agree so we wouldn't have to talk about this any more.

"Sure." He stood and held out his hand to help me up. He pulled me effortlessly to my feet and draped his arm over my shoulders as we walked back to the car.

We drove home in silence. I was lost in my thoughts, and Owen knew that when I needed to think, he wouldn't get much conversation from me. He'd learned just to let me be. He parked in the driveway at my dad's, and as we walked up the steps to the house, Owen slipped his hand into mine and stroked his thumb over the back of my hand.

I smiled. Owen always knew how to reassure me without words. He could sense when I was upset or stressed and knew the right way to comfort me with a smile or a gentle touch.

The house was dark, and once inside, we walked quickly and quietly up the stairs so we didn't disturb my dad.

"I'm going to have a quick shower," Owen said. He kissed my forehead and disappeared into the bathroom.

I went into the bedroom, changed into my pajamas, and climbed into bed. I thought back over the past few hours, and I felt myself becoming angry. I couldn't believe how Cameron had behaved. I'd never seen him so angry, and it unnerved me. Why did he even care if I was with Owen? He'd decided long ago he didn't want *me* anymore. Hadn't he? I still couldn't believe he'd mouthed those words to me as we left. And I never would've guessed his silent words could affect me so much.

In my mind I saw his lips again and watched as he mouthed *"I still love you."*

I sighed and rolled onto my side, cuddling the spare pillow to my chest. The bedroom door opened, and Owen walked in wearing a towel wrapped around his waist.

"Hey," he said with a smile.

"Hey yourself," I said, pushing the thoughts of Cameron away.

He had a wicked glint in his eye, and I knew immediately what he was thinking. He stalked toward the bed like he was hunting me and dropped the towel before climbing onto the bed on his hands and knees.

"What are you doing?" I giggled, squirming as he laid his body on top of mine and kissed my neck.

"Claiming what's mine," he growled.

He worked his way up my throat to my mouth, and I parted my lips for him. Our tongues moved together for a moment, but I froze when I heard a creak on the stairs. Suddenly I was painfully aware of my father in the next room. I pressed my hand to Owen's bare chest, pushing him off me.

"Owen."

"Mm-hmm?" Undeterred, he reached down to unbutton my top.

"Can we…not?"

He looked confused before lying down next to me with a disappointed look on his face. I almost reconsidered, but the ick factor was just too strong.

"Why?" he asked, running his fingers through my hair splayed out on the pillow.

"It's not that I don't want to—you know I do. It's just…well, my dad is in the next room."

Owen chuckled and pulled me into his arms. "You're twenty-eight years old, Char. I think Michael knows you've had sex," he said, laughing.

"I know that. It's just…well…what if he heard us?" I asked, mortified.

Owen kissed me lightly and climbed under the blanket, snuggling against me once he was settled.

"Okay, but when we get our own place, we're going to do it every single night for a month."

"Deal." I tilted my head back and pressed my lips to his.

"I love you," I whispered.

"Love you more," he replied.

Owen often replied to my declarations of love that way, and it made me wonder if it was true. Did he love me more than I loved him? I wasn't sure.

"Goodnight, baby," he said, kissing the top of my head and reaching over to switch off the bedside lamp.

"Goodnight," I whispered as I snuggled into his chest.

⁕

I walked along a beach. The wind was warm, which was unusual for this time of year, but it was so nice I didn't question it. The sun shone in a bright purple sky, and the white sand was fluffy beneath my bare feet, as if I walked on clouds.

"I love you," a voice whispered. I looked over to find Owen walking next to me.

I smiled at him and looked down. His fingers were entwined with mine, but I didn't remember him taking my hand.

"Isn't it beautiful?" I asked him, dropping his hand and spinning around to take in the view.

Owen nodded and watched me twirling in the sand.

"Look how beautiful the water is," I said, running to the shoreline.

The water lapped at the white sand, and the sun's rays bounced off the surface, shooting tiny rainbows through the air.

"Don't go near the water," Owen called in an alarmed voice.

"But it's so pretty. I'll just walk in the shallows," I assured him, taking a step forward and allowing the waves to lap at my feet. "The water is warm!"

"Charlotte, please come back up here with me where it's safe!" Owen begged, tears streaming down his face.

I turned to look at him, confused by his reaction, but it appeared to be very important to him that I stay out of the water, so I lifted my foot to walk back onto the dry sand.

Suddenly, the sky went dark, storm clouds swirled overhead, and the water turned ice cold. It swelled around my feet, and I wasn't able to step up onto the sand.

"Help me," I called to Owen.

But he just looked at me sadly and shook his head.

"I warned you," he whispered.

The water rose quickly around me, and I shook from fear and cold. The icy water was now up to my waist.

"Owen, please! I need you!" I called, holding my arms out, begging him to save me.

"I love you," he called sadly, dropping a single violet-colored rose in the sand.

"Owen!"

The water moved toward my shoulders, and my feet no longer touched the bottom. The current threw me around, and I had no control. My legs thrashed wildly beneath me, but I couldn't swim to shore. Owen was just a small dot on the horizon now.

The freezing, salty water sucked me under, and I held my breath to stop it from flooding my lungs. I swam fiercely, and my head broke the surface. I looked frantically for Owen, but he was gone.

The current pulled me under again, and I could feel myself sinking, no matter how hard I tried to kick back to the surface. My lungs were burning and in desperate need of oxygen. I held my breath as long as I could, but the burning was too much. My lips parted, and icy water rushed into my lungs.

I woke suddenly and gasped for breath before I realized my lungs weren't filling with ocean water, and I was safely tucked into bed. Owen still slept soundly next to me. I shifted to get into a more comfortable position and lay on my back, looking up at the ceiling, the dream still fresh in my mind.

What did it mean? Why hadn't Owen tried to save me? I looked at his sleeping form next to me. He was so peaceful—his eyelashes fluttering slightly and his chest rising and falling rhythmically.

I traced his stubbly jawline with my fingers, allowing them to run softly over his lips and then down his throat. He sighed, and his arm came around me, pulling me against his body, our legs entwining. I closed my eyes as I lay against his chest and allowed myself to fall back to sleep.

CLICK CLICK CLICK

I opened my eyes and looked around the room, confused. I could hear Owen's deep breathing next to me, and I relaxed slightly. I snuggled into his side, thinking the noise must have been an insect outside or the creaking of the loose floorboard on the staircase.

CLICK CLICK

Okay, that was definitely a noise. I rolled out of Owen's arms and sat up as quietly as I could. While I looked over my shoulder to make sure he wasn't waking up, I swung my legs over the side of the bed and stood. Owen rolled over and clutched my pillow to his chest, burying his face in the softness.

CLICK CLICK CLICK CLICK

The noise seemed to be coming from the window, and I walked over slowly to see if there was a branch tapping the glass. Just as I reached the window another *CLICK* sounded, and I saw a small object hit the glass.

I looked out and saw a single violet-colored rose on the lawn, directly below my window. My breath stilled in my throat as suddenly it all seemed familiar—the sound, the rose…

…CLICK CLICK

I threw the blankets off and grabbed my robe, tying it on as I rushed over to the window. I pulled it open and stuck my head out into the cool night air. I smiled when I saw, directly below my window on the lawn, a single violet-colored rose.

"Cam?" I whispered into the night, trying not to wake my parents who were asleep in the next room.

He stepped out from behind a tree with a bunch of roses, which he held up in the air as if presenting them to me.

My heart beat frantically in my chest at the sight of him, just as it did every time he was near me. Seeing him standing with a bunch of roses gave me hope that he might like me as much as I liked him. I'd been hoping for weeks that our friendship might progress into something more intimate, but every time I thought he was about to kiss me, he'd pull back. I'd been starting to lose hope — until now.

"I'll come down," I whispered, a joyous grin breaking over my face.

I couldn't believe I was so happy about Cameron sneaking over. We'd met a few weeks earlier in a coffee shop in Hartford when we were forced to share a table because it was so busy. We'd done the polite chit-chat thing and discovered we both lived in Fairfield. His family had moved a few months before, and even though he was twenty-one and could have stayed in San Diego alone, he'd decided to move with them.

We'd agreed to see each other again for coffee the following week, and we got along very well. Being with Cameron was easy, and I found myself telling him things I'd never shared with anyone. I fell for him quickly and had been in a state of near-constant happiness since we started seeing each other daily.

I was almost a year out of high school and hadn't really found any direction in my life. My mother was pressuring me to start college, and my father was trying to convince me to go to the police academy. College had sounded like a pretty good idea until I found Cameron, but now the thought of leaving Fairfield for four years was unbearable.

I opened my bedroom door as quietly as I could. It made a slight creaking sound when I had it about half open, so I held it steady and squeezed myself through the gap without opening it any further. Tiptoeing down the stairs, I brushed my fingers through my hair and tried to make it look neat before opening the front door and slipping outside.

Cameron stood on the steps with a big grin to match the one on my face.

"What are you doing here?"

"I had to tell you something," he said, taking a few steps toward me and handing me the roses. Their sweet scent floated up around me, and I breathed it in deeply.

"What is it?" I took a step closer so we were only a few inches apart.

Cameron looked down into my eyes and cupped my face in his hands. A shiver ran down my spine as I stared up at him, completely mesmerized.

"I…um, I think I love you. Well, I know I do." He took a deep breath. "I love you, Charlotte," he finished with a goofy smile.

I stared up into his beautiful face, stunned. I'd never dreamed he might be feeling the same way.

"I love you, Cameron."

His hands fell from my face and wrapped around my waist, pulling me to him. I could feel his warm breath on my cheek. We gazed into each other's eyes as his lips moved achingly slowly toward mine.

"I want to kiss you," he said breathlessly, turning his face slightly so our noses wouldn't bump. His lips stopped only an inch from mine.

I nodded eagerly, and my eyes fluttered closed just as his soft lips pressed against mine. My whole body melted into his, and my legs turned to jelly. If his arms hadn't been holding me so tightly, I knew I would've fallen over. Our mouths moved together hungrily, and when my lips parted slightly, I felt his warm tongue moving across my bottom lip. As it slipped inside my mouth, he let out a low moan, and I let the roses drop to wrap my arms around his neck, weaving my hands into his hair and pulling his face as close to mine as possible.

I'd kissed boys before, but I'd never experienced anything like this. It was as if we were communicating, expressing ourselves more clearly than we could with words.

When we finally broke apart, he peppered tiny kisses on my lips, my cheeks, and my eyelids before pulling away completely.

"Does this mean we're going steady now?" he joked…

I stared down at the rose, knowing it could only mean one thing: Cameron was outside. I felt anxious anticipation shiver up my spine as I opened the window.

"Cam?" I whispered as quietly as I could so as not to wake Owen.

He stepped out from behind the tree and gave me a small wave. He appeared to be nervous. His shoulders were hunched, and he wasn't making eye contact.

"What are you doing here?" I hissed angrily.

"I need to talk to you."

"No. Just go away. You'll wake up my father."

"Please, Char, two minutes," he begged.

I didn't know what to do. I could go down there and talk to him or I could close the window, go back to bed, and risk him knocking on the door and waking everybody up, which would make the whole situation much worse.

With a sigh, I decided I should go talk to him, if only to tell him to leave and not come back. But I was pretty sure that wasn't what I'd say. For some reason, whether I wanted to admit it or not, I longed for Cameron's company. I shook my head to focus and pictured the huge scene that would play out if Cam woke up Owen and my dad.

I grabbed some shoes and a coat and tiptoed to the bedroom door. I opened it as quietly as I could, and when it started to creak, I squished myself through just as I'd done the last time Cameron left a rose under my window.

I tiptoed down the stairs and stood in the hallway for a moment, preparing myself. Then I put on my shoes and coat, I opened the door, and walked outside. Cameron stood on the steps.

Folding my arms over my chest like a protective barrier, I let out a sigh. "What are you doing here?"

"I need to tell you something. Will you come for a walk with me?"

I thought about it for a moment and nodded. If I yelled at him, which was highly probable, I didn't want to wake up Owen and my dad.

"A short walk around the block," I agreed harshly, pushing past him onto the lawn and down the driveway. I didn't wait for him, but he soon fell into step next to me.

"What do you want to say?" I asked, my arms still folded over my chest.

"I wanted to tell you how sorry I am for ruining your dinner tonight. I honestly didn't know you'd be there, and I also didn't mean to be so rude to your boyfriend."

"Fiancé," I corrected.

"Excuse me?"

"You called Owen my boyfriend. He's my fiancé."

Cameron nodded and looked down at his feet. "Right, sorry. I just didn't want you to think I went there on purpose. When I saw him sitting there next to you in my parents' home, like he was part of the family, I just lost my mind a little. I truly am sorry."

I nodded as we turned the corner and walked toward the small park at the end of the street. I still felt so much anger toward him, but I also felt sympathy. I could remember exactly how it felt to see Cameron and Lucy together, so I knew how hard it must have been to see me with Owen.

"I'm sorry I slapped you."

Cameron rubbed his cheek and smiled. "I deserved it. That and a lot more."

We walked into the park in silence, and I sat on one of the swings, slowly moving back and forth with my feet still on the ground.

"Are you happy, Charlotte?" Cameron asked. He stood in front of me with his hands in his pockets.

"I really am. I wasn't for a long, long time. But I'm finally doing okay."

"Only okay?" he asked, taking a step toward me and placing his hands on the chains on either side of my head.

I pushed the swing back and ducked out from under him. I was not at all comfortable being that close.

"I'm great." I plastered a smile on my face that I didn't really feel.

Cameron looked down at his shoes, but I could see he was smiling.

"I'm really glad," he whispered. "I want you to be happy."

An uncomfortable feeling washed over me, and I looked around for something to do so I wouldn't be standing there staring at him. I moved over to the monkey bars and started to swing across. Once I made it to the other end, I dropped down into the sand and found Cameron watching me with a smile.

"I've missed you," he said simply.

I looked at him. I didn't look for the man he was when I fell in love with him or the man who'd shattered me. I saw him as the man he was today, and I realized I'd missed him too. I missed the ease of my life when I was with him, how carefree and happy everything seemed. I missed when he was the last person I'd see before I fell asleep every night and the first person I'd see every morning

In that moment, I didn't want to say something that would hurt him. Right now we were Cameron and Charlotte. The past didn't matter.

"I've missed you too," I said softly, meeting his gaze.

His eyes burned into mine, and for the first time since we started our walk, the sadness was gone, and he looked like he had some hope. But that hope in his eyes terrified me, and I wondered if it'd been a mistake to meet him tonight.

"I better get home," I said, turning to walk out of the park. Cameron jogged after me.

"Let me walk you back," he said softly, standing a little closer to me than I found comfortable.

"No, I'm fine. Thank you for your apology. It's accepted. Goodbye, Cam."

I jogged down the street and around the corner. I didn't stop until I was safely inside the house. Then I slumped against the inside of the door, sliding all the way to the floor.

My fingers ran through my hair and gripped it tightly in frustration. What was I thinking? Did I really tell Cameron I'd missed him and talk to him like we were friends? As if nothing happened?

I banged my head back against the door. I'd been back in Fairfield for only a week and already Cameron had entwined himself in my life. I knew it wasn't a good idea to come back. In the morning I'd talk to Owen about living in Hartford, I decided. We'd still be close to my dad, it would be way more convenient for Owen's work, and I wouldn't have Cameron in my face every day.

This decision made, I felt much calmer as I stood and quietly went back upstairs. I crept silently into my room and discarded my shoes and coat. I climbed back into bed and Owen rolled toward me, spooning me from behind.

Chapter Seven

Everything and Nothing

"I didn't hear you kids come in last night, how was your dinner?" Dad asked, putting a forkful of eggs into his mouth.

Owen coughed and spat toast crumbs all over the table.

"It was fine," I replied hesitantly.

"David and Ellen are very nice people," Owen said stiffly, brushing crumbs off the table around his plate.

"I'm glad. To be honest with you, I was worried it might be an awkward night." Dad chuckled. He finished his eggs and stood to rinse his plate in the sink. "See ya tonight, kiddo."

"See ya, Dad," I called as he ruffled my hair and disappeared out the front door.

Owen and I finished our food without speaking. I wasn't sure how to broach the subject of living in Hartford with him, or if I should be honest about my reasons.

"Can I talk to you a second?" I asked as Owen stood up.

"Sure." He sat back down and reached his arm across the table to stroke my hand. "What's on your mind?"

"I was thinking…it doesn't seem right for you to have to drive an hour to work every day. Why don't we just live in Hartford? We're still close enough to Fairfield that we can visit my dad whenever we like, but it will be more convenient."

"I've already told you that I don't mind the drive. Fairfield has always been your home, and I want you to be happy."

"I'll *be* happy in Hartford. Fairfield used to be my home, but I left and moved on with my life. I don't think I belong here anymore." I was going to try as hard as I could to explain this without dragging Cameron into it. I didn't see any point in making Owen feel insecure when there was nothing for him to worry about.

"I don't know—we already put the application in on that house," Owen mused.

"I know, but we can withdraw it and look for a place in Hartford. Please just think about it?" I asked coyly, raising the tone of my voice slightly and looking up at him through my eyelashes. I knew that was a low thing to do, but I hoped his sexual frustration would play in my favor.

"I guess it wouldn't hurt to look. The sooner we get our own place, the better."

"Great! I know this will be much better for us," I told him cheerfully. I was sure a one-hour buffer was all I needed to stop thinking about Cameron.

Owen and I spent the day together, lazing on the couch and watching some of Dad's old black-and-white movies. I groaned when Owen dug out the home movies but allowed him to watch as a much younger version of me danced across the screen at my school recital, unwrapped Christmas and birthday presents, and then graduated from high school. I didn't even realize my dad had kept all these, but it was nice to know he had a part of me with him.

Just after Dad came home from work, Owen set off on his drive back to Boston. He had to be back at work the following morning. I couldn't wait for the next three weeks to be over so he could be with me all the time.

⁂

My hands gripped the steering wheel as the car swerved over the road. I tried to hold the wheel steady, but it wasn't obeying. Quickly I pulled over to the side of the road. Rain poured down and water sprayed up on either side of the car as I stopped at the curb and turned off the engine.

I got out of the car and was drenched within seconds as I walked all the way around it to find a flat tire.

"Shit," I swore under my breath.

I opened the trunk and stared at the spare and the tire iron. How the hell was I supposed to change the tire? I'd never done it before and didn't even know where to start.

I jumped back in the car and pulled out my cell phone to dial my dad's work number.

"Fairfield Police Department, how my I direct your call?" the nasally female voice asked.

"Hey, Margie, it's Charlotte. Is my dad around?"

"Hey, sugar, he's out on a call, but I can take a message."

"Can you please ask him to call me on my cell when he gets back? It's important."

"Sure thing, honey."

As I ended the call, my car shook with the force of the wind blowing off a passing vehicle. I groaned, having no idea what I was going to do. My dad might not call back for hours. Then another car came up the highway, slowed down, and pulled over onto the shoulder just in front of me.

The car door opened and a man climbed out, holding his jacket over his head. He ran up to my window and knocked, so I rolled it down. With the rain-spattered glass out of the way, I realized who it was.

"Cam?"

He peered through the window at me. "Charlotte," he said with a smile.

"What are you doing out here?"

"I'm driving to Hartford for a dental conference. What about you?"

"I was driving to Hartford to look…for a house…" I trailed off.

His smile fell briefly, but it was firmly back in place almost before I could register it had been gone. "You're not staying in Fairfield?"

"Owen and I were thinking of moving to Fairfield, but we're also looking in Hartford."

"Do you need a hand?"

"I'm all right. I just have a flat."

"Let me have a look," he said, turning to examine my tires.

I got out of my car and ran through the puddles to stand by him while he examined the damage.

"You don't have to help. My dad will probably call me back and be here soon."

"Well, I don't think I can change the tire with this much water on the road anyway, so why don't I take you home, and then your dad can change the tire for you later tonight?"

I looked at the car and at the water on the road, weighing my options. I didn't really have many, but I didn't want help from him. I decided I'd rather sit here in the rain than take a ride with him. I went back around to my door.

"Thanks for the offer, but I'll just wait for Dad," I called as I climbed in and slammed the door.

I closed my eyes and willed him to leave, but I knew that wasn't likely.

Cameron knocked on the window and yelled something I couldn't hear through the glass. I ignored him and turned on the radio, hoping he'd get the hint. But like the stubborn man I remembered, he kept knocking until I finally gave up and rolled down the window.

"What?" I yelled over the sound of the rain.

"Stop being stubborn! I'm just trying to help you!" he shouted, putting his hands on the open window edge.

"I don't want your help, Cam."

"Fine! You can give me gas money if that makes you feel better." He threw his hands up in frustration.

If I gave him money for gas then it wasn't really a favor. I'd be paying him for a service—I could think of him as a taxi driver.

"Come on, Charlotte, you know I'm not going to leave you out here alone, so you make the choice. Either you let me take you home, or I'll just stand in the rain until your dad gets here."

I thought about leaving him to stand in the rain all afternoon, but I liked the idea of being home…and dry. So I grabbed my handbag from the passenger seat and got out of the car, back into the pouring rain. I made sure the doors were locked before running over to Cameron's car and climbing inside.

The warm air from the heater sent shivers down my spine as I settled into the seat and pulled my seatbelt across my chest. Cameron climbed in as well and pulled back out onto the street. He made a quick U-turn to head back toward Fairfield.

"What about your conference?" I asked.

"I'll tell them I couldn't get through because of flooding on the road."

That sounded like a favor to me, and I scowled. *Gas money. Right!* I pulled out my purse and grabbed a twenty, slamming it down on the dashboard.

"That's too much! It wouldn't even be five dollars' worth of gas to get you back to Michael's house."

"The other fifteen is for your inconvenience."

"Whatever makes you happy, Char," Cameron said, chuckling and shaking his head.

I held my hands up in front of the heater, allowing my gloves to dry and fingers to defrost.

"Can I ask you a question?" Cameron asked.

"No," I shot back a little too quickly.

"Well, I've got you trapped in my car," he said, laughing. "So I'll ask it anyway, and you can decide not to answer if you choose."

I kept my eyes on the heater.

"Why did you leave?

I turned to stare at him incredulously. Had he *really* just asked me why I left town?

"Are you serious?"

"Completely. I never understood why you left without even talking to me. Didn't you want to hear anything I had to say? Or even say goodbye?" His voice was full of sorrow, and I felt the same sympathy for him I had the other night in the park. "After everything we'd been through together… how much we loved each other, I thought I at least deserved a goodbye."

"I left because I saw you sucking face with your mistress, and I was angry with you!"

An unidentifiable emotion flashed over Cameron's face before he turned off the highway toward Fairfield. "I wasn't *sucking face* with her. It was a peck…and she wasn't my mistress," he said, finishing so softly I could barely hear him.

I opened my mouth to yell but thought better of it. I crossed my arms firmly over my chest to stop myself from slapping him again. "I don't want to talk about this right now!" I seethed before turning my back to him and staring out the window.

"This was always our problem."

I spun around to face him again, furious. "And what is *that* supposed to mean?" I demanded.

"This," he said, waving his hand between us, "is exactly why we didn't work out. We never communicated."

"Really? I always thought we didn't work out because you liked putting your dick in my friend," I snarled before turning away again.

Cameron was silent, and I smiled, knowing I'd won that round. When he didn't say anything for several minutes, I got curious and turned slowly to look at him over my shoulder.

He gripped the steering wheel, his jaw clenched.

"You don't know what you're talking about," he said as we turned onto my dad's street.

"Is that so? So, you *weren't* fucking Lucy while we were married?" I shot back as he pulled up in the driveway and turned off the car.

He turned in his seat, looked me straight in the eye, and sighed. "If you'd allowed me to explain this five years ago, things might be very different."

How would talking about the details have made me accept his affair? He wasn't making any sense.

He must have noticed my blank stare because he continued without waiting for me to speak.

"I know it won't change anything now. I can see you've moved on, and I'm honestly happy for you, but don't you want to know what really happened with us, Charlotte? Don't you have any curiosity or sentimentality at all? Have you been able to forget what we had so easily?"

I sat in silence and processed his words. "What do you mean when you say *what really happened?*" I asked cautiously.

Cameron sighed again and braced himself on the steering wheel.

"This isn't the place to talk about it. Will you meet me later tonight?"

"I can't," I said automatically.

Cameron gave me a half-smile. "Is your big policeman afraid of us spending time together?"

I laughed. "Hardly! He's the one encouraging me to speak to you, so I can put the past behind me."

"You mean, put *me* behind you."

I didn't say anything. We both knew he was right, and at the moment I didn't feel like rubbing it in his face.

"He's not good enough for you, Charlotte," Cameron whispered.

My anger resurfaced, and I turned quickly to face him. "Owen has nothing to do with this. If you want to talk about our past, that's one thing. But you can't talk about my present life!"

"I do want to talk about the past, and I'm more than happy to leave Owen out of any future conversations. Trust me — he's not my favorite topic."

"Good." We sat in silence for a moment as I stared at my father's house.

"So will you listen to what I have to say?"

"I'll admit that I'm curious about what you want to tell me. I don't know what could possibly make me think differently about all this," I told him. "I'll let you know when I can meet you."

I could have met him that night, but I didn't want him to think I'd just drop everything whenever he wanted. Cameron could adapt to my schedule.

"Here's my cell number," he said, handing me a business card from his wallet. "Call me anytime."

I looked at the card and flicked the corner of the cardboard with my fingernail.

Dr. Cameron Harper, D.D.S.
Harper Allied Health Clinic

Below this was a phone number and email address. I stared at the card for a long time. The first emotion I felt was pride. He'd done it — finished school and gone into partnership with his father, just like he always said he would. Something nagged at the back of my mind as I stared at the card, and I clenched my jaw as I remembered.

Harper Allied Health Clinic. He worked with his father, who worked with Lucy.

My chest tightened, and I crumpled the card in my hand, a hard lump forming in my throat.

"What is it?" Cameron asked.

"Nothing."

"Charlotte, please. Lack of communication has always been an issue for us. Please, just this once, tell me what's upsetting you," he begged, touching my arm.

I jerked away from him and took a deep breath, then another.

"You work with your father."

Cameron gave me a confused look. "Well, not exactly. We work in the same building, but my office is three floors above his."

"Your mother told me Lucy works for your Dad," I added, gauging his reaction.

His eyes hardened instantly at Lucy's name, and I couldn't work out why that would be. Maybe they'd broken up, maybe she'd broken his heart, maybe…he still loved her.

I wasn't sure why it bothered me. I was with Owen now. It shouldn't matter if Cameron had feelings for someone else…but it did.

"I'm sorry about that. I didn't want her to work there, but I don't have any say about who my father hires. Bonnie, Sarah, and Lucy are still friends, and Dad hired her as a favor to my sister. I don't ever speak to her, or even acknowledge her when I see her in the building," he said, giving me an intense stare.

He doesn't speak to her? I felt compelled to ask him what had happened between them, but I knew the answer would probably hurt more than I was ready to deal with. I'd have to prepare myself.

My cell phone rang, and Cameron and I both jumped in our seats. I picked up the phone and stared at it, as if looking would answer it, before I remembered to press the button and put the device to my ear.

"Hello?"

"Char, is everything okay? I was told you called and it was urgent," Dad said, a hint of panic in his voice.

"Yes, I'm fine, Dad, really. I got a flat tire, and I was hoping you could pick me up and change it."

"Sure, where are you? I'll come right away," Dad replied, sounding relieved.

"I'm at home actually. Ca—a man picked me up and dropped me here so I wouldn't have to wait in the rain."

"I don't like that, Charlotte. Getting into a car with strangers can be dangerous."

I rolled my eyes and gave my dad a grunt of acknowledgement. I wasn't in the mood to be lectured, especially not with Cameron sitting a few feet away.

"I'll be right home, and we'll go get your car," he said before hanging up.

I pulled the phone from my ear and turned to Cameron, unfastening my seatbelt. "My dad's on his way."

"We still have a lot to talk about," Cameron said, an urgency in his voice.

"I'll call you when I'm ready," I said, holding up the crumpled card.

"Thank you."

"It really means a lot to you that we talk about this, doesn't it?"

He nodded. "It does."

"It won't change anything."

"Maybe it won't. But it might change everything," he replied. "Goodbye."

"Goodbye, Cam. Thank you for the ride," I said, surprised that there wasn't the slightest hint of anger or resentment in my voice as I said his name.

"Anything for you, Charlotte."

That smile used to melt me into a pile of goo. Now it pulled on my heart strings and made me feel sad.

I stepped out and watched as he drove off down the street. Not one minute after Cameron left, my dad's police cruiser turned the corner and drove toward me.

⁂

"Hello?" I said cheerily into the phone as I sat on the couch flicking channels, looking for something to watch.

"Hey, baby, sorry I couldn't call yesterday. How are you?" Owen asked. He sounded tired.

"Not bad. I took my car to the shop this morning to have my tire replaced. I got a flat yesterday."

I had a feeling Owen wouldn't mind that I'd seen Cameron, but I didn't think he'd want to hear about him being my knight in shining armor, saving me from being stuck on the side of the road in a storm. Nothing had really happened, so it wasn't worth mentioning.

"I have some bad news. A couple of guys called in sick, and they need me to work a double shift. So I won't be able to call you again tonight."

We'd gotten into a routine of talking on the phone for about an hour just about every night while we were apart. We didn't talk about anything important, just what we'd been up to that day, but it allowed us to feel together, and it eased the ache his absence caused in my heart.

"Oh, I'm sorry. Won't you be tired?"

"I'll be fine. You have a good night, and I'll call you in the morning."

"Okay, don't work too hard," I said as I stood up and went into the kitchen and leaned against the wall. "I love you."

"Love you more," he replied before hanging up.

The smile that appeared at the sound of Owen's voice slowly slipped away as I remembered a similar situation from a few years ago…

…I'd heard footsteps coming down the hall and rolled over in bed as a crack of light appeared in the doorway and Cameron slipped into the room.

I sat up and rubbed my eyes.

"Oh, damn, I didn't want to wake you," he whispered, sitting on the bed and stroking my hair and face.

"What time is it?" I asked groggily.

"Almost three in the morning. You should go back to sleep."

"Are you just getting home? Doesn't the library close at eleven?"

Cameron often stayed at the library late to study for his exams, and I'd gone to bed thinking he was studying.

"Yeah," he said, chuckling nervously as he rubbed the back of his neck. "I fell asleep at the desk and woke up when the janitor started vacuuming."

"You poor thing, you study so much. Did you have dinner?"

"Ah, no," he replied as he got up from the bed to undress.

I threw the blankets off and stood up.

"What are you doing?"

"I'm going to make you something to eat. You work so hard, and I don't want you getting sick or starving," I told him, walking down the hall to the kitchen.

"No, go back to bed, sweetheart. You must be tired." He followed me down the hall in his boxer-briefs.

"I don't mind, really. I want you taken care of."

Cameron sighed and looked down at me with love in his eyes. I realized I hadn't seen that expression for a while. He leaned down and pressed his lips to mine softly.

"I love you," he said…

At the time it had seemed so ordinary, but in retrospect, he'd probably been out with Lucy that night.

The same anguish and despair I felt when I first found out about the affair washed over me again, and I knew nothing Cameron could say now would make things better. Nothing.

But I was still curious. Curiosity overcame sadness, and I pulled his card out of my pocket, staring at the number.

"I'm going out, Dad," I called as I grabbed my coat and went to the car.

I sat with my hands on the steering wheel and stared at my knuckles. I was so conflicted. If Owen was here he could calm me down and make me feel safe. Then I could forget all about this. But he was in Boston, and I felt completely unsure about what to do.

With a sigh, I leaned my head back on the car seat. The only way for me to get closure—and satisfy my nagging curiosity—was to know the whole story. There was only person who could help me with that.

I pulled my cell phone out of my bag and dialed the number, listening to the phone ring and almost losing my nerve a few times before it stopped.

"Hello?" he answered.

"I'm ready to talk," I blurted. "Can you meet me now?"

"Yes," he replied eagerly.

I was dreading this conversation, and he was happy about it?

"Where?" I asked.

I didn't mean to be rude, but my hands were shaking, my voice was quivering, and I just wanted to get off the phone as quickly as possible and get this night over with.

"You know where."

I did know. I supposed it was only right; we'd gone there to express our love several times, so it seemed fitting to go there to discuss the end of it.

"Ten minutes," I said before hanging up.

I steered the car to the highway that left town. I tried to concentrate on driving and not on the many possibilities of what Cameron had to say to me. Just past the exit I used to get to the harbor, a small dirt street came into view. I pulled up in a clearing to find Cameron's car already there.

I got out and walked into the forest. As a child I'd loved playing in these trees, running over the logs and jumping from rock to rock. The forest had always been a happy place for me. But right now it seemed eerie, frightening even. I looked up at the gnarled branches and jumped whenever a bird screeched.

I made my way through the trees slowly, being careful not to trip, and I breathed a sigh of relief when my destination became visible.

Cameron smiled when he saw me. He stood next to a fallen tree covered in moss. It was our tree. We'd come here many times to sit and talk when we were dating; we'd made love right in the very spot where Cameron stood right now. He'd also brought me here the day before our wedding to remind me that being married wasn't going to change our love or our commitment to each other.

He'd been wrong.

I walked over and sat on the log. He sat beside me.

"Thank you for coming," he said with a smile.

I crossed my arms firmly over my chest. "Where do we start?"

Cameron stood and sat instead on the mossy ground so we were facing each other. He looked up at me. "Would you like me to just explain what was happening for me or do you have specific questions?" he asked, his voice nothing but calm.

"Why don't you start, and I'll stop you if I have questions," I suggested, shifting nervously.

Cameron nodded and took a deep breath before looking up at me again. "When did you first notice a problem with our relationship?"

I wanted to say it was when I read Lucy's text message, but after years of thinking about it I knew that it was long before that—it had been right around the time my mother left. I hadn't made love to Cameron for months, and I'd spent most of my time with my father for about six months before I knew anything about the affair.

"I suppose about six months before I found out about Lucy."

Cameron nodded. He had a far away look in his eyes, like he was lost in the memories he was about to describe. "After your mother left, you just disappeared," he said. "I knew you were hurting, and I tried to be there for you, but you just didn't seem to want me around. You spent all your time with your father, which I understood, but you never wanted me to come visit him with you. You just shut me out."

He paused to breathe, and I gently stroked the side of his face. I wasn't sure what made me touch him, but it felt right. Cameron's eyes shot to mine quickly, but then he appeared to relax, and he leaned his cheek into my palm.

"I'm sorry I acted like that. I was so lost." I *had* checked out emotionally, but that still didn't justify cheating.

"I wanted so much to be there for you, and I tried for a long time, but over and over you rejected me, ignoring my requests to help you and pushing me away. We barely even talked."

I dropped my hand from his face and wrapped my arms around my body again for protection.

"I loved you so much, Charlotte. Do you know how hard it was for me to see you in so much pain and not be able to help you? You grew more and more distant, and no matter what I tried to do to connect with you, you'd resist. It was like I could see your trust in me fading."

I nodded, acknowledging that everything he said was true. I remembered him holding me as I cried, rocking me as I fell into restless sleep, and always being there. I also remembered my emotional detachment, my withdrawal from our physical relationship, and my telling him I was fine—to stop fussing over me. I *had* pushed him away, and that realization was terrifying. Looking back, I knew it was because if my mother could do that to my father, I thought Cameron could it to me. So I distanced myself, putting up walls to protect my heart.

A sinking sensation settled in my stomach as he continued to speak.

"I was lost, hopeless and desperate to make a connection with you, but you didn't even notice. I didn't need you to support me, but I did need you to let *me* support *you*. I was convinced you didn't want me anymore, that you didn't need me around and had fallen out of love with me—"

I gasped loudly, cutting off his speech.

Cameron looked down at the ground, ashamed. "Nothing I've said is an excuse for what happened. I'm not trying to make excuses. What I did was very wrong, and I know that, but this is how I was feeling."

"You thought I wasn't in love with you anymore?" I asked as I grasped his hand.

"Yes," he whispered, his eyes on the ground. He squeezed my hand tightly.

"Cam," I cried as I slipped off the log and sat in the dirt with him. "I never stopped loving you. Never." I wanted to show him he was wrong, to prove I'd still loved him, but I couldn't think of a single example to give him.

We stared into each others' eyes for a moment, and all the things Cameron had said rolled around in my head. The sinking feeling in my stomach now rose to my chest. I doubled over, hugging myself again.

"Charlotte, what is it?" He placed his hand on my shoulder.

Suddenly Cameron's words from yesterday afternoon made sense. What we'd talked about *had* changed nothing; he'd still cheated, but it had also changed *everything*. I finally understood.

"I drove you away. The affair was my fault," I whispered as tears ran down my cheeks.

Chapter Eight
The Safe Coffin

He was right. I'd pushed him away, over and over. I'd been there for my father as much as I could, but I'd neglected my husband. And I never really let him back in after that. I was too afraid of how much he was capable of hurting me.

"No! Charlotte, no!" Cameron took both of my trembling hands in his. "The betrayal was completely my fault. You needed me to be there for you, and I wasn't. I *should* have been there, even when you pushed me away. I should have stayed. There's no excuse for my behavior."

I was sure he meant the words he was saying, but they didn't change our situation. Cameron had tried to support me, and I'd pushed him to the point where he didn't even believe I loved him anymore.

"Charlotte, say something," he begged.

"I'm sorry."

"You have nothing to apologize for. I was the one who went to Lucy."

At the mention of Lucy's name, the guilt I was feeling dried up. How could I have forgotten about *her?* No matter what I did to him, no matter how hard I'd pushed him away, he shouldn't have sought out my best friend.

"Lucy," I said, my voice cold and hard as I wiped the tears from my cheeks. I moved away from him, standing up and ripping my hands from his.

He sighed and leaned against the log with his knees bent. "Do you want to know about her? My association with her is not what you think it was."

I balked at the word "association." It was too cold a term for an act of such intimacy.

I turned to face him. "I've come this far." I knew I needed to hear this, but I was terrified of the emotional ramifications.

Cameron nodded and patted the ground next to him, but I shook my head and sat on the log, as far from him as I could get. He gave me a sad smile.

"Lucy was…a distraction. She wanted me and made me feel needed. She was someone to talk to, someone to listen who wouldn't push me away. That's all she was—wh-where are you going?" he asked as I stood up, brushed the dirt off my jeans, and started back into the trees.

"I thought I was here to listen to your version of what happened between us," I said, turning back to glare at him, my arms over my chest. "I'm not going to sit here and listen to your lies."

"I'm not lying!" Cameron protested, scrambling to his feet and coming toward me.

"You chose her over me!" I threw my arms up in the air. My voice echoed around the trees and Cameron looked at me, shocked. "You stood in front of me, while we were still married, and told me you cared about her. You can't tell me now that she didn't mean anything to you!"

Cameron sighed and ran his hands through his hair, tugging on it before pacing through the clearing. His face fell into shadow as moved under the trees.

"I never wanted her more than I wanted you… I was so confused." He sighed. "She gave me something I needed, something I craved, something I wasn't getting from you. I loved that she needed me. I loved that she made me feel wanted, but I never loved *her*. I've only ever *loved you*. Does that make sense?"

I slowly walked back to the log and sat down.

"You cared about her enough to throw me away."

"I honestly never meant it to go as far as it did. But it really wasn't what you seem to think it was. It was not a sexual relationship…until after you left."

He took a deep breath and sat down next to me. "You were growing further away from me every day, and I tried to talk to you about it. I wanted to make you trust me again. But over the weeks you remained distant, and you even stopped saying you loved me. At night I'd reach out to hold you in bed and you'd shrug me off, as if you didn't even want to touch me. Do you know how painful that was? One night I went for a walk down by the harbor, and I ran into Lucy. We sat on the sand and talked for hours. I cried, and she was there for me. I told her how I missed you and how I didn't know how to make you love me again. I shared my pain, and it made me feel better. It made me feel close to her. That night we shared a kiss. It was *one kiss*, Char, nothing more than that, I swear. And after that kiss I felt sick. I couldn't believe I'd done it, and I never wanted it to happen again."

I stopped myself from blocking my ears and singing *LALALALALA* in my head until he stopped talking.

"You remained so isolated, and the guilt I felt from kissing Lucy just grew," he continued. "But I swear, apart from that one kiss it was only an emotional relationship. I never let it become sexual…until after you moved out." He looked down at the ground, and I could tell he was ashamed.

"Emotional betrayal is so much worse than physical…so much more hurtful," I said, trying my best to hold in my tears.

Cameron didn't say anything more; he just looked down at the ground.

"I don't think I can listen to any more right now," I told him, standing again.

"There's still so much you don't know. Everything that happened after you left, how I ended it with her, and how my family reacted… Please, you have to hear the whole story before you can understand."

"I can't. You have no idea what it does to me, what it's doing to me right now, listening to you. This hurts me more than you can know."

I swiped the drops from my face with my sleeve. "I have to go home. I can't listen to any more tonight," I said and began to move away from him, back toward my car. The moonlight cast eerie shadows through the trees, and I watched as the silvery light danced over my skin.

"Don't you want to hear the rest?"

"I need some time to process everything you've said. This is a lot to take in." I could hear Cameron following me. "I'm so sorry I pushed you away. I never meant to hurt you," I said softly as I reached the cars.

"And I never meant to hurt you."

"You were right," I said, turning and giving him a weak smile.

He cocked his head to the side.

"What you told me changes everything I thought I knew, and yet nothing between us has changed. I'll call you when I'm ready to talk again," I explained before turning and closing the remaining distance to my car alone.

I got in and started the engine but didn't drive away. I sat in the car and cried. I'd been wrong about so many things, and the truth was much more bitter than I'd been expecting. This was almost as painful as when the wounds were fresh.

I looked up to see Cameron getting into his car. He stopped and gave me a wave and a smile. He fucking *smiled.*

Rage boiled inside me. The crushing defeat I'd been feeling dissolved when I saw his smile. He smiled at me like everything was fixed between us now, like I'd forgiven him. He was wrong.

I opened the car door and ran, almost falling over my own feet as I raced across to his car.

"Don't act like everything is okay with us!"

"Huh?"

"Just because I was distant doesn't justify you sneaking around with my best friend! *You broke me, Cameron!* You broke me!"

"I'm sorry," he said, reaching out to pull me into a hug.

"*No!*" I screamed, pushing his arms away. "You can't touch me! You have no right to touch me!"

Cameron's mouth fell open, and he flinched as if I'd struck him.

I hated myself for crying, but I couldn't stop. I stumbled back and leaned against Cameron's car for support.

He stayed a few feet away, for which I was grateful.

"You have to forgive me," he whispered.

My eyes shot up to meet his. "And why do I *have* to do that?"

"Because we're meant to be together, Char. You can't deny that!" he said, thoroughly convinced.

"*We* aren't meant to do anything. Do you understand what you did to us? You completely destroyed any chance for us to be together ever again. You lied to me and snuck around behind my back, even after what happened with my parents. Can't you see that I'm not capable of trusting you now? Do you take this seriously at all?"

"You won't understand until you hear the rest of what I have to say. Do you want to hear it?" He offered a tentative hand to me.

"No! I'm going home!" I pushed myself off his car and walked back around to mine.

"I'll be here when you're ready to listen. I'm sorry I'm still hurting you."

I looked over, saw his crushed, defeated body language, and almost gave in. I *almost* walked back over and told him it was okay, that I was as much to blame as he was, and it would all work out for the best. But I didn't.

He deserved to suffer the way I'd suffered, and as immature as it was, part of me was happy to see him crushed. With one final look, I opened my car door and was about to climb inside when I heard him say the words I couldn't handle hearing right then.

"I love you," he said.

My anger flared again. "Don't you say that to me! Don't you *dare* say that!" I slammed the door and drove out of the clearing as quickly as I could.

I cried all the way home—great heaving gasps that echoed in the car. I drove past the "Welcome to Fairfield" sign and slowed as I turned down the main street. I wiped my eyes and took a few deep breaths to calm myself.

At home I parked the car and crept into the house. I took a shower so hot that steam filled the bathroom and my skin was pink when I got out. I changed slowly into pajamas and climbed into bed. I was on autopilot, going through the motions but not really experiencing anything.

I pulled the blankets over my head and tried to block out Cameron's words. I didn't want to think about how all this had been partly my fault. I didn't want to think about the hurtful words I'd said to him, and I certainly didn't want to think about the three words he'd said before I left.

In the safety of my bed, my reaction in the forest now seemed a bit extreme, and I felt a little guilty for yelling at Cameron. What he'd said had hurt me. I was honestly surprised that he hadn't cheated on me physically, but emotional betrayal was just as bad, I told myself. Though maybe I just wanted to feel less guilty about not listening to him all those years ago.

I decided to make myself a safe place where thoughts of Cameron weren't allowed. I lay on the bed and straightened out my arms and legs. I imagined I was lying on a warm, soft cushion, and I added walls around the cushion: one above my head, one below my feet, and one on either side. Then I lowered a roof onto my safe box and smiled.

I lay in my imaginary safe box for a few moments, feeling quite relaxed until a disturbing thought crossed my mind: I'd put myself in a coffin.

I shook my head. Was that how I saw a life without Cameron? A death sentence? I pulled Owen's pillow over from the other side of the bed and clutched it tightly to my chest, letting out a long sigh.

I closed my eyes and thought of all my favorite memories of Owen: the night I came home and found him standing in the rain with flowers, the first time we made love, when he asked me to marry him, and our trip to Italy last year. I slowly calmed, and my breathing regulated as I drifted off to sleep.

⚜

Bang! Bang! Bang!

My eyes flew open, and I rolled over. Owen was lying in bed next to me with the same shocked expression on his face I was sure was on mine. He had dark circles under his eyes and looked exhausted. He'd driven through the night and arrived at two in the morning so we could spend the whole day together today and go to Hartford to look for houses. A few days had passed since my confrontation with Cameron in the forest, and I still hadn't made much sense of things. I was grateful to have Owen here now to help me keep everything in perspective.

"Where is she, Michael?" I heard from downstairs. I groaned, recognizing the voice.

I heard footsteps coming up the stairs, and I pulled the blanket up over our heads in an attempt to hide.

"What's going on?" Owen asked.

I was about to answer when there was a soft knock on the bedroom door.

"Char?" my dad called through the door. "Bonnie is here to see you."

"*Charlotte Grace Barnes!* Get out of that bed right now!" Bonnie yelled from downstairs.

Owen threw off the blankets and sat up. "Who the hell is that?"

"My friend Bonnie," I said carefully, getting out of bed and putting on my robe. "I'll go see what she wants."

I followed my father downstairs where I found Bonnie in the living room, hands on her hips, foot tapping impatiently.

"Hello, Bonnie."

"*Hello, Bonnie?* After five years that's all you have to say to me?" she asked incredulously.

I tapped my chin in faux thought and gave her a smile. "Yep, that's it!"

"Ah, I've missed you!" Bonnie said, laughing and launching herself at me. She hugged me tightly, all signs of anger gone.

"I've missed you too!"

"When Mom said she saw you, I couldn't believe it. You're not so great at answering the phone, so I had to just come over," Bonnie said raising her eyebrows pointedly.

"Well, you could've *tried* calling," I said with a scowl. But she did have a point. "And I've been a little overwhelmed with Harpers the last few days. I ran into Ellen in the grocery store, and Ryan was here for my dad's policemen party—"

"Wait! Ryan saw you before I did?" she shrieked, anger flashing in her eyes.

"Uh, yeah," I said, trying to hide my smile.

I looked her over. Bonnie's hair was darker and shorter, and her makeup was less intense than it had been when she was nineteen. Even though she was apparently just as spoiled as I remembered, I still loved her.

"How do you know Ryan?" Owen asked, suddenly appearing behind me.

I cringed. Poor Owen had been face to face with too many Harpers already.

"He's my brother. Is that okay with you?" Bonnie asked with more than a little attitude.

Owen shook his head and kissed my temple. "I'm going to take a shower," he said, heading back upstairs.

Once Owen had left the room, I slapped her shoulder playfully. "Be nice to him, please!"

She rolled her eyes dramatically. "Yeah, yeah, Mom told me the deal. We all have to be nice to the new guy."

"His name is Owen, and if you gave him a chance you'd see he's a really good guy." I smoothed my hair and pulled my robe tighter around me.

"I don't care if he's Jesus reincarnated. You belong with my brother. You know it, I know it, and even the new guy knows it," Bonnie said, smiling.

"Just butt out of it, Bonnie," I said, my tone bordering on rude. I was sick of being told who I should be with. I was more than capable of making my own decisions.

"So, what are we going to do today?" Bonnie asked, sitting on the edge on the couch.

"Well, I don't know what you're doing, but Owen and I are going to look at houses in Hartford."

She pouted and folded her arms across her chest. "You can look at houses anytime. Why don't we spend the day catching up?"

"Owen made a special trip from Boston to spend time with me. Why don't you and I catch up later in the week?"

Bonnie sighed dramatically and stood up.

"Fine. Saturday afternoon. You and me, lunch at the diner."

I nodded and gave her a hug. "I'll see you there. Now, you better take off before Owen comes back."

"Yeah, yeah. I'm still not happy about the new guy," she said as she headed out the door.

Not long after I went back upstairs, Owen reappeared with wet hair, wearing old sweat pants and a T-shirt.

"Is she gone?" He looked around as if she might jump out from behind the closet door.

"Yes. Sorry about that. I guess Ellen told her I was in town."

"There sure are a lot of them."

"A lot of what?"

"A lot of *his* family. New ones keep appearing out of nowhere. Should I be prepared for more?" he asked sarcastically.

I walked over to run my hands under his shirt and stroke across his chest. I couldn't imagine how hard this was for him, and he was handling it so much better than I would have in his place. It made me appreciate him so much.

"I think that's all of them now," I assured him, kissing his chin softly.

"Are they always going to be around?" He wrapped his arms around my waist.

"Well, Cameron won't be, but would you mind the others?"

Owen released me and walked across the room. "I'd prefer if they all just left us alone."

"I have a past. I'm sorry about that, but you were the one who wanted to move back here. I haven't initiated contact with any of them, but the fact is, they're like family to me, and I don't want to turn them away."

This was a first. Owen and I had never raised our voices to each other. We always talked about issues before they got to the "blow up" stage.

"They *were* your family. They aren't your family anymore. You seem to have trouble making that distinction."

I didn't want to yell at him; he hadn't done anything wrong. In fact, he'd been *more* than accepting of the Harpers since we came here. I walked over and rested my hands on his chest, wanting to make things right.

"Bonnie isn't a threat to our relationship"

Owen sighed and looked down at me. "I know that. I don't know why I'm acting so irrationally."

"Are you transferring your concerns about Cameron to his whole family?"

Owen nodded. "I just feel like he's never going to be out of your life as long as his family is around. You'll always be reminded of him, talking about him, and it'll increase the chances of you seeing him."

"Cameron is my past," I whispered. "I'm in love with you."

"I want to believe that," he said, and both our bodies stiffened.

"I didn't mean that," he said quickly. "I do believe you. I know you love me."

"I'm sorry if you feel like I don't love you enough. I'm giving you everything I can!" I exclaimed, turning away from him.

Owen's arms wrapped around me from behind, and he pulled me tightly against his chest.

"I believe you. I don't know where that came from. Being here is just much harder than I thought it was going to be. Your ex-husband is everywhere, and I'm terrified he'll steal you away," he whispered into my ear, his warm breath sending a shiver down my spine.

"I'm not going back to him. I'm with you."

"I know you are. I know you are," he whispered, kissing my neck. "I'm sorry I said that."

I stood silently in Owen's arms for a few minutes, unsure of what to say. Everything was going so badly. I'd screamed at Cameron, and now I was having a fight with Owen, who didn't think I loved him enough.

Cameron had also thought I didn't love him. Why couldn't I express love to the men I cared about? Was I that dead inside? Had my mother's betrayal somehow turned me into a dry husk? A million questions ran through my mind in an endless loop. I wasn't sure how I could show my love to Owen in a more effective way, but I was going to try.

◦❦◦

The next day, Owen packed up to leave early in the morning. He was working the night shift and needed to get some sleep before he reported for work.

As planned, we'd spent the previous day house hunting in Hartford. But after three houses, lunch at a lovely Thai restaurant, and a few hours in the car, we decided to stop. There just wasn't anything that seemed like it would work for us. Unfortunately this made the house in Fairfield seem all the more perfect.

I stood at the front door as he loaded his overnight bag into the trunk. Even though I was managing fine here with Dad, I missed Owen every minute he was away. He came back up the porch stairs to kiss me goodbye.

"Do you have to leave?" I asked. "Stay, please."

"I wish I could, but we only have another two weeks of this. Then I'll be here all the time."

"I know. I just miss you so much when you're gone."

"Two weeks," he promised, cupping my face gently. His lips pressed against mine, and I automatically sunk into his chest.

"Drive safely," I whispered when our mouths parted. He kissed the tip of my nose and then my forehead before walking away.

❧ ⁕ ☙

"Charlotte!" Bonnie called when I walked into the diner the following Saturday afternoon. I was a little sweaty from the walk from my house, but the diner wasn't really that far, and it felt invigorating to be out in the sunshine.

She sat in a booth in the corner with a noticeably pregnant Sarah next to her. I smiled when I saw Sarah; she'd been very special to me when we were both partners of the Harper sons.

Sarah was stroking her large abdomen in soothing circles, but she stopped when she saw me and waved. I walked over and sat down across from them in the booth.

"Hey, Sarah," I said with a smile.

"It's good to see you."

"Um, what about me?" Bonnie asked.

"Sorry, Bonnie, it's good to see you too," Sarah said, laughing, though Bonnie looked annoyed.

"How've you been, Bonnie?" I asked, giving Sarah a wink.

"Oh, I've been so good! I have a boyfriend now. His name is Alex, and he's so wonderful! And the sex, oh, God! Let me tell you, that boy…" She raised her eyebrows, but thankfully left the rest of her thought unsaid.

"We all know how amazing Alex is in the sack," Sarah said with disgust. "I want to hear about Charlotte."

Bonnie smiled and leaned over the table. "Yes, how is *your* sex life, Charlotte? Is the new guy any good? He must be if you're going to marry him!"

Sarah rolled her eyes, and I burst out laughing.

"What? We have to get through this stuff quickly before Mom gets here!" Bonnie exclaimed.

"Ellen's coming?" I asked.

"Yeah, I told her we were meeting, and she wanted to come. We've only got a few minutes before she arrives. Just enough time to do some girly, dirty talking. Now, spill about the new guy," Bonnie said, giggling and leaning forward in her seat.

"Um, well…he's good."

"Oh, come on! We need something juicy!" Sarah begged.

I shifted in my seat uncomfortably and thought about what I could say. I was never really into the whole dirty-talk-with-my-friends thing, and especially not with my ex-husband's family. How awkward. But I supposed I should try…

"Okay, well, when we make love Owen is always really adoring. Like, he strokes me and kisses me the whole time. It's nice."

"So when do we get to meet this Owen?" Sarah asked.

"I've already met him," Bonnie boasted. "Saw him naked too!"

Sarah's mouth fell open, and I jumped in. "Bonnie burst into my house while Owen and I were still asleep, and she saw him *topless*, not naked."

"And?" Sarah asked.

"And…he's hot!" Bonnie wailed, covering her face and pretending to cry.

"Why is that a bad thing?" I asked with a giggle. It was surprisingly nice to talk to people about my relationship with Owen. I'd never really done that.

"Well, I was hoping he'd be ugly. Then it would be easier for me to get you back with my brother! Owen's a hottie, so that makes my job harder," she said, as if it was the most obvious thing in the world.

"I'm not with Owen because he's hot!" Did she think I was that shallow? "I love him."

Sarah and Bonnie looked at each other quickly and nodded with sympathetic looks in their eyes.

"What's this about?" I asked, pointing to their nodding heads.

"Nothing!" they said at the same time.

"Sarah?" I asked, knowing she was my best bet for finding out what they meant.

"Well, it's just that everyone knows you were meant to be with Cam," she said while Bonnie nodded her head vigorously.

I sighed and leaned back.

"Well, Cam doesn't seem to agree with you. Maybe you should be having lunch with Lucy."

Bonnie and Sarah looked at each other again, confused this time.

"What are you talking about?" Bonnie asked.

I wasn't sure I wanted to delve into the details of my failed marriage, especially since it appeared Cam had left them in the dark. As I pondered what to say, I was thankfully interrupted by Ellen.

"Oh!" she exclaimed as she walked up to the table. "My three favorite girls in the whole world, all together!"

Ellen sat next to me and wrapped her arm around my shoulder.

"So what are we chatting about?"

I was about to say something neutral like "Oh, just catching up…" when Bonnie jumped in.

"Charlotte was about to tell us what Lucy has to do with her divorce."

At the mention of Lucy, Ellen's face hardened, and she gripped my shoulder. "I don't think that's something that we should talk about here," she scolded, looking from Sarah to Bonnie.

I patted her hand, a silent thank you for her consideration.

"Okay, well, let's go home then and have a good chat about this. It's long overdue," Bonnie said, grabbing her purse and heading for the exit.

Ellen, Sarah, and I just stared at each other, not sure what to do.

"Come on, I'll drive," Bonnie called, pulling her keys from her handbag.

We got up and followed her outside.

"We don't have to talk about this if you don't want to," Ellen assured me as we found Bonnie's car in the lot. I got in and gave Ellen a smile before she turned and went to her own car.

We hadn't been driving long when a siren blared behind us and flashing lights filled the car.

"Dammit! I was only *just* speeding," Bonnie grumbled as she pulled over and lowered her window.

The policeman approached, and Bonnie groaned when she saw him in the mirror.

"License and registration, please," the deep voice said.

I had to hold back a giggle when I recognized Ryan's voice. "Hey, baby," he added when he saw Sarah in the passenger seat.

"Ryan, I wasn't even speeding," Bonnie protested, handing her brother the documents.

"Do you know how fast you were going back there, ma'am?" Ryan asked in his deep, authoritarian voice.

"Oh, cut the act. Are you going to give me a ticket or not?"

"Don't speak to an officer like that, miss, or I'll have to arrest you," he said, chuckling and handing her the papers back. "How's the morning sickness today, babe?"

"Not too bad," Sarah replied, smiling as Bonnie rolled her eyes.

"Ryan, stop being an idiot!" Bonnie whined.

Ryan bent down to look into the car. "Oh, hey…Charlotte?"

"Hey, Ryan," I said with a small wave.

"Okay, I'm going to let you off with a warning this time, miss, but watch your speed," Ryan said, winking at me and walking back to his car.

"Stupid Ryan," Bonnie grumbled, pulling the car back out onto the road.

As nervous as I was about the conversation we'd have when we arrived at Ellen's, I was smiling—a real, genuine smile. It had been so long since I spent time with these people I loved, and who I knew loved me too. It was nice. It was just a shame Cameron came with the package.

After we pulled up behind Ellen's car in the driveway, I helped Sarah stand and guided her and her growing midsection into the house. I sat on the same loveseat I'd sat on the week before with Owen and waited. I wasn't sure if I was ready to go through the whole explanation and the undoubtedly explosive reaction Bonnie would have, but their lives had all been affected by Cameron's actions too.

"So…Lucy?" Bonnie asked, once everyone was seated.

I sighed and glanced at Ellen, who gave me an encouraging look.

"Lucy and Cam were seeing each other while we were married," I whispered.

Bonnie and Sarah both gasped loudly, and Bonnie shot out of her chair to pace around the room. Sarah mumbled something under her breath that sounded like swearing, but I couldn't quite make it out.

"While you were married? You mean *before* you left him?" Bonnie clarified. "Because we knew they dated after you left."

I nodded. "Yes, she was the reason I left."

"That fucking bitch!" Bonnie yelled.

"Bonnie!" I scolded, looking at Ellen and silently apologizing with my eyes.

"No, she's right. Lucy is a fucking bitch," Ellen said.

"You knew about this?" Bonnie asked her mother incredulously.

"Charlotte told me last week when she came for dinner with Owen."

"Well, I'm going to talk to Cam about what a moron he is," Bonnie said firmly.

"I've already done that, dear. It didn't change anything," Ellen told her.

"What did you say to him?" I asked. "You both looked so sad when you came down the stairs."

Ellen sighed and shifted in her seat.

"I asked him what he'd been thinking. He didn't really want to give me any answers; he just kept saying he needed to talk to you before he could explain anything to me. So I told him I was disappointed in him and he'd broken my heart."

"You let him off easy. I would have yelled and thrown things," Bonnie said, continuing to stomp around the room.

"I'm sorry, Ellen," I whispered.

"No, I'm sorry, Charlotte. I'm sorry my son treated you so badly. I didn't raise him to behave that way, and I'm deeply ashamed of him."

"What did he tell you happened between us?"

"He didn't say much. We asked him over and over what had happened, and all he would say was that he'd 'messed up.' He wouldn't give any details."

"I know Ryan tried to talk with him as well but got a similar response. All he would say was he wished he could make it right," Sarah said, rubbing her hand over her swollen abdomen.

"That's it. I'm going to talk to him right now!" Bonnie threatened, walking back over to the couch to get her purse.

"He's at work. You can't interrupt his appointments," Ellen said firmly.

Bonnie thought for a moment before an evil smile broke over her face. She grabbed her cell phone and quickly dialed a number.

"Hello, I need to see Dr. Harper today. I have a terrible toothache," she said into the phone. "I'm his sister Bonnie…See you then…Thanks very much."

She hung up and smiled.

"He had a cancellation at two o'clock, and they can see me right away. I now have a whole hour booked with him, and no one will interrupt," she said smugly.

"Now hang on—" I began, but Sarah was trying to stand, and I stopped talking as I rushed over to help her.

"Let's stop in at Dad's surgery on our way and give Lucy a hard time too!" Sarah laughed.

"Oh, why didn't I think of that?" Bonnie squealed.

Bonnie and Sarah walked out the front door, and I heard Bonnie's car start.

"We'd better go with them to make sure they don't get into trouble," Ellen said, heading for the door.

I stayed on the couch, not really wanting to watch the drama that was about to unfold. I couldn't think of anything I wanted less than to see Lucy. Just the thought of it had my palms sweating and pulse racing.

Ellen looked back over her shoulder and saw me still on the couch.

"Everything okay, dear?" she asked.

"I think I'll just go home. The walk will do me good. I don't want to be involved with whatever's going to go on."

Ellen sat down next to me on the loveseat. "I know Cameron and Lucy are probably the last people you want to see, but maybe it will help you put this behind you if you can confront them."

I considered that she might be right. It *would* give me a chance to evaluate the situation after the conversation Cameron and I'd had in the forest.

I nodded and Ellen took my hand.

"If you want to leave, just let me know and we'll go right away," she assured me as we stood and went out to her car. We followed Bonnie and Sarah to Cameron's office.

As we drove into town, I closed my eyes. I wasn't as concerned about seeing Cameron as I was about facing Lucy. I hadn't seen her since that day at the grocery store five years ago, and I was terrified that all those emotions would come flooding back as soon as I saw her. Lucy and I had such a history. We'd been best friends since grade school and a part of me missed the friendship I'd had with the Lucy who hadn't stolen my husband.

Sooner than I would have liked, we pulled up outside the clinic. I scanned the parking lot and saw Cameron's black car a few spaces over, its metallic paint glittering in the sun. I looked up at the building and felt a shiver run through my body. Cameron was in there right now, and so was Lucy. They were in there together every day.

It didn't seem fair that after all the history I had with each of them, *I* was the one isolated. I still remembered the day they met…

…"You're going to love Lucy!" I'd gushed as I pulled Cameron toward the diner.

"Well, I'm sure I'll like her just fine, but you're the only one I love," Cameron growled, pulling me to his chest and kissing me fiercely.

"It's really important to me that you like her. She's my best friend," I told him, resting my cheek on his chest.

"Don't worry, love, I'm sure we'll get along fine." He grasped my hand tightly as we walked into the diner.

Lucy smiled as we approached the table. Of course she'd heard me gushing about Cameron for weeks, but I hadn't been ready for them to meet until I was sure what I was feeling for him was real.

"Hey, Char," she called, waving us over to her table. I saw the way she was running her eyes over Cameron, and I possessively put my hand around his waist.

"Lucy, this is Cameron," I said proudly when we reached the table.

"Hey," she said with a smile.

This was a new experience for us. We'd been best friends for as long as we could remember and neither of us had had a serious boyfriend before. I knew Lucy was jealous of the time I'd been spending with Cameron, but I hoped now we could all hang out together.

"Hi, Lucy," Cameron said, pulling me close to him in the booth and picking up a menu. "What do you want to drink, babe?"

"I'll have a vanilla Coke," I said, smiling at him.

I looked over at Lucy and raised my eyebrows, questioning what she thought of him. She nodded and licked her lips, our code that she thought he was hot. I giggled.

"So, Cameron, is Charlotte your first-ever girlfriend? You look like a guy who's had a bit of experience."

My eyes narrowed. What she was trying to do?

Cameron shifted awkwardly and cleared his throat. "No, Charlotte isn't my first girlfriend. But I wouldn't say I've had a lot of experience. I dated a few girls in high school — nothing serious."

"It's okay. You don't have to explain yourself," I said, giving Lucy a firm stare.

"I'm just looking out for you, Char. I want to make sure you're with a good guy," Lucy said, crossing her arms over her chest.

"I need to go to the bathroom, excuse me," I said to Cameron as I stood up. "Join me, Lucy?"

She made a big drama about getting up before following me through the diner to the bathroom.

"What are you doing?" I asked as soon as we were through the door.

"Nothing. I just don't think he's good for you. He looks like a player. He's probably just going to cheat on you — or dump you because he gets bored."

I stared at her for a moment, but then I understood. "You're jealous!"

"Am not!"

"Yes, you are! You think he's attractive, and you don't know what he's doing with me," I elaborated. I knew Lucy always thought of herself as prettier than me, and we'd had a similar argument when Ethan asked me to the prom.

She gave me a smug look. "You'll see, and I'm the one who'll have to pick up the pieces when he breaks your heart, just like I did with Ethan."

Maybe she was looking out for me. My anger quickly dissipated. "I need you to like him. I love him, and he loves me, and he's going to be in my life."

She rolled her eyes. "Okay, I'll be nicer," she promised, giving me a hug.

We walked back through the diner, and I smiled when I saw Cameron waiting for us to return. I could tell he was nervous because his leg was bouncing and he tapped his fingertips on the table. I wished I could run my hands through his thick black hair and calm him down.

"He is fucking hot!" Lucy said as we returned to the table…

"I don't know about this." Suddenly the idea of seeing Lucy was making me ill.

"What do you mean? Don't you want to get back at her?" Bonnie asked. "Ooh, I know—you should walk into the office, pretend you don't recognize her, and say you need to see *David* because you're pregnant with his son's child!"

I rolled my eyes. "Yes, and *that* information wouldn't fly around town at the speed of light and give Owen a heart attack when he heard it from a stranger at the gas station."

"Oh, right," Bonnie replied, looking disappointed.

We rode up the elevator to the second floor and got out. The sign on the door said *D. Harper, Chiropractor*, and Ellen strolled in as if she owned the place. We all followed. I kept my head down so Lucy wouldn't see me right away.

"Hello, Mrs. Harper. David is in with a patient, but he'll be free to see you in a few minutes," Lucy said pleasantly.

When I heard her voice I felt bile rise up in my throat. How could Cameron have ever cared about her?

"Actually, Lucy, we're here to see you," Bonnie said.

Lucy looked curiously at Bonnie and Sarah, and her eyes almost popped out of her head when she saw me standing behind them.

"Ch-Charlotte?" she asked.

I opened my mouth to say something, but I couldn't get any words out.

"Don't you speak to her," Bonnie threatened.

"I'll say whatever I like to her. Charlotte and I were friends long before she ever met you!"

"Yeah, well, you aren't friends anymore! And neither are we! I can't believe you could do this to Charlotte…to all of us! You destroyed our family," Bonnie said. I could hear in her voice that she was close to tears.

"You can't come in here and talk to me like this!" Lucy said, standing behind her desk.

"How could you hide this from us all these years?" Sarah asked, stepping forward to face Lucy.

I watched their interactions silently. They'd remained friends with Lucy all this time, and she'd lied to them every day.

"Are you going to let them talk to me like this?" Lucy asked Ellen in desperation.

"Yes. You deserve this and much more. If I could think of a work-related reason to dismiss you from this position, I would. Just count yourself lucky that you're good at your job."

"Do you have anything to add?" Lucy asked, turning toward me.

If I was ever going to confront Lucy, I knew this was the time. But I was shocked to find I didn't have anything to say to her. The only reason to talk it out would be to mend our relationship, and that was the last thing I wanted to do. I just shook my head and turned away.

"I'm not just going to stand here and take this—tell David I wasn't feeling well," she said, grabbing her purse.

"Coward," Bonnie said under her breath.

Lucy shot her a warning glare. "At least I can satisfy a man in the bedroom," she snarled at me as she walked past.

An image of her and Cameron entangled invaded my mind, and I bit my tongue, turning so she wouldn't see me cry. I wished I was strong enough to say something, but I knew I'd just start blubbering. She didn't deserve the satisfaction of seeing my pain.

Just before she walked out, Lucy turned and looked at me. "You know, Charlotte, it's a shame we couldn't stay friends. After all the things Cameron told me about you, I really feel like I know you better than anyone," she said with a smirk.

Rage clouded my judgment, and before I knew what I was doing, I'd slapped her hard across the face. "Shut up!" I yelled before clamping my hand over my mouth in shock.

Lucy stumbled back, clutching her cheek.

"Go, Charlotte!" Bonnie cheered as Lucy ran out the door.

Ellen's arms were around me before I could really comprehend what had happened. "Are you okay?"

I nodded and took a moment to calm myself. The office phone rang and we all looked at each other. Ellen released me and walked over to the desk.

"David Harper's office," she said politely into the phone as she sat down in the chair.

"Let me just check for you…Yes, I have your appointment for three o'clock…Okay, see you then, Mr. Carter…Goodbye."

I sat down in one of the waiting area seats and replayed what had happened. I felt like I floated out of my body and watched myself slapping Lucy. Did I really do that?

"Lucy, can you please make a return appointment for Mr. Gr—Ellen? What's going on?" David asked, coming out of his office, a man trailing behind him.

"Hello, dear," Ellen said, smiling from behind the desk. "I have everything under control."

"Hello, Daddy," Bonnie said with a wave.

David looked around his waiting room in shock as he registered that every woman in his family was there, plus me.

"Charlotte, what's wrong?" he asked.

I shook my head, unable to put into words what had just happened.

"We talked with Lucy, and she walked out," Bonnie said.

David sighed, and his jaw tensed as he turned back to Ellen, who was scheduling a return appointment for the patient.

"Thank you. See you next week," Ellen said pleasantly as the man left the office.

"Okay, now let's do Cam!" Bonnie said, clapping her hands and jumping like a child about to get ice cream.

"I have my hands full here," Ellen said as she tapped on the keyboard.

"Do *what* to Cam?" David asked.

"Don't worry, Dad. I'm just going to talk to him."

"I think I'll stay here. This is all too much excitement for me," Sarah laughed, picking up a magazine. "Stop back and pick me up when you're ready to go."

"Come on, Charlotte," Bonnie said, pulling me out the door and into the elevator.

The metal doors closed, then opened, and we exited into a hallway identical to the one outside David's office. A similar plaque adorned the wall: *Dr. C. Harper, D.D.S*

Chapter Nine

The Last Honest Smile

Cameron's secretary looked up and smiled as we entered his office. "Hello, Bonnie" she said. "Good to see you again."

"Hey, Connie. Is Cam ready for me?"

"Sure, just go through to the waiting room, and he'll will be with you shortly," she said before looking back at her computer screen.

Bonnie and I walked through another door and entered a small, sterile room with chairs along the walls and a table covered in magazines.

"Your sister has no right to talk to me like that! What did you say to her about me?" Lucy's voice screamed, seemingly from behind one of the exam room doors.

Bonnie and I looked at each other curiously as the voice continued. "And that *bitch* ex-wife of yours—"

"Don't you *ever* talk about Charlotte like that!" Cameron's voice roared, cutting her off.

Bonnie's lips set in a hard line, and she marched up to open the door where the screaming was coming from. She stepped inside and closed it behind her.

Bonnie's voice joined the ruckus as I sunk down into one of the chairs and closed my eyes, trying to block out my name being yelled over and over again. I felt sick to my stomach and—more than anything—I just wanted to go home and pretend this day had never happened.

First Lucy would scream something about how I'd never really loved Cameron and he was better off without me, then Cameron and Bonnie would yell at her in a jumble of cursing. Periodically Bonnie would switch gears to yell at Cameron for being a moron and letting me go.

"Just go, Lucy, and don't ever come back!" Cameron finally said, loud enough for me to make out clearly. The door opened, and I stiffened in my seat as Lucy appeared in the waiting room. It seemed to take her a second to realize it was me, but when she did, an evil grin appeared on her face. She sat in the chair next to mine and leaned in close.

"I'm going to tell you this because we were friends once. You can't trust Cameron. Whatever he's telling you, don't believe it. He's been chasing me the whole time you were gone. I know all about your problems — how you wouldn't fuck him and you ignored him and basically treated him like shit. All I'm saying is you're better off without him because instead of trying to get you back, he kept running to me for comfort. That's not what someone who loves you does."

I sat in silence as her words sunk in, my nausea intensifying. Cameron was chasing her? Why did he tell me he didn't talk to her at all? I jolted in my seat as the exam room door flew open again.

"Charlotte's *here?* Now?" Cameron asked as he stepped into the waiting room, his face softening when he saw me. The expression was short-lived, however. It turned to ice when he saw Lucy sitting next to me.

"I told you to get the fuck *out!* Now!"

Lucy stood and wiggled her hips a little as she walked over to him. I watched with disgust as she trailed a finger down his chest.

"Ooh, you know I love the dirty talk, baby," she cooed.

"Now!" He pushed her hand from his chest and walked over to me.

Bonnie held the door open for Lucy to leave. I watched her disappear and looked at the magazines on the table so I wouldn't have to see Cameron's face.

"Charlotte," he said, sitting in the chair Lucy had just vacated.

I tried to hold it all in and be strong, but all this was too much for me. My hands began to shake.

"What did she say, Charlotte?"

I shook my head and closed my eyes, trying to block him out. I felt a small hand on my back and looked up to see Bonnie standing next to me. She rubbed comforting circles on my shoulder blade, but I could tell she was agitated because her foot tapped furiously on the floor.

"Just leave her alone, Cam," she hissed.

"Bonnie, can you wait outside, please?" Cameron asked. He was trying to be calm, but I could hear the tension in his voice.

"No way!"

"It's okay, Bonnie. I'd like to talk to him," I said, speaking for the first time since I entered the room. I had to ask him about what Lucy said. I wouldn't be able to think about anything else until it was explained.

I stood up and walked into the room the others had just come out of, with Cameron following close behind.

"I'll be right here if you need me," Bonnie sang out before Cameron closed the door.

"What did she say to you?" he asked again as I took a seat and looked around the room.

What I'd thought was an exam room was actually Cameron's office. He had a large mahogany desk with models of teeth lined up in front of his computer. The shelves behind the desk held rows of books, his framed diploma, and some family photographs.

I smiled when I saw the happy faces of the Harpers, but then I noticed several other frames around the room. My breath caught when I saw on his desk, only a few feet away from me, a picture of Cameron and me at the harbor. It was only half-turned toward me, but I'd know that photo anywhere: it was our wedding day. We were barefoot, and the wind blew our hair around. The sun set behind us over the water, creating beautiful colors in the ripples as we embraced. Love radiated from Cameron's eyes, and the smile on my face wasn't forced or fake. I couldn't remember the last time I'd smiled that honestly. Well, actually I could…

…"I present to you, for the first time, Mr. and Mrs. Cameron Harper," the minister had announced as I watched all of our friends and family cheer and smile at us.

Cameron's arm wrapped tightly around my waist, and his nose rubbed against my cheek as he pressed a soft kiss just below my ear. He exhaled slowly and my skin tingled as his warm breath flowed over it.

"You're mine. Forever," he whispered, and my heart swelled at his words. There was nothing more in the whole world that I wanted than to be his.

Cameron guided me slowly down the aisle past our loved ones. As the large double doors of the church closed behind us, we found ourselves alone for the first time since being named husband and wife, and my whole future swam before my eyes: Cameron and me with our own home, with our children, traveling the world, with our grandchildren… Every possible event in my future life was tied to Cameron.

I smiled up at him and pressed my lips softly to his. "I love you," I whispered.

"I will love you for the rest of my life," he vowed…

I looked at our faces in the picture and wondered if I'd have gone through with that day, had I known the eventual outcome. I honestly couldn't say.

"Charlotte?" Cameron called, pulling my attention away from the photo. "Please tell me what she said."

I used all of my resolve to look at his face and into his eyes. I suspected Lucy was lying, so I needed to see his reaction. I believed I knew him well enough to tell if he was lying…although I hadn't done so well in the past.

"Lucy said you're still chasing her," I said flatly, studying his face as he stood on the other side of his desk.

His eyes opened in shock, then narrowed to slits. He looked very angry. I could see his chest heaving, and he closed his eyes and scrubbed his hands over his face. His reaction seemed genuine, and I wanted to believe it was, but I couldn't be sure.

I watched him sit in his large leather chair. He leaned forward, placing his arms on the desk.

"Charlotte, I know you don't have any reason to trust me—in fact you have every reason *not* to trust me, but I promise you with everything I am, I have *not* been in contact with Lucy since I ended things with her five years ago."

He looked me directly in the eye as he spoke, and I couldn't help but believe him. I released the breath I'd been holding and nodded.

He sighed loudly and leaned back in his chair, looking as relieved as I felt. We sat in silence: Cameron watching my face and me trying my hardest not to look at our wedding picture again.

Finally, Cameron leaned forward and cleared his throat. "Have you thought at all about our conversation?"

I shook my head and Cameron frowned.

"It's a lot to think about. I'm going to need some time." My throat felt hoarse, dry, and a little sore. I was sure I looked as bad as I felt.

"I understand," he said, walking around his desk to lean on the mahogany surface in front of me. "But, I *have* been thinking about it — about one thing in particular, actually — and I have a question."

I looked up at him. "What is it?" I cleared my throat and swallowed, trying to coach my voice back to normal.

"You said something, something I'd like some clarification on," he said, crouching down in front of me, only inches away.

Looking into his eyes was like coming home — and it unsettled me. I shifted in my chair and broke eye contact, looking down into my lap.

"What?" I whispered.

"You said you never stopped loving me…what…I mean, ugh." He shook his head and ran a hand through his hair.

I knew what he was about to ask me, and my foot tapped nervously on the floor as I waited for him to finish. I looked over his shoulder, trying to focus on something else, but my eyes focused again on our wedding photo.

"What I mean to say is…do you still love me?" he asked, his voice dropping to a whisper.

My eyes were glued on my happy face. I missed that girl — how carefree she was, how happy she'd been. She was happy because of Cameron. I looked at the Cameron in the photo and saw the expression of love on his face. I chanced a glance at the Cameron in front of me now and was startled to see that same love in his eyes. His expression was sad, but the love was still there.

I knew in that moment I did still love Cameron, and I would never stop loving him, no matter what he did or said or how much he hurt me. I closed my eyes and nodded slightly.

"I love you too," he whispered, his thumb brushing the tears from my cheek. I jumped back from him, startled.

"I'm sorry," he said, pulling his hand back quickly.

I could see the smile he was trying to hide, and his happiness at my declaration annoyed me.

"Nothing has changed, Cameron. I'm still with Owen, and I'll stay with him."

His smile fell slightly, and his eyes pierced into mine. "Do you love him? *Really* love him?"

I wanted to jump from my seat and scream that I loved Owen and always would and that Cameron didn't matter, but I knew that wasn't true. I did love Owen, absolutely, but it was different. Cameron was my first love. What I felt for him was eternal, was all-consuming, and despite what we'd been through, the flame was still burning. But Owen was safe. He was respectful, grounding, and supportive. Owen was better for me.

And Cameron needed to know I loved Owen, so I nodded in answer to his question. "But not like I love you," I blurted. The words were out of my mouth before I'd even thought them, and I clamped my hands over my mouth in shock.

Cameron's eyes darkened, and as if in slow motion, his face moved toward mine. His hands came up slowly and cupped my face, tilting it slightly to the side. My hand fell away from my mouth as his face got closer, and I watched, frozen, as his eyes closed. He was going to kiss me.

Alarm bells sounded in my brain, and just before his lips reached mine I pushed back from him, my chair skidding along the floor.

"Don't," I said.

"I'm sorry. I shouldn't have done that."

I could see he was hurt, but my devotion to Owen kept me from comforting him.

"It's just all so much. I can't deal with this right now," I said, backing toward the door. I was completely overwhelmed by the past twenty-four hours.

"Don't run…*please*," he begged as he took a step toward me. "You always run."

"Bonnie's waiting for me." It was all I could think to say as my hand grasped the doorknob.

I heard Cameron sigh as I walked back out into the waiting room. Bonnie looked up from the magazine she was reading and smiled.

"You okay?"

"Yeah, let's get out of here," I said quickly, walking to the door.

"I just want to talk to Cam. I haven't gotten to say my piece yet. I won't be long."

"Just leave him alone, Bonnie. It's been a long day for all of us."

I was relieved when she nodded and grudgingly followed me out. My mind started racing as soon as I was free of his office. I was angry that he'd tried to kiss me, but I *had* just told him I loved him. I groaned and shook my head. Everything was so muddled. I couldn't blame Cameron for being confused about my twisted messages. I really had to sort myself out before I spoke to him again.

We rode the elevator down in silence and got out at David's office. When we walked in, Sarah was still sitting and reading her magazine.

"How did it go?" she asked when she saw us.

"The skank was there!" Bonnie told her, eyes wide. "But we got rid of her."

"Did you slap her again, Charlotte?" Sarah said, giggling.

"No." I wasn't really listening—I couldn't get the picture of Cameron's face as he tried to kiss me out of my mind.

Sarah stood and covered her mouth as she yawned. "That bitch. I can't believe she was with him."

I shook my head, unable to come up with a response. I was just ready to go home.

"Why don't you take Sarah home?" Ellen called from the desk. "She's looking pretty tired."

We said our goodbyes to Ellen, and I followed Sarah and Bonnie out to the car, helping Sarah into the front seat again before climbing into the back. Bonnie drove us to Ryan and Sarah's house and dropped her off before turning around and driving back to town.

"Will you come over? We haven't even had lunch. We can grab some take out on the way," she asked without taking her eyes off the road.

I really just wanted to go home, but it was three o'clock already, and I hadn't eaten since breakfast. Besides that, Dad wouldn't be home for a few hours, and if I was left alone, my brain would go into overdrive. The last thing I wanted to do was dwell on the almost-kiss with my ex-husband. Spending the afternoon with Bonnie would be a good distraction.

"Sure."

We stopped at a drive-thru in town and quickly ate our burgers in the car, both of us ravenous.

I was gathering our garbage and not paying attention when Bonnie turned down a familiar street. I looked in horror as the house where I'd lived with Cameron came into view. No matter how much I wanted to look away, I couldn't.

The last time I was here I'd packed my belongings and left my wedding ring on the table. That was one of the saddest memories of my entire life.

But as Bonnie drove closer, I started to relax, which surprised me.

The house looked just as I remembered it, and it wasn't scary at all. The landscaping was a little overgrown, and the shutters looked worn, but apart from that, it looked like my house.

"What's wrong?" Bonnie looked over at me with concern. "Oh, this was your house," she added when she saw where I was looking.

I nodded and turned to look back over my shoulder as we passed.

"He still lives there, you know. Dad keeps trying to get him to sell it and get an apartment in town, but he won't."

I was surprised by that bit of news and not sure what to make of it. But I had enough Cameron on my mind already to delve too deeply into it.

After a moment Bonnie turned another corner and pulled up in a driveway in front of a red brick house with a perfectly manicured lawn.

"Home sweet home," she said.

I followed her inside. Her house was lovely: all of the furniture was new, but not modern. Everything had a classic elegance about it, and the rich colors in the carpets and curtains reminded me of royalty.

"I did all the decorating," she said proudly. She plopped down heavily on the couch and curled her legs under her.

"It's beautiful. So, when do I get to meet this Alex I've heard so much about?"

"Soon!" she gushed, patting the couch next to her. "He'll be home from work in a few hours. Maybe you could stay for dinner and meet him?"

"That sounds nice."

I walked slowly across the room, looking at the photos and books on the shelves. I wondered if I could talk with Bonnie about her decorating in an attempt to keep the conversation off Cameron.

"What made you decide on this color scheme?" I asked, examining the wall closely. I felt completely transparent and hoped my attempt at distraction wasn't too obvious.

"Oh, well, I prefer cool colors because they relax me," she responded, waving her arm toward the pale blue wall.

"Do you find suede hard to keep clean?" I asked, turning toward the couch and trying to keep an interested look on my face.

"It's not too hard as long as it doesn't get wet…and this isn't going to work, you know," she said with a smile.

"What isn't going to work?" I asked innocently.

"You're not going to distract me."

I sighed and sat down next to her in defeat.

"What happened, Charlotte?"

I was struck by how different she was from earlier in the day. The loud, boisterous girl was gone, and in front of me sat a woman who was ready for some real answers. I took a deep breath and told her my story.

I started at the beginning—how I'd acted after my mother left. I told her about my distance from Cameron, his late nights at the library to study. She nodded, but never interrupted me, for which I was grateful. Then I told her about Christmas.

Bonnie gasped when she learned about the text message from Lucy. She was obviously pained when I described how I'd felt, being with the family on that Christmas Day, and I watched her shift uncomfortably in her seat as I described moving out.

"But what about Lucy?" she blurted after I told her how Cameron called me several times a day after I moved in with my father.

"Exactly. That's why I didn't answer any of his calls. There was no point in talking because he couldn't change what had happened with her."

"Continue, please."

I settled back into the couch cushions before explaining how I saw Lucy and Cameron kissing in the grocery store, and I watched Bonnie's hands ball into fists. I explained the pain and all-consuming sorrow and how leaving seemed my only option, so I just packed everything into my car and left the next day. I told her how I'd had no idea where I would go, so I just drove, and when I passed over the state line from Connecticut into Massachusetts, I felt a weight lift from my chest. I stayed at a motel in Boston for a week before I managed to land a waitressing job. Then I'd rented a cheap apartment.

Then I told her about meeting Owen and how he'd pursued me. I was glad to see her face soften once she'd heard the story of our romance and how we fell in love. I skipped forward and ended my tale with Owen wanting to move to Fairfield.

Bonnie seemed very interested in Owen's reason for the move, so I explained how he wanted me to make peace with my past before we committed ourselves to a marriage, and how he was concerned about how much I missed my father.

"Didn't you know you'd see all of us? I mean, this is a small town."

"I know. I guess a part of me *was* hoping to see you all. When I lost Cameron, I also lost all of you, and that was hard." I tried my best to stop the tears prickling behind my eyes.

"It was hard for us too," Bonnie whispered, picking at the lace edging on the pillow. "We were all so hurt… You didn't—you didn't even say goodbye."

I pulled Bonnie into a hug, no longer able to hold in my tears. I could feel her body shaking and heard soft sniffles as she let out her own tears.

"I'm so sorry about that," I whispered. "I know I should have said goodbye. I should have explained…but I was so hurt, and the only thing I could do was to run. I had to protect myself. I couldn't bear the thought of anything that reminded me of Cameron." I rested my head on Bonnie's shoulder.

She pulled back but kept her hands on my shoulders, holding me still.

"We didn't understand, and Cameron didn't give us any explanation. All we saw was that you were gone, and he was very quickly spiraling downward. He didn't leave his house for weeks. Mom would take food over for him, but he barely ate it. We were all really worried, but…slowly he started to face the world again. I don't really know what happened for him in that time. I guess only Cameron could tell you that." She let go of my shoulders and sat back. "We found out later that he'd dated Lucy for a while, but neither of them would give us any details, and we didn't push it. I suppose we should've put two and two together…"

I was shocked that Cameron had been so affected by my leaving. For so long I'd assumed he made a happy home with Lucy and didn't think of me at all. This piece of information confirmed the story Cameron told me and made me believe the other things he'd said might be true as well.

"What happened when you moved back here? Was it hard to be home?" She dropped the pillow back onto the couch and pulled her knees up to her chest.

I shifted in my seat and picked up the pillow Bonnie had discarded. I described what it was like to see Ellen at the market, and I cringed as I told her about grabbing the contraceptive jelly.

Bonnie giggled, and the brightness returned to her sad eyes. The lightness of the moment didn't last long, though, as I told her the rest of what had happened since my return to Fairfield.

"His excuse was that you were distant and trying to look after your father after your mother left?" she shrieked, immediately standing.

I nodded. I couldn't elaborate because I couldn't really justify his reasoning either.

"Right. I was going to let this drop, but I just can't. Tonight after he gets home from work, I'm going to go over there and—"

"No!" I said, cutting her off.

Bonnie looked at me questioningly.

"Just leave it alone, Bonnie. This doesn't have anything to do with you"

She stared at me for a moment. Bonnie was used to getting her way, and from what I remembered, she wasn't above a tantrum.

"He's my brother. I have a right to talk to him if I want to."

"Yes, you do, but I'm asking you to please just let this go. I think enough of a mess was caused today without you adding to it. Cameron has already told me he's sorry. There's nothing else to be said, so you yelling at him won't do any good," I practically shouted. I didn't mean to be so angry, but I was.

I didn't regret what had happened with Lucy today. I was glad to finally confront her, but I didn't want it to go any further. I just wanted to forget.

Bonnie pouted, and I could see she was going into the sulking routine.

"I wasn't going to do anything bad. I just want to tell him I think what he did was wrong and explain how much he hurt everyone with his actions," she said, looking at me sadly.

I sighed. "I know you don't mean any harm, Bonnie. But he knows all of that. Why do you think Cameron didn't tell you all of this himself? You talking to him is only going to make him feel worse. Please, I'm asking you to just let this go."

Bonnie folded her arms across her chest. "Fine!" she huffed, throwing herself down on the couch.

"I know you want to help, but right now Cameron and I both need some time. We don't need anything else making things more complicated then they already are. Can you respect that?"

She didn't reply or even look at me, so I took that as my cue to leave. I'd spent quite enough time with her today and could feel a slight headache coming on.

"I think I'm going to head home. I'll take a rain check on dinner and meeting Alex." I collected my handbag from the counter.

"I'll drive you," Bonnie said as she stood up.

"It's okay. I think I'd enjoy the walk. I need some fresh air."

I looked over my shoulder and called out a goodbye as I opened the door. Bonnie lay on the couch with her arms folded, but she didn't respond, so just pulled the door closed behind me.

As I moved at a brisk pace down the street, I thought about the past twenty-four hours. I now had more information about my breakup with Cameron, more details about how everyone in my life was feeling about it, and more insight into my own feelings than I'd gained the whole five years I was gone.

My mind raced as I thought over my recent conversations with Cameron. I didn't excuse his cheating. His reason didn't make what he did okay, and nothing he could say would change my opinion. But maybe that didn't matter. Maybe I didn't need to forgive him because I was fine without him. I really had moved to a point where I was okay *not* being with Cameron.

But then why the freakout in his office?

I remembered that Cameron had tried to kiss me only a few hours ago, and my stomach turned. No matter how much I loved him — and I did love him very much; I could admit that to myself now — I wasn't able to completely let go of what he did. I couldn't trust him again.

I turned the corner onto the street where I used to live and moved silently down the block. I kicked pebbles along the sidewalk and slowly looked up when I stopped in front of the house. Cameron's house. My house. Our house.

I looked at it objectively. It was a beautiful home. I remembered how much I'd loved living there and how excited we were when we first moved in. I'd missed this house for a long time after I moved to Boston. The apartment there had never really felt like home. *Because Cameron wasn't there*, said a little voice inside my head. I quickly shook that thought away.

My gaze fell on the driveway, and I noticed several oil stains on the concrete — some old and dried and others darker and more recent. Was Cameron's car leaking oil? Not that it mattered to me. I gazed over the landscaping and realized the flowerbeds were almost the same as I remembered. The plants had grown and flourished in my absence, although they could use a little trimming. Looking around me, I stepped across the grass and walked up to the front window.

I knew it would be a mistake, but still I wanted to see inside the house. I cupped my hand to the glass to stop the reflection from the sun and peered through the window. It was dark inside, but as my eyes adjusted, I was able to make out some shapes.

As far as I could tell, the living room looked just the same. The furniture was exactly where I remembered it being, as if five years hadn't passed.

I stepped back from the window and quickly returned to the sidewalk and my walk down the street. I didn't need to see any more. My mind was flooded with images of Cameron and me snuggled on that couch.

As I walked, I tried to focus on the cracks in the pavement and the sounds of the birds singing in the trees above, but the only thing I saw was Cameron's face slowly moving toward mine, his eyes closed and his lips slightly parted.

I finished walking the mile and a half into town and thought further about the insanity that had been my day with the Harper women. Had all of that really happened? I came to the conclusion that Ellen, Bonnie, and Sarah weren't the same people I remembered, just as I wasn't the same person they knew from before.

I was sure my divorce from Cameron had had a negative effect on the entire family, but I never realized they might need closure as much as I did. When I thought back to the events at David's office, I was surprised at my own behavior as well. When Lucy was in my face, I just couldn't hold myself back.

I felt guilty for a moment, and I allowed it to sit there, feeling I deserved it — if not for what happened with Lucy, then at least for Owen. I owed him some serious explanations.

Finally my dad's house came into view. I finished my walk, headed up the driveway, and slowly walked inside, still thinking. I'd have to talk with Owen when he called. I hated the fact that he was affected so much by all of this, but I wanted to be honest with him about everything that happened.

I pulled out my cell phone and typed him a text message, sending it before I lost my nerve.

Hey you, Having a good day at work?
Need to tell you some things.
When is a good time to call? Love you. xx

I waited very impatiently for him to text back, staring at the phone until — after what felt like hours — the screen lit up, and it vibrated in my hand. I read the message quickly while holding my breath.

Getting off work early!
Want to meet in Hartford for dinner?

I was overjoyed at his suggestion. Spending time with Owen was exactly what I needed.

Sounds great. Where?

I ran upstairs and to look through my closet. I wanted to wear something nice for him. I had excitement butterflies like I did when Owen and I had first started dating. I heard my phone beep and ran back downstairs to read his reply.

How about that Thai place
where we had lunch when we were there? @8?

See you there.

⁓❦⁓

The hour drive to Hartford flew by, and my nerves about the conversation ahead were forgotten until I stepped out of my car at the restaurant.

"It's so good to see you," Owen said happily, pulling me into his arms and swinging me around. His voice was normal, but he held me just a little tighter than usual, and I could sense some tension in him.

"I missed you." I sighed happily. It had only been two days, yet it felt like an eternity.

"Let's get some food. I'm starving." He pulled me into the small Thai place. The aromatic scent was overwhelming as we walked through the door, and I heard Owen's stomach grumble.

We ordered quickly, both knowing exactly what we wanted, and once the waitress left, we were alone.

"So, you wanted to talk?" Owen asked, sipping his water.

"Yes, about Cameron."

"This is all very cryptic. I'm nervous."

I smiled, trying to assure him nothing was wrong, but when I opened my mouth to speak, I couldn't get anything out. Instead I reached under the table and patted his knee.

"Are you still upset about me spending time with Bonnie?" I asked, thinking it might be safer to ease into the conversation.

"No. I know I was upset the other day, but I understand. I feel like an idiot for overreacting to her visit." He pulled his chair around to sit next to me instead of across from me. He brushed his lips softly against my forehead, but his hands were shaking slightly, and his voice was tense.

Taking a deep breath, I looked right into his eyes. "I have to tell you some things."

His smile faded, and he let out a long breath. "If you're going to break my heart, Charlotte, please do it quickly," he said, refusing to look at me.

"What? Owen, no!" I grabbed his chin and pulled his face to look into mine. "I love you. I'm going to marry you."

"Then what is it?"

The pain in Owen's eyes burned me like rays from the sun. Suddenly all my emotional turmoil over the last twenty-four hours seemed trivial. My past was over. What mattered now was right here in front of me.

"I spoke with Cameron," I said, not knowing how else to start.

Owen nodded but didn't say anything. He understood better than anyone how difficult it was for me to talk about things, and I knew he wouldn't interrupt me.

"He told me he had some things to explain and — I don't know — curiosity got the better of me, I guess, so I met him and we talked. He told me his reasons for being with Lucy, but he swears there wasn't an affair, and he said he was very sorry."

I wanted to be honest with Owen, but now that I'd said all this out loud, I was terrified he was going to leave me.

Owen looked into his lap, but he was nodding. "What reasons did he give?"

"He said I was distant after my mom ran off, and he thought after months of me pulling away that I…didn't love him anymore," I said. "He said he only kissed Lucy once and the rest of the affair was just emotional, not physical. He said he talked to her because he couldn't talk to me." I said that last part with some difficulty. It was still hard for me to process that.

Owen lifted his head and looked at me curiously. "What did you say to him?"

"I said — well, I yelled — that my being distant wasn't justification for what he did, and I didn't accept his apology. It wasn't a very nice conversation."

I looked Owen right in the eye to judge his reaction. He was calm, but I could see sadness in his eyes.

I knew I needed to tell him what else Cameron said the other night before I left, even if it would be hurtful.

"Here you go," the waitress said in an overly cheery voice as she put our plates down in front of us.

"Thank you," Owen said politely, never taking his eyes off of me.

We were silent until she walked away, and I looked down at my plate, picked up my chopsticks, and started to push noodles around. Taking a deep breath, I counted to ten in my head, then exhaled slowly.

"He said he still loves me," I whispered.

"I knew it."

The people at the next table looked at us nervously as I reached out and stroked Owen's arm to soothe him. I could only imagine how difficult that was for him to hear. I hadn't even told him about my feelings yet.

"Nothing happened. I promise you. When he told me that, I yelled at him and drove away. I swear to you…" I trailed off when I saw a tear welling in his eye.

"I trust you, Charlotte. I do, but this worries me. I've felt you pulling away, and I'm terrified."

I could see the despair in his eyes, and I felt my heart break for him. "Have I pulled away?"

Owen nodded sadly, and my mind started to race.

I tried to think back over my behavior, but I couldn't find anything I'd done to make him think I was leaving. In fact, I recalled telling him over and over that I would stay.

We sat in silence for a few more minutes before Owen started to eat. I continued to push my noodles around, having lost my appetite.

"That's why I was upset when you said you *hoped* I loved you. Cameron told me he felt unloved, and I felt like you were saying the same thing. I honestly don't know what I've done to pull away from you," I said, my voice sounding slightly panicked.

Owen stayed silent. He just shook his head slowly and kept his eyes on his plate.

"What do I have to do to prove how much I love you?"

Owen looked at me, and his face softened, his head cocked slightly to the side.

"Nothing," he whispered, his hand cupping my cheek. "I believe you."

"But?" I asked, knowing he was holding back.

He sighed. "But…you've been acting differently since you got home. It's natural, and I understand it must be so hard to be back there, but I think it's important for you to find yourself again—your true self, not some façade you wear so people don't see your pain. And as much as I hate the thought of you spending time with him, maybe resolving things with Cameron can help you with that."

I marveled at how selfless he was and how lucky I was to have him. I snuggled against his chest, as close as I could get.

"I know who I am," I assured him. "All he'd be able to tell me is who I was." But a small voice in the back of my head whispered that I'd always carry Cameron with me.

"I hate that he knows a part of you that I never will."

I didn't know what to say because he was right. Part of me that would always belong to Cameron. But that part of me was my past—my whole future belonged to Owen, and Cameron wouldn't know the future me. Unfortunately, that thought kind of upset me.

I still hadn't told Owen about my second conversation with Cameron in his office today, or about my declaration of love, but the more I thought about it, the more I questioned the need tell him at all. Hearing that I still loved my ex-husband would only hurt Owen, and nothing good would come from it. As long as I knew the feelings I had for Cameron wouldn't jeopardize my relationship, maybe it was better to spare Owen that pain.

I'd carried these feelings for Cameron the whole time I'd been in love with Owen. I just never realized it. The two men could share my heart, but only one of them would be in on the secret.

Owen and I sat in silence while I let my thoughts run freely and when I looked up, he was watching me expectantly. "Are you going to eat?"

I looked down at the food and shook my head. "Sorry, I'm not really hungry."

"Okay, let's get out of here and go for a walk," he said, dropping a few bills on the table.

We walked out of the restaurant and down the street past our cars. Owen rubbed his thumb slowly over the back of my hand as we strolled in silence.

Soon we came to a park and walked over to a pond with a small waterfall. Owen sat down on the grass and pulled me next to him, throwing his arm over my shoulder.

"We're going to be fine," he said softly. I wasn't sure if he was talking to me or just reassuring himself.

"Yes, we are." I kissed his cheek. "I love you."

Owen pulled me into his arms and leaned down to me. I lay back in the grass with his warm body pressed to mine.

He moaned as our lips moved together, and I felt his erection pressing into my thigh. My body automatically reacted. I pressed my hips against his. Owen moved his hands down my body and stroked my breasts through my shirt, his lips trailing down my throat. Once his mouth left mine, I found myself gasping for breath and realized just how turned on I was. It seemed the sex ban in my dad's house was having just as much of an effect on me as on Owen.

"Yes," I whispered as I felt my jeans being undone and his fingers slipped below the waistband.

Owen's lips never left my neck, but he let out a guttural moan when he felt how aroused I was.

Suddenly, we froze as the sound of people talking echoed through the parking area behind us. Owen started to chuckle and sat up, removing his hand from my jeans. I pouted at the loss of his touch.

"I can't win," he said with a sigh as we watched a couple walk hand in hand down to the water.

"Time to go home?" I reached over to stroke his arm.

Owen nodded and helped me stand. We brushed off the loose grass and walked back up to our cars. Our goodbyes were short — although Owen did linger a bit longer to kiss me than he usually did. Fortunately his next trip to see me was only a few days away.

The whole drive home I thought about Owen and Cameron — and whether I had the courage to face my past once and for all.

Chapter Ten
The Ties That Bind

I awoke the following morning to my phone beeping on the nightstand. Groaning, I rolled over and grabbed for it several times before my hand finally found it. I pulled the phone over to my face and squinted at the screen. I had a text message from Bonnie.

> I'm sorry for interfering in your life.
> You were right. Not my place.
> I'll back off, I promise!
> Please don't be mad! xx

I smiled, knowing it must have been hard for Bonnie to admit she was wrong. I quickly typed a reply.

> I'm not mad. I know your heart's in the right place,
> but I appreciate you backing off.
> It'll make everything easier.
> Also, I have a question…

Because we were thinking of moving to Fairfield, Owen and I had been hesitant to start planning our wedding. We didn't even know for sure where we'd be living. But now that we'd finalized the move, it was time to get serious about planning. This would have the added benefit of reassuring Owen of my commitment to him, and Bonnie was the perfect person to help me plan my wedding.

> What?

Her text came back almost immediately, and I laughed as I typed back to her, suspecting she would scream when she read my note. I hoped Alex wasn't trying to sleep.

> I'm going to start planning my wedding
> and wondered if you'd help.

She didn't reply, and after five minutes I decided I wasn't going to wait any longer. I got out of bed and went to take a shower. As I stood under the warm water and watched the soap suds swirl around the drain, I thought about marrying Owen. I'd already done the big, romantic day, and Owen knew I didn't want to do all that again.

We were both happy with the idea of a small ceremony — just close friends and family — and I thought it might be nice if we went to New York City. My dad could drive down, and Owen's family could make the trip from Boston. Plus, I wouldn't be reminded of Cameron everywhere I looked.

Once I'd dried my hair and dressed, I went back and looked at my phone. I'd missed a call and a text message. I redialed the missed call first.

"Hello, Fairfield Realty. How can I help you?" said a voice on the line.

"Hello. I missed a call from this number."

"Name?"

"Charlotte Barnes."

"Yes, Ms. Barnes, I'll put you through to the agent who called. One moment please," she said before switching me to music. The music stopped almost as soon as it started, and a man's voice answered cheerily.

"Charlotte, good to speak to you again," he said as if we were old friends.

"Good to speak to you too. Do you have some news on our application?"

"Yes, your rental application been approved," he reported. "You can pick up the key and give us a deposit next week and move in any time after that."

"That's great! I'll let Owen know, and we'll come in next week to finalize everything," I told him excitedly before hanging up.

We had a house!

I squealed and dialed Owen's cell number with shaking fingers. His voicemail answered.

"You've reached Owen Cooper, please leave me a message."

"Owen!" I yelled. "Our rental application was just approved. We can move in next week! Call me back."

I hung up and remembered I still had an unread text message. It was Bonnie's reply.

I'd love to help!
Maybe we can get together next weekend?

Next weekend? That was unlike Bonnie. I'd expected her to be on my doorstep wanting to plan that very minute. Maybe she needed some time to adjust to the idea of me marrying someone who wasn't Cameron. I was just glad she was willing to help. I shrugged and typed "Sounds great!" in response before looking around the room to see if there was anything I could start packing for the move.

Ten minutes later, I was still standing in the middle of the bedroom staring into space. Aside from the clothes in the closet, which I still needed, there was nothing to pack. I'd never really unpacked when I arrived.

With a sigh, I went downstairs to make breakfast. Maybe I'd drive by the new house later and plan a makeover of the landscaping or something. When had my life become so mundane?

I tried to think about how I could occupy my days for the upcoming weeks and months. What did other people my age do during the day?

They had jobs, of course.

I sighed and put two slices of bread in the toaster. I'd worked for the past few years, but I never had the motivation or desire to choose a career, so my jobs were minimum wage and transitory. It was easy to give notice at the restaurant and be free when Owen and I had decided to move, but it left me with no idea about what to do next. I thought of my dad telling me I'd regret my decision to forgo my scholarship to NYU to stay in Fairfield with Cameron.

I closed my eyes, remembering with perfect clarity how I'd stood in this kitchen and yelled at him that he didn't understand what it was like to be in this much in love. I'd told him I wasn't going anywhere without Cameron. Dad had chuckled and patted my shoulder. He said one day I'd be disappointed with the decision, but it was my mistake to make.

Looks like that day had come. As much as I'd hated him that day—and I did—he'd been right.

I poured myself a cup of coffee and spread peanut butter on my toast before sitting at the dining table in front of the newspaper Dad had left behind. I flicked through the pages until I came to the job listings. A couple of sales jobs seemed interesting, so I circled them and kept reading. After a few more minutes and not finding anything else relevant, I closed the newspaper and picked up my cell phone. Owen hadn't called back yet, so I supposed he was busy.

I thought about the night before and how he'd told me again that I should talk with Cameron, despite how it clearly made him crazy. I knew he was right, and so selfless to demand I do this for myself, but I was scared. I wasn't going to learn anything I didn't already know, I told myself. Nothing Cameron said mattered anyway because I was with Owen now.

I also figured I could leave if Cameron upset me, and with a surge of courage, I decided to suck it up and do it. I found the card Cameron had given me and dialed his work number.

"Harper Dental Clinic, how can I help you?" a cheerful voice said.

"Hello, I'd like to speak with Doctor Harper, please."

"May I ask who's calling?"

"Charlotte Barnes."

"Just a moment. I'll see if Doctor Harper is available," she said, her voice clear and professional.

"Charlotte?" Cameron's voice came on the line.

"Hi, Cam…um…how are you?" I asked, suddenly losing my courage.

"I'm fine, and you?" he asked, his voice sounding cautious.

"Oh…I'm good." I wasn't asking him out on a date. Why was I suddenly so nervous?

"Were you calling for any particular reason? Not that I mind if you just called to chat—you're welcome to call me whenever you like…for any reason. I just thought there might be a specific thing you wanted to discuss," Cameron rambled.

He was as nervous as I was, which actually helped me relax a little.

"Charlotte?" Cameron asked again.

"I'm ready to talk…well, to listen, actually. You'll talk and I'll listen… about Lucy…" I trailed off and smacked myself in the head for not being able to form a coherent sentence.

Cameron was silent for a moment. "Now?"

"Um, no. Whenever is good for you. Should I make an appointment to see you in your office?"

I didn't want to be anywhere public where I might be seen crying or anywhere too relaxed where he might try to make a move. I thought about how he'd tried to kiss me in his office, but I'd just make sure to keep a safe distance between us.

"Yeah…uh…that should be fine. Can I call you back after I've had a chance to look over my appointment book?"

"Sure. Talk to you then," I said before hanging up.

What the hell was that?

I put my phone down and ran my fingers through my hair in frustration. I couldn't believe I'd acted so stupidly. I'd known Cameron for ten years, had spoken to him on the phone hundreds — if not thousands — of times, and yet when I wanted to appear strong and confident, I came across as a bumbling fool.

A few minutes later my cell rang.

"Hello?" I asked, grinning when I saw Owen's name flash on the screen.

"We got it?" Owen's voice ripped through the phone, and I laughed at how excited he sounded.

"Yeah, we can collect the keys next week!" I was feeling as excited as he seemed to be. "Do you want to accept it, or should we continue look in Hartford?"

"Well, I love that house, but to be honest, I don't know how comfortable I am about us living so close to Cameron. I was okay with it until he said he still loves you… Now I just don't know if it's a good idea."

"I've had similar thoughts. That's why I suggested looking in Hartford in the first place."

"I hate to just give it up. Why don't we take the house in Fairfield on a month-to-month lease, if we can, and see how it goes? If Cameron becomes an issue we can look at moving to Hartford."

I thought about that for a moment. I wasn't feeling the need to run from Cameron anymore. "I think that's a great idea. I'll call the guy back and ask about a month-to-month lease."

"This is so great," Owen said. "We're really settling down. You know, I was thinking…maybe we should start getting some ideas for the wedding."

"I was thinking the exact same thing! I've already enlisted some help in the planning. We'll be starting next weekend," I told him proudly.

"Ah, you're the best! I love you," he sighed into the phone.

"I love you," I echoed just before there was a beep from my phone. I looked at the screen. "I have another call. Do you want me to call you back?"

"Nah, I better get back to work."

"Have a good day," I said before hanging up and answering the second call. "Hello?"

"Hello again," Cameron responded, sounding surprised.

"Oh, hey. Sorry I took so long to answer. I was on a call with—I was on another call," I said.

"No problem. So I was looking at my appointments, and I have all afternoon free on Tuesday next week. Maybe we could have lunch first so we could catch up. Nothing about the past—we'll just talk about what's happening now, and then when we're feeling a bit more comfortable we can talk about the past… What do you think?"

I felt rather uneasy about sitting and chatting with him like we were old friends, but I decided to agree for now. If I changed my mind, I'd simply call and cancel.

"Sounds good. What time should I be there?"

"Why don't you come by the office at about twelve-thirty, and I'll order something in?"

"Okay, see you Tuesday," I told him with a bit of formality in my voice. We weren't friends, and I wanted him to remember that.

"Have a good weekend."

"Goodbye," I said as I hit the *end* button on my cell. *Did I do the right thing?*

⁓⊰ ♡✦♡ ⊱⁓

I never could decide for sure if this was the right course of action, but the following Tuesday I found myself walking toward the building with shaking hands. I'd been a nervous wreck all morning, and I considered calling Cameron and canceling the whole meeting. But when Owen had visited over the weekend, he'd encouraged me to just get it over and done with. Once I knew what Cameron had to say, I could move on with the plans for our wedding.

Thinking of Owen, I walked into the building with a new determination. When I stepped through the door into Cameron's office, his receptionist gave me a polite smile.

"Are you Ms. Barnes?"

"Yes, but please call me Charlotte."

"Doctor Harper is ready for you. Please go through." She held her arm out, indicating the waiting room.

I entered the empty waiting room and saw Cameron's office door standing open. I could see him sitting at his desk, tapping his fingers lightly on the keyboard. He looked so calm—wasn't he nervous at all? I walked over and knocked to announce my arrival, even though the door was open.

Cameron looked up and smiled. "Come in," he said, gesturing to one of the chairs in front of his desk.

I took a seat and noticed a delicious smell in the room.

"I ordered Chinese. I hope you don't mind." He closed the door and sat in the chair next to mine. I could smell his cologne. It smelled good. *Shit!* I was in trouble already.

I turned my chair to face him, but also moved it slightly away. The scent of his cologne was much softer in this new position, and I relaxed a little.

"Fried rice?" He held out a box and a pair of chopsticks.

"Thanks." I put some of the rice on the plate he'd laid out on his desk before picking up another container and adding chicken and vegetables. I grabbed one of the bottles of diet soda he'd provided, smiling when I realized he remembered what I liked to drink.

"This looks great," I said awkwardly. After that I was at a loss. I was relieved when Cameron started to speak.

"How was your weekend?" he asked casually before scooping rice into his mouth.

"Busy."

He cocked an eyebrow.

"Owen and I spent the weekend in Hartford picking out furniture for the house we're moving in to."

If the news upset him at all, he didn't show it. He kept his expression neutral and gave me a smile. "That's great."

I nodded and took a few bites of my food, but I didn't enjoy it. Our upcoming conversation was making me anxious. I put the plate down and picked up my soda.

"How are things with you?" I asked.

He sighed and stirred the rice around on his plate. "Dad is really pushing me to sell the house…our house," he said, looking up at me.

"Do you want to?"

"No…well, maybe."

"What do you mean?"

"I've been thinking about moving my clinic. There just isn't a large enough pool of people here for me to be as successful as I could be, and there doesn't seem to be anything holding me here anymore except…" He stopped talking and looked down at his food.

"Except the house?"

He nodded, and I chewed on my lip.

"Why have you kept it so long?"

Cameron jerked his head up, surprised. "You can't tell?"

"Because of me?" I asked, hoping I was wrong.

His eyes filled with sorrow, and he nodded again. "I'm sorry," he almost whispered. "I know it was *me* who wanted to talk to you about everything—to lay it all out—but now I'm finding it really difficult."

"It's okay," I said, resisting the urge to stroke his hand. I knew touching him right now would be counterproductive.

"No, it's not." He straightened up, and I could see a definite change in his demeanor. "I'm fine now."

He looked down at my plate of half-eaten food and then at his own. "I'm not really hungry," he said, standing up to dump his plate in the trash.

"Me either," I agreed, handing him my plate as well.

"Do you want to get started, then?"

I nodded and moved over to the couch on the other side of the room. Cameron watched me cautiously. I patted the couch cushion next to me, and he hesitantly came and sat down. I slid to the far side and leaned on the arm so we weren't in danger of touching.

"Do you still want to do this? You seem uncomfortable," I said.

"I think it's important that we do this."

"Okay."

"Do you have questions?" he asked, his posture very rigid.

I sighed. "Cam, I can't relax if you're so tense."

His body slouched a bit, and he ran his hands through his hair. "I'm sorry," he said, meeting my eyes. "It's hard for me to admit all the things I did wrong. I know I did them, and I can admit them to myself, but it's hard to say them to you when I know it's going to cause you pain."

"Well, why don't you let me worry about me? I can look after myself. I promise to let you know if I can't take any more, okay?"

His face relaxed a little, and he nodded, then narrowed his eyes. "You won't just get up and run out of here?"

"No!"

"Okay. What's your first question about Lucy?"

My mind was racing with all the questions I wanted to ask, but I didn't know if I really wanted the answers to any of them. I looked down at the hem of my denim skirt, picking at a frayed edge.

"When did it start?"

"You told me the other night that you knew when things started to go wrong between us," Cameron said thoughtfully. "Well, my involvement with Lucy initially started about five months after your mother moved away."

I gasped. I'd assumed he'd been seeing Lucy for much longer than three months.

"When *exactly* did it start?" I wasn't sure why, but now that I had the option of learning the details, I was eager to know everything. I'd gotten the length of the affair wrong—what else was I wrong about?

"Well, I told you about running into her at the harbor that night," Cam said, looking at the floor. "But I guess when I first started talking to her... Do you remember—before that—when we all went to Hartford and ended up in that nightclub?"

I recalled a night, the September before I left, when Cameron and I had an argument before we went out—about something I couldn't remember now. We'd gone to dinner with his family and ended up dancing at a club. I also recalled Cameron sitting in the corner sulking most of the night while everyone else danced.

"I remember."

"While you, Bonnie, and Sarah were dancing, Lucy approached me and..." He stopped talking and ran his hands over his face. "This is hard for me to say to you. Sorry."

"It's hard for me to hear," I said, returning his weak smile. "Go on." I could feel my heart pounding as I waited for him to start speaking again.

"She asked me if I was okay. I told her we were just going through some things, and she asked if I wanted to talk about it. We left the club and walked around talking for over an hour, and when I got back you were still dancing—as if you hadn't even noticed I was gone..." he trailed off and stared at me, waiting for my response.

A hard lump formed in my throat, and I tried to swallow it down as best I could. It was true that I hadn't known he was gone for an hour. How could I have cared so little about my husband? And it disgusted me that my so-called best friend had taken advantage of the situation.

"I'm sorry," Cameron whispered.

"Go on," I choked out. I knew he mistook my pain for something he'd caused, but I didn't have to words to tell him I was upset with myself. I closed my eyes as he continued to speak.

"You'd been so distant, and I hoped that if we got out and had some fun like we used to, it would make us close again. I just wanted us to be like we were before, but you pushed me away again. It hurt even more when I saw that you appeared to be acting perfectly normal with Sarah and Bonnie. I watched you dancing with them—smiling and laughing—and I assumed the distance between us wasn't about your mother after all…but just that you weren't in love with me anymore."

The lump in my throat sank into my stomach, and I started to feel a little sick. For so long I'd thought only about my own pain. What Cameron had been feeling was something new to me…and it was hard to hear.

"What are you thinking?" he asked.

I wiped a few stray tears from my face before looking into his eyes. I felt awful that I'd ever made him feel neglected and unloved.

"I'm sorry," I said with a sniffle.

"You have nothing to be sorry for!" He reached across and rubbed my leg. I leaned away from his touch, and he moved his hand back to his lap.

"I'm sorry I'm not handling this better. I don't want to cry." I breathed for a moment. "I'm fine. Was there anything else?"

He shook his head. "I'm sorry," he said for the millionth time that day. His apologies were starting to annoy me. "Are you all right?"

I pushed my shoulders back and nodded. But I kept my mouth clamped shut because I knew if I tried to speak I'd either burst out crying or scream at him, and I didn't want to do either.

"For days after that I was really confused. It felt good to have someone I could confide in, but it also felt wrong to be talking to someone else behind your back," he continued. "Over and over I tried to tell you, but every time I'd get up the courage to start a conversation, you'd tell me you needed to be alone or you were dealing with too much to listen. I understood that—I really did—but it just reinforced my feeling that you didn't want me anymore."

My deep breathing was not keeping me as calm as I'd hoped as I allowed Cameron's words to settle in. Was it betraying Owen to still feel so strongly about all this?

I noticed Cameron opening his mouth a few times, as if he were going to start speaking, but he never said a word. I knew I had to pull myself together or we'd just sit there in silence all day. So I mentally gave myself a slap.

"Okay." I took a deep breath and noticed my voice wasn't shaking as much. "How long did it go on?"

Cameron leaned back on the couch and rested his head against the top, covering his face with his fingers. I heard him exhale before he moved his hands down to tap nervously on his thighs.

"After that night in Hartford, I was always on edge whenever Lucy came over. It was like we had a secret from you, and it didn't feel right. That thought plagued me, and one night I went down to the harbor to think. But instead of clearing my head, I just got pulled in further because she was there."

I nodded.

"Well, after that, we'd meet every few days to talk. It felt so good to have someone to share my thoughts with, someone I could talk to about my concerns for you and my loneliness, and someone who needed something back from me. She made me feel wanted, needed, and cared for, and I started to look forward to our time together. Over the weeks I started to feel closer to her, and at some point I did believe I loved her."

I cleared my throat. I didn't mean to interrupt him, but it was a reaction I couldn't control.

"I was wrong about that," he continued. "But I didn't know until later on. Not long before Christmas, she told me she loved me and, without even really thinking, I told her I loved her too. I felt so guilty for that, but part of me honestly believed I could love her. I knew it wasn't the same as the way I loved you—I'll never love anyone the way I love you—but it was a type of love all the same."

I gasped again, not from shock this time, but from understanding. What he described was exactly the same as the thoughts I'd had the previous week while trying to justify my feelings for both Owen and Cameron. While I absolutely could not condone his feelings for Lucy, I found myself softening to his dilemma because I was going through the same thing.

"By that point, I was so disgusted with myself, and I was trying so hard to hide it from you. I usually deleted any trace of contact with her from my home life, so when you showed me that text message on my phone…" He paused and looked at me. "I was so angry with myself for being careless, but it was also a huge relief to have it out in the open. Now you could punish me the way I deserved—you could hurt me and yell at me, and then we could work through it. I wasn't at all prepared for you to walk away without a word. That just confirmed that you didn't care. If you could walk away so easily, you must not have loved me, just as I feared."

"It wasn't *at all* easy for me to walk away from you…from us," I interrupted harshly. "It was the hardest thing I've ever had to do."

Cameron watched me sadly. "Watching you drive out of that grocery store parking lot after you saw me with Lucy was the hardest thing I've ever lived through."

"You didn't answer my question…how long did it last?" I reminded him, refocusing the conversation to avoid a pity exchange.

"Right, sorry. After you left, things changed. I was so angry with myself—repulsed by my actions. But I started seeing Lucy more. I tried to convince myself what I felt for her must be real…it *had* to be real or else I'd ruined our relationship for nothing."

"So…you had a relationship with her to prove to yourself that you'd made the right choices?"

"I don't know. At the time it made sense, but looking back I can see how ridiculous it was. I wanted to make it work with her—I really did—but after you left I lost my reason for everything. I was like a zombie, going through the motions of a relationship with her, but without any emotion. I just completely shut down."

"Did you have sex with her?" I braced for the answer before the question even left my mouth.

"I fucked her," he clarified. "It was *just* sex. The physical release was there, but it was just that—a release. No gratification or emotional enjoyment."

Revulsion hit me like a brick wall, and I slid back as far from him as I could without falling off the couch.

I must have had a horrified look on my face because he paused and backpedaled a little. "I never hurt her or anything! I was just completely detached emotionally."

I tried to pull myself back together. "And how long did that go on?" I asked, my nausea increasing. I'd spent that month hiding from the world, trying to put my broken heart back together, and he'd been having regular sex.

"Until that day at the grocery store. Lucy was fed up with coming to the house and not having any food to eat, so she demanded we get some groceries. I didn't care whether I was eating or not at that point, but I went along, grudgingly. As I'm sure you remember, I called you constantly during that time, but you never answered your phone. I even went to your dad's house a few times, but he never let me in, and one time he threatened to arrest me for trespassing, so I stopped coming. When I saw you in the grocery store, I was so happy. I felt some hope for the first time in months."

He took a breath, and I fiddled with the frayed edge of my skirt as I imagined Lucy making herself at home in my house…in my bed.

"I was horrified when I realized you saw Lucy kiss me, and I knew I had to act fast to talk to you before you left my life forever. I tried to get you to listen, but you were so angry. I was actually relieved that you were angry. If you hadn't cared about me anymore, you wouldn't have had such a strong reaction. So when I saw how furious you were, I knew there was still love in your heart, and that made me feel good—even if I was still feeling wretched for what I did to you."

I nodded, remembering the day clearly.

"Even though you drove away from me, I was left with a sense of hope that you still cared about me. If you still loved me, there was a chance for us. I held on to that for a long time. After you left, Lucy approached me, furious that I'd left her in the store to come running after you. She started yelling, but I felt so rejuvenated at the thought that you must still love me… My interest in her completely fell apart, and I broke things off with her for good about two weeks later. I've barely spoken to her since," he said, running his fingers through his hair and sending it in all different directions.

"It was all so selfish. Everything was for your own needs… You treated her terribly."

Cameron gave me a guilty look and nodded. "I used Lucy to give me what I wasn't getting from you, and then I used her to try to make myself feel better. I do feel guilty about that, but on the other hand, I couldn't care less about her feelings—it was hurting *you* that affected me. It's only your feelings I care about," he said, sounding a little petulant.

I looked at Cameron and realized he wasn't the man I thought he was. I'd never thought *my* Cameron was selfish or would use another person for his own reasons. Right now he was like a stranger to me.

"It was that day that I realized I wasn't good enough for you," he said, almost mirroring my thoughts. "I hadn't been patient, hadn't waited for you and had faith in our love when you needed me to do that the most. That made me take a long, hard look at myself. I knew I'd have to become a person you could be proud to be with, who was worthy of your love. That's why I didn't pursue you for a long time, and when I *was* ready and believed I *could* be a person worthy of you, I came to see you, but you were gone."

"You looked for me?" I always assumed Cameron didn't care.

"Yes. The details aren't important, but I did try."

I wondered why he didn't want to tell me more, but I didn't push. I'd already learned so much that my brain was on overload.

"I *am* a good man now," he said, looking at me through his long lashes.

I nodded but didn't say anything. I wanted to believe he was a good man, that I hadn't married someone capable of doing the things he'd done. Maybe the last five years had changed him—I just wasn't sure.

He smiled and looked into my eyes. "I can be what you need now."

I shifted in my seat. Cameron's gaze never left mine, and the intimacy of his stare combined with his words made me extremely uncomfortable. I could avoid his flirting and innuendo, but a direct question would be difficult to evade. I hoped he'd never ask me to come back to him. I decided to lay out my position out so it was clear. Yes, it was true he hadn't technically cheated, but did that even matter anymore? Regardless of the past, I was with Owen now, and I was happy.

"Cameron…" I said slowly.

"I like it better off," he said with a small smile.

"Huh?"

He pointed to my hand. "I like it better off," he repeated.

I looked down to where he was pointing and saw I'd been sliding my engagement ring on and off my finger. I stared down at the diamond Owen gave me and placed it back in position.

"This is where it belongs."

The smile left Cameron's face, and his knee began to bounce as he rubbed his hands up and down his thighs nervously.

"All I can offer you is friendship," I said. I tried to say it nicely, with a soft tone and a half-smile, but the grimace on Cameron's face told me my words hurt him.

"I know," he said. "I just wanted you to know you have options."

I nodded and stood up. "I should go."

"No! Please stay!" he blurted. Then, after a moment, he sighed. "I'd rather have your friendship than nothing at all."

I doubted whether friendship was truly possible for us, but he looked so hopeful, and I did like the idea of having him in my life.

Although I felt better knowing the details of his relationship with Lucy, I still hadn't processed everything. It was a relief to confirm that there'd been no true affair, but he *had* slept with her after I moved out. Was I okay with that? Could I accept it? I didn't know.

I tried to think of something to say to lighten the mood before I left. I glanced at him and again noticed the hint of wrinkles around his eyes. They reminded me how much of each other's lives we'd missed.

"I can't believe how old you are!" I said suddenly.

"Excuse me?" he asked with a chuckle.

I laughed while trying to cover my tracks. "I mean, how old we both are. When I'm around you I feel like I'm still twenty-two years old. And then I look at you now and…my God, Cameron, you're *thirty!*"

"And you're twenty-eight," he said with a shrug. He obviously wasn't seeing what I found so astonishing.

"When we met I was only eighteen. We were just children then. We're getting older, I forget that," I said, and he smiled. "Can I give you some *friendly* advice?"

"Of course."

"Sell the house."

He studied my face for a moment, and I gave him a smile.

"It's holding you back, keeping you stuck. I think it would be good for you," I said.

He nodded sadly. "I'll think about it."

Suddenly his head popped up. "Do you want to see it again?" he asked.

I nodded. "Sometime."

I was curious about the house. Peeking through the window had been almost surreal. I needed to say goodbye to that house properly—and goodbye to the person I was when I lived there.

"Why not right now?" he asked, walking across the room to his desk.

"Don't you have work to do?"

"It's almost the end of the day, and I had the whole afternoon blocked out for your visit, so I can take off a little early." Then he used the intercom to tell his receptionist she could pack up and head home.

I looked at my watch in surprise. We'd been talking for almost three hours.

"Ah, sure. Okay," I said, mostly because I couldn't think of a reason to say no. I'd just get all of the past out of the way in one day.

⊷≺ ☙❀☙ ≻⊶

A short time later I pulled up in the driveway behind Cameron. I waited for him to get out and open the front door before I came to follow him inside. I needed the extra time to prepare myself. I took in every detail as I stepped through the door and allowed my eyes to get accustomed to the indoor light.

Cameron kicked off his shoes and stood by the couch, watching me as I slowly made my way around the room, touching things softly and smiling to myself.

"It looks just the same." I turned to face him, inhaling deeply and allowing the smells to take me back to the time when this was my home.

He shrugged. "Yeah, I never really changed anything. I like it how it is."

"Can I?" I asked as I pointed down the hallway toward the bedrooms.

"Sure," he replied, standing to walk down the hall with me.

My hand hesitated over the bedroom door handle before turning it and pushing the door open. The blinds were all drawn, so I could only make out shapes. Cameron's hand slipped past me and switched on the light, brightening the room.

It was a little different than I remembered, but still familiar. The bed was in the same position, but the bedspread was different. There was now a large flat-screen TV on the wall opposite the bed, and the bookcase that had once been filled with dentistry text books now held novels of all shapes and sizes.

I let out a long breath and stepped into the room hesitantly. My gaze moved to the walk-in closet, and I opened the door and stepped inside. Cameron's clothes were all still on one side and the other side—my side—was empty, apart from a few storage boxes stacked against the wall.

I could feel him standing behind me, his warm breath on the back of my neck, and I remembered being in this same position on Christmas Day, five years ago, when he pressed me against that wall and kissed me. I stared at the wall as if to bring the memory to life, but then shook it off and pushed past Cameron so I could get out of the closet. I suddenly felt suffocated.

Standing in the bedroom again, I saw something on the bedside table glint in the light. I walked over and picked up two gold rings: my engagement and wedding bands.

"You still have these?"

Cameron gave me a sheepish look and grabbed them from my hand, shoving them in his pocket.

"Sorry. I look at them sometimes," he mumbled.

You keep them by your bed? I let it drop. He looked embarrassed, and I didn't want to make him feel any worse.

I turned to look at my old bed, the wrought-iron frame so familiar. A smile spread on my lips as I remembered how much I'd loved that bed, until an unwelcome thought entered my mind: I wasn't the last woman to sleep there.

"Would you like a drink or something to eat?" Cameron asked, unaware of my thoughts. I followed him out of the bedroom and through the large archway into the kitchen.

"No, thanks. I should be going. Dad will be getting home from work soon, and I need to start on dinner," I said, still thinking about Lucy in my bed.

Why had he kept those rings all these years? I knew I shouldn't be surprised. He'd kept the house and had our wedding picture up in his office, so it wasn't out of character. But there was something more personal about the rings.

"Oh, right, well…we don't want to keep him waiting."

I smiled at him. He was trying to make this friendship work, but I knew it was hard for him. And it was just as hard for me.

"Are we okay?" he asked, looking solemn for a moment. "About all the Lucy stuff?"

I thought about his question. Was I okay with the fact that he'd gotten involved with Lucy? No. Was I okay with our conversation today? I thought so. "We'll be fine," I told him with an encouraging smile.

Cameron followed me out and waved as I drove off down the street.

I wasn't sure how Owen was going to feel about it, but I felt like I owed it to myself, to my younger self, to give it a try. I was going to be friends with Cameron.

Chapter Eleven
Turning the Tables

"Should I put these boxes in the bedroom?" Owen called loudly.

I stuck my head around the doorway to see which ones he was holding. "Yeah, just put them in the closet, and I'll unpack them when I'm done in the kitchen," I called before going back to organizing the pots and pans.

"I think this is the last of it, Char," Dad said, placing a large box on the counter.

"Thanks for helping, Dad. We really appreciate it. You should come over for dinner tomorrow night, and we'll celebrate."

"Sounds good, kiddo," he said with a smile.

"Why don't we wait until the weekend and make it a housewarming party?" Owen added. "I might invite some of the guys from work." He'd arrived from Boston the day before, just in time for our move, and he'd start work in Hartford the following week. I was so relieved to have him here all the time—and in our own place!

"Yeah, sounds good." I buried my head in the cabinet to put the last few things in place.

"I don't know—Hartford boys?" Dad joked. "We'd better have some Fairfield guys too."

Owen punched him in the arm and opened the fridge. "Sure." He handed Dad a beer and got one for himself.

"Think we can get it organized for this weekend?" Owen asked.

I nodded, and Dad charged full steam ahead.

"I'll call all the boys tonight and set it up," he said. "You just get the food."

Owen came over and kissed the top of my head, offering me a sip of his beer. I took the bottle from him and swallowed a mouthful before giving it back.

"This is a great house," Dad said, taking a long drink from his bottle.

"Yeah, I think we'll be happy here," I said.

Owen slipped his arms around my waist and kissed my cheek. I felt a little uncomfortable in front of my father, but Dad's smile made me realize he was happy. I smiled back and leaned back into Owen's chest.

"I'm exhausted, so I might leave you kids to it," Dad said, placing his beer on the counter.

"Are you sure? We're gonna order some pizza," Owen said, releasing me to pull his cell phone out of his pocket.

"Nah, you relax and get used to your new place," he replied, giving me a hug. "'Night, Char."

"Thanks for all your help today," I said, hugging him back.

"Thanks, Michael," Owen called as I walked Dad down the hallway and out into the yard.

"I'm glad you're going to be around for a while," Dad said when we reached his car.

"And only around the corner!"

"That's even better."

"Thanks again, Dad. Today would have been much harder without your help."

"Let me know if you need anything else."

After I watched him drive away, I turned and smiled at the house. It was great to finally have a place that was mine and Owen's. Since my conversation with Cameron at his office, everything was going really smoothly. Owen seemed okay with the idea of Cameron and me being friends, as long as we didn't hang out together alone, and that seemed like a good compromise.

I hadn't seen Cameron since I left his house, but Bonnie had told me yesterday that he seemed happier than she'd seen him in a long time. I took comfort in that. I hoped he felt better because he'd gotten everything off his chest. He'd been carrying it around for so long. Surely he felt freer now.

I walked back through the front door looking for Owen, and I screamed when he picked me up and ran down the hall with me over his shoulder.

"We have half an hour before the pizza will be here," he said, laughing and running to the bedroom, slamming the door closed behind us. The sex ban was officially over.

⋯⊱ ☙❈❧ ⊰⋯

I looked in the shopping cart and raised my eyebrows at Owen.

"What's all that?"

"We need everything!" he replied.

"Really? We need…" I counted the items in the cart. "Fourteen bags of potato chips?"

"Cops eat a lot," he chuckled. "I want people to have fun at our party, and fun means plenty of food."

"I agree we need to have enough food, but this is ridiculous!" I exclaimed as I pulled bags of chips out of the cart and placed them back on the shelf. "We'll keep six bags."

"Okay, six bags, but then can we also get pretzels?"

I laughed and nodded as he selected several bags. I loved how simple things were with Owen. He was easygoing and carefree, and I felt the same when I was around him. This was how I wanted to feel all the time.

"Charlotte, is this the replacement?" I heard from behind me. I turned and saw Lucy heading down the aisle with a menacingly fake smile plastered on her face.

I sighed and grabbed Owen's arm to steer him away, but Lucy wasn't having any of that.

"Hi," she called out to Owen. "I'm Lucy, a friend of Charlotte's from high school."

"Nice to meet you," Owen said cautiously.

"You're being a little rude, Charlotte," Lucy whispered.

"Owen, this is Lucy, my *ex*-best friend. Lucy, this is my fiancé, Owen," I said stiffly, looking around to see if anyone was watching.

Living in a small town had many perks, but the fact that everyone knew everyone's business was a drawback. The last thing I needed was gossip about Lucy and me getting around town, so I'd be polite, but get away as quickly as I could.

Owen gave me a curious look, and I nodded. I'd told him all about Lucy.

"Lucy," Owen said, looking her up and down with a sneer. "Char, don't we have to be somewhere?"

I gave him a smile and nodded. I was so grateful he was trying to help.

"Are you having a party?" Lucy asked innocently.

"Excuse me?" I asked.

"Oh, all the pretzels and stuff—unless, is that what you normally eat?"

"We just got our own place, and we're having a housewarming party," Owen said defensively, wrapping his arm around me tightly. I knew he was trying to be civil and defend my eating habits, but I groaned internally because I knew what was coming.

"Oh! I'd love to come and warm your new home."

Owen and I stared at her. Was she serious?

"Sorry. I think you warmed Charlotte's previous home a little *too* much, and I'm not in to skank," Owen said before pushing the cart around to the next aisle.

He left Lucy and me standing in shock. I'd *not* been expecting that. A smile formed on my face, and Lucy scowled.

"I can't believe he just said that to me!" she gasped.

"I can." I followed the path Owen had taken and left her standing in the chips.

"That's her?" Owen asked when I caught up with him.

"Yep."

"*Her?*" he asked again.

"Yes," I said, not sure what he was getting at.

"Sorry. I just can't seem to wrap my head around this. Cameron had *you*—you were his—and he cheated on *you* with *her?*"

I nodded.

"What the fuck was he thinking?" Owen laughed, shaking his head and throwing his arm over my shoulder.

❧ ❈ ☙

A few hours later our backyard was full of people, and I was doing my best to be a good hostess, refilling drinks and bringing around snacks.

"Can you pass those chips?" one of the Hartford guys called loudly.

Another man threw the bag of chips across the backyard, and the guy caught it like a football and did a touchdown dance. I rolled my eyes and walked into the house to get more drinks.

With Owen's new colleagues, as well as my dad and some of his work friends, it was like a police function in my backyard. I was grateful when the doorbell rang because it gave me an excuse to get away from the testosterone overload.

I opened the door and stepped back as Ryan pushed his way into the entryway followed by Sarah, Bonnie, a tall dark-haired man I didn't know, and Cameron. I looked at them in confusion and Ryan gave me a sheepish smile.

I suspected Ryan would be coming since he worked with my father, but I didn't know he'd be bringing the entire Harper clan along.

"Hi," I said awkwardly. I knew Owen would lose it the second he saw Cameron. He'd agreed to me seeing Cameron in groups, but I doubted he meant in our own home.

"Hope you don't mind—these guys tagged along," Ryan said as he swung his case of beer up onto his shoulder and looked around. "Nice house."

"It's fine," I said with a tight smile.

There was a chorus of hellos from everyone as we made our way through to the kitchen. Our sink was filled with ice, which I pointed out to Ryan so he could add his beer to the pile.

"The house is gorgeous, Charlotte," Sarah gushed as she ran her fingers along the marble counter.

"Thanks. We like it."

"This is Alex," Bonnie squealed when I turned to her.

He was very handsome, not that I would have expected anything else from a guy Bonnie was dating, but he was *exceptionally* attractive. His dark hair was a bit longer than Cameron's and curled slightly at the ends. His square jaw was covered in short stubble, and his green eyes sparkled when he looked down at Bonnie. He had a pair of thin-rimmed glasses balanced on his nose. He was much taller than Bonnie, but with his arm around her, it was easy to see they fit together.

"Nice to meet you, Alex," I said, smiling warmly.

"Nice to meet you too. Bonnie talks about you all the time," he said with a friendly smile. He took the beer Ryan handed him.

"Well, the party is out in the yard, so make your way out whenever you're ready." I pointed to the back of the house.

I tried to catch Cameron's eye but he was absorbed in looking around the room. Butterflies flapped viciously in my stomach as I tried to envision Owen's reaction.

"Can we have a tour?" Bonnie asked.

"Sure." I held my arms out wide to showcase the room. "This is the kitchen." As I walked through the house indicating the different rooms, Bonnie and Sarah oohed and ahhed, and Alex kept whispering in Bonnie's ear. But Cameron hadn't said a word since entering my house.

I looked over to him, and he smiled. Then just as we stepped into the living room, I heard my name being called.

"Charlotte?" Owen's voice rang through the house. "Where'd you put the lighter for the grill?"

Bonnie groaned and rolled her eyes as Owen entered the room. I shot her an annoyed look, but she just gave me an innocent smile.

"Char…" Owen came into the room and saw the people standing around. His eyes fell on Cameron and went cold before flicking to me angrily.

"Why don't you guys go get a drink while I help Owen?" I tried to maintain an aura of calm, but inside I was nervous.

Cameron gave me a quick look before following the others back toward the kitchen. Once we were alone, Owen walked quickly across the room to me.

"What is *he* doing here?" he demanded, pointing his finger after the retreating Harpers.

"I don't know! Honestly, I didn't invite any of them. Ryan brought them along."

"I'm not happy about this," he said in a warning tone.

"I know. I'm sorry. Do you want me to ask them to go?" I asked, hoping he would say no.

Owen sighed and took a deep breath. "No, I wouldn't ask you to do that," he said, sounding defeated.

"I didn't invite him."

"It's okay. There are so many people here I'll probably forget he's around anyway. Why did we think this was a good idea?" he chuckled as he sat on the couch.

"You wanted to invite some of your work friends, and then Dad was excited, and it kind of got out of control."

"Right. Let's *not* do this again."

"Deal," I agreed with a laugh.

"How long until you think everyone will leave?" he whispered in a suggestive tone.

"Well, most of them have only just arrived, and we haven't even fired up the grill yet."

"So a while then?"

I punched his shoulder playfully. "A while, yes."

"Come here, you," he said, pulling me down to his lap.

I giggled and leaned down to kiss him softly, but he wrapped his arms around me and pulled me against his chest, deepening the kiss. His tongue swirled with mine, and he groaned as I shifted in his lap.

A cough behind us made me jump. I pulled away from Owen and turned to find Cameron in the doorway.

"Can we help you?" Owen asked, sounding annoyed.

"Sorry…ah, Bonnie wanted me to ask if you minded if she started getting the food ready," Cameron said.

His eyes never left mine as he spoke, and I remembered how it felt when I saw him kissing Lucy. I immediately stood up and moved away from the couch so he wouldn't have to stare at me sitting in Owen's lap.

I glanced back at Owen, who folded his arms and stared at Cameron. This was not good. I had to get them away from each other.

"Why don't you and I go help her?" I asked Cameron, walking out of the room and tugging on his shirt so he'd follow me.

I knew Owen would be angry, but I wasn't going to leave them alone.

Cameron was silent as he walked behind me, and I searched for something to say. I knew seeing me with Owen must have hurt him, but this was my home. Owen was my fiancé, and I refused to feel guilty. Besides, I hadn't invited him, and he had to know when he decided to crash the party that he'd see Owen and me together. He was pushing this friendship thing a little too hard.

But having experience with seeing the person I loved kissing someone else, I felt a certain amount of sympathy for him.

"I'm sorry you saw that," I said when we reached the kitchen.

"It's okay. I think I needed to see it. Maybe that's why I came today."

"What?"

"It makes me face reality," he said quickly before moving away to help Bonnie with the food.

"Oh, Charlotte, good. Can I use this pineapple juice for piña coladas, or did you buy it for something special?" she asked, holding up the can from the fridge.

"You can use it," I said as I watched Cameron.

I wasn't sure how I was feeling. I only knew Owen must be angry with me now, Cameron was hurting, and I had a house full of guests I needed to entertain.

"Do you want one?" Bonnie called over the sound of the blender.

"Huh?"

"A piña colada. I'm making real ones for us and a virgin for Sarah," she clarified.

"Oh, yeah, sounds good." I continued watching Cameron carefully, wondering why he didn't just go home. I couldn't understand why he wanted to torture himself like this.

"Ugh! Reason number forty-seven!" Sarah huffed from her barstool.

"Reason forty-seven for what?" I asked. Bonnie and Cameron rolled their eyes, and I assumed they were well versed on the other forty-six reasons.

"Reason forty-seven why I can't wait to *not* be pregnant! I want a *real* cocktail!"

"Only a few more months," Alex said, coming in with several empty beer bottles. He threw them in the trash as Sarah sighed and took a sip of her mocktail.

"You don't have to clean up," I told Alex.

"I like to help out." He shrugged before placing a kiss on Bonnie's cheek and taking a fresh armful of beers out of the ice.

"I'll go make sure Ryan's not getting into any trouble," Cameron said, following Alex out.

"Thanks, Cam," Sarah called, taking another sip of the creamy drink. She grimaced and put down the glass. "It's not the same without the rum."

I took a sip of my cocktail and felt the burn on the back of my throat. Normally I wasn't much of a drinker, but I knew I'd need it today.

"Shall we?" Bonnie asked, picking up the drinks and walking out the door, followed by Sarah.

I grabbed a fruit platter and headed toward the door as Ryan walked in. He gave me another sheepish smile.

"Are you mad at me?" he asked.

"No… but maybe slightly confused and annoyed. Owen, however, might want to hit you."

"I think I can handle him," Ryan chuckled. He flexed his large biceps, which caused me to giggle.

"Seriously, though, what were you thinking, Ry?"

"I don't know. I guess I didn't really think. Cam told me you guys were going to be friends, so when I heard you were having a barbeque I assumed it would be okay for everyone to come."

I sighed and punched him lightly on the arm. "Do me a favor, okay? Next time you want to invite people over, can you let me know first?"

"Deal."

We shook hands and walked out to join everyone in the yard.

"Thanks, Char," Dad said as I placed the platter in the center of the table.

"I'll get the grill started in just a second," Owen said, brushing past me with a meaningful look as he headed toward the door.

I followed him back into the house, and I could feel Cameron's eyes following me. I hoped he wouldn't interrupt us again.

"He has to leave," Owen said as soon as we were alone.

"Let's not make a fuss. He's just spending time with his family and some of your work friends. It's not a big deal. He's barely even said anything to me. You don't have to worry."

"It *is* a big fucking deal! He keeps looking at you," Owen said, sneering.

I rolled my eyes. "Everyone was looking at me because I was carrying food."

Owen shook his head and cupped my face with his hands. "He was *looking* at you."

I knew arguing with him wasn't going to solve anything, so I freed myself from his grasp and pulled the fridge door open to get the steaks.

"You don't have anything to worry about. We're just friends. Why don't we just relax and enjoy the party, and you can ignore Cameron?"

Owen's nostrils flared, and he looked furious, but seemed to have lost the will to argue any more.

"Keep him away from me," he said through gritted teeth before walking back outside with the meat.

I quickly grabbed the oil, barbecue tongs, and some paper towels before following him.

Once the meat was cooking, most of the guys went to stand around the grill and drink beer. I couldn't believe how cliché it was, and I chuckled to myself when I saw my dad, Ryan, and Owen right in the middle of a male-bonding session.

I sat down at the table where the remaining Harpers were chatting and laughing together. I felt a little like an outsider. They were all family, and I wasn't a part of that anymore. I downed the rest of my drink before deciding I should probably go and make the rest of the food before the meat was ready.

I walked back into the kitchen and pulled out the ingredients for garlic bread, quickly making a loaf and placing it in the preheated oven. I turned back to the fridge, pulling out vegetables and stacking them on the counter so I could make the salad. I went to the pantry to grab an onion, and when I turned back around Cameron was leaning against the wall.

"Hey," he said with a smile.

"Hey," I replied, starting to rip the lettuce into small pieces. I was a little rougher than I normally would have been.

"I just wanted to tell you I'm sorry if I've caused any trouble between you and Owen." He selected a knife from the block on the counter and started slicing one of the tomatoes.

"Oh no, we're fine." I could hear the strain in my voice, and when Cameron cocked an eyebrow at me, I knew he'd heard it too. "Okay, well, maybe there's a little trouble. But it's fine."

I washed the lettuce and shook the excess water from it before placing it in a large bowl. Cameron put his sliced tomatoes in and picked up a cucumber.

As I chopped an onion, I could feel my eyes tearing up.

"Sorry about the tears…stupid onion." I laughed as I wiped my cheek with the back of my hand.

Cameron chuckled softly as he put the sliced cucumbers into the bowl. He washed his hands in the sink as I grabbed a paper towel to wipe my eyes.

"What's going on?" Owen demanded from the doorway.

Cameron and I spun around to look at him.

"Nothing," I said. "We're just making a salad."

"Nothing? Then why are you crying?" Owen pulled me into a protective hug. "What did he say to you?"

"I didn't say anything," Cameron said, looking confused.

"Right, so Charlotte is just crying for no reason?"

I leaned back from him. "I was cutting up an onion for the salad. Really, Cameron didn't do anything."

"Right, he's so innocent," Owen said sarcastically.

"Is there a problem here?" Cameron asked. He was getting defensive.

"Yes, *you* are the problem here."

I rolled my eyes and pulled out of Owen's grasp, taking a step backward and slipping on something. I tried to steady myself, but my arms flailed wildly as I fell backward.

The next thing I knew, a pair of strong arms came around my waist, preventing me from falling flat on my back. Since Owen was in front of me, the warm body behind me could only belong to one other person.

"Are you okay?" Cameron asked.

"Get your hands off her!" Owen roared. He quickly ushered me behind his back before swinging his fist into Cameron's face.

"*Owen!*" I screamed in a mixture of shock and anger. "What the hell are you doing?"

Before he could answer me, Cameron regained his footing, turned, and with a furious look on his face, pulled his arm back.

"Cam, don't!" I yelled.

But he swung his arm and hit Owen in the jaw.

Owen grunted and curled over in pain. I thought that was going to be the end of it, but then Owen pushed forward and wrapped his arms around Cameron's waist, pulling him down to the floor.

"Stop it! Stop it!" I yelled as I watched them roll around, each landing the occasional punch. I reached down to pull Owen off of Cameron, but strong arms clasped around my waist from behind, holding me back.

"You'll just get hurt by accident," Alex said as my Dad and Ryan dove in to rip the two men apart.

"What's going on here?" Dad yelled in his policeman voice.

Owen shrugged off my father's arms and turned to me. "Are you okay?"

"No, I'm not okay!" I pushed out of Alex's arms and stomped down the hall to the bedroom. I slammed the door behind me.

I was furious with both Owen and Cameron. I'd never seen Owen be physically violent before, and I never expected him to just attack someone. I'd always considered him one of the calmest, most level-headed people I knew.

As for Cameron, I'd thought of him as a placid person as well. I'd only seen him fight one other time in the ten years I'd known him. It was shortly after we started dating, and he'd done it to protect me…

…The cool wind had blown my hair around my face, and I pulled my coat tighter. Where was Cameron? It wasn't like him to be late. I looked up and down the street for any sign of him, but there was no one around. I pulled my cell phone out of my pocket to see if I'd missed a call from him and found an unread text message flashing on the screen.

Sorry, got held up in class.
I'll be about 15 minutes late.
See you soon.

I felt myself relax, knowing he was on his way. I searched through the phone's menu until I got to the games and started a new game of Snake. Lucy and I often challenged each other, and since she usually beat me, I could use this time to practice.

I'd only played for about a minute when I heard footsteps.

"Hey there."

I glanced up from my game and saw someone I didn't know. "I'm Craig," he said pleasantly.

"Hi," I said before looking back at my phone and directing the small snake around the screen.

Craig's hand rested on my shoulder, and his index finger brushed my neck. "That was rude."

"Excuse me?" I stepped away from him.

"I introduced myself, and you didn't tell me your name. It was rude. Now, let's try that again. I'm Craig."

"Ch-Charlotte." I took another step back as he stepped toward me.

"Charlotte," he said with a smile. "There, now was that so hard?"

I shook my head and looked back over my shoulder to see if there was anyone else around. Surely someone was about to see the same movie as Cameron and I, but the street in front of the theater was empty. I started to panic.

"Where are you running to?" Craig asked as I started to back away. When I looked at him again he was standing right in front of me. His hands grasped my shoulders firmly. I struggled against him, but he wouldn't let go.

Up close, he smelled of beer and cigarettes, and I silently prayed Cameron would arrive and Craig would just walk away.

"My boyfriend is coming," I blurted.

He smiled maliciously. "But he's not here now, is he?"

He stepped forward, forcing me to stumble backward until I was pressed against the wall.

I opened my mouth to scream, but he clamped his hand over my lips. "Uh-uh, none of that. I don't want to hurt you," he whispered into my ear before his moist lips pressed against my neck, and he pushed his body hard against mine.

Hot tears ran down my cheeks, and suddenly he was gone. I opened my eyes and saw Craig and Cameron circling each other, both with furious looks on their faces.

"What the fuck are you doing?" Cameron yelled.

"Just lookin' after your girl," Craig taunted.

Cameron launched himself at Craig, and I could only stare as his fist made contact. I heard a loud crack as Craig screamed in pain and blood sprayed on my shoes.

"Cam, be careful!" I yelled. He turned to me, a startled look on his face, as if he'd forgotten I was there. His expression instantly changed from incensed to concerned as he ran over to me.

"Are you okay?" He surrounded me in a hug and stroked his fingers through my hair.

"I'm fine. Can we just go?" I pleaded.

"Yeah." Cameron looked back over his shoulder at Craig, who was jogging away.

As soon as Craig's retreating form turned the corner, I relaxed. Once we were safe in Cameron's car, I ran my fingers gently over his knuckles. I could see the bruise forming.

"Did he hurt you?" Cameron asked.

"No." I shook my head. "Are *you* hurt?"

"As long as you're safe, I'm perfectly fine," Cam said, giving me a smile…

I lay down on the bed and pulled a pillow over my head. I couldn't believe Owen and Cameron had just been in a physical altercation. It seemed so juvenile and ridiculous.

I could hear talking and the door opening and closing, and I knew people were leaving. I hated being a drama queen, but I didn't feel like I could face Owen or Cameron right then. Hopefully our guests would understand.

I stood up, walked over to the window, and pulled the curtain back so I could peek outside. Several of the cars were already gone, and I saw Bonnie, Alex, and Cameron walking toward Bonnie's car. Then Cameron looked back at the house for a moment.

I shook my head as I watched Bonnie's car pull out of the drive and wondered why I'd yelled at Owen and run away instead of staying and talking to him. I thought for a minute, and I realized it was what I always did when a problem came up. I ran. It seemed to be almost an instinctual reaction to difficulty, but I didn't want to be afraid to talk with my fiancé. Owen had been trying to teach me to talk through our issues, and it seemed I still had a long way to go.

I walked toward the bedroom door with a newfound determination. Running away from my problems hadn't helped me in the past, so I'd try to face this issue head on and sort it out before it became any bigger.

I opened the door and walked through the house, surprised to find it completely empty. I headed out into the backyard and found Owen cleaning the grill.

"Hey," I said.

"Hey, you," he said with his back to me, continuing to work the brush over the grill.

"What happened in there?" I sat on one of the outdoor chairs and curled my knees up to my chest.

Owen sighed loudly and spun to face me. I could see the beginnings of a black eye, and I shook my head. Cameron probably had a similar bruise on his face.

"I'm sorry—" Owen began.

"Don't apologize," I interrupted. "Just tell me what you were thinking."

"I don't know. I walked into the kitchen and you were alone with him, and you were crying, and then he had his arms around you, and I just lost it."

I was silent for a moment, looking at the sadness and remorse in his eyes. "Are you injured?" I asked.

"A bit of a sore jaw and my knuckles are swollen."

I stood up and ran my fingers lightly down his jaw, but I pulled my hand back when he winced at my touch. I got up on my tiptoes and gently kissed his sore chin.

"I'll apologize to him," he sighed, his arms slipping around my waist and holding me to his chest.

I could tell he wasn't happy about that prospect, and I didn't expect him to really do it. It was enough for me that he'd offered. But I didn't get a chance to tell him that because the phone rang inside the house.

"I'll get that," I said, pulling out of his grasp and heading to the study.

"Hello?"

"Charlotte, are you okay?" Cameron's voice asked, sounding relieved.

"Cam?" I was unsure how he'd gotten my new phone number.

"Yeah. Bonnie gave me your number—I hope that's all right."

"What were you going to do if Owen answered?"

He was silent for a moment. Then he chuckled softly. "Hang up," he admitted.

I rolled my eyes.

"So are you okay?" he asked. "Is Owen angry with you?"

"I'm fine. We talked about it. He said he was sorry he hit you, and he knows he shouldn't have done it. I'm really sorry, Cam. Are you badly hurt?"

"I'll probably have a black eye, but apart from that I'm fine. I was concerned that he'd take it out on you after everyone left."

"That would never happen. Owen treats me really well. There's no need to worry," I told him, a little insulted.

"Okay, well…I just wanted to check in. I'm glad you're okay. Will I talk to you soon?"

"Yeah," I said, not really knowing when that would be. Now that we'd talked about everything and the past was out in the open, I couldn't see much of a reason.

"Maybe we could have lunch next week. Just as friends?"

"I'll let you know," I said vaguely before hanging up.

I was going to have to think more about Owen's feelings and talk to him about how he *really* felt about Cameron and me having a friendship before I took it any further. It was time for me to be serious about my relationship and think about Owen's needs. Having Cameron in my life was going to more of a problem than I'd originally thought.

Chapter Twelve
Goodbye, My Love

"Come in, Bonnie," I called from the kitchen when I heard her knock. Footsteps echoed down the hallway before Bonnie's smiling face appeared next to me, and her arms wrapped around my waist.

"You're going to be a bride."

I laughed and hugged her back. "I know! Hey, Alex." I looked over Bonnie's shoulder as I saw him enter the room.

He nodded and sat down on one of the barstools.

"Coffee?" I asked, switching the percolator on and taking cups from the cupboard.

"I'd love a coffee," Alex said.

"Not for me. I'll just start looking through your magazines," Bonnie replied, looking around the counters. "Where are your magazines?"

"What magazines?" I asked.

"The *bridal* magazines, so we can plan!" she said, as if that were the most obvious thing in the world.

"I didn't buy any. I've already had a big wedding, and Owen and I agreed to have a small ceremony," I explained, grabbing the milk out of the fridge.

Bonnie scrunched up her face as if she smelled something bad and spun around to face Alex. "Will you be okay here?" she asked him. "I'm just going to run to the store. I'll be right back."

"Sure," he said as I handed him his coffee.

"Bonnie—"

"We *need* magazines, Charlotte. Even if you don't want a big wedding, we still need some inspiration for your dress," she said anxiously.

I shrugged and sat down next to Alex. "Okay, but don't take too long."

"Be right back," she sang as she disappeared down the hall.

After the front door closed, Alex and I sat in silence, drinking our coffee. It dawned on me that I was sitting with a virtual stranger, and I felt a little uncomfortable. I took a long drink from my cup.

"So…" Alex said.

Our eyes met, and I opened my mouth to reply but couldn't think of anything to say. I just looked at the countertop and drank more of my coffee. Alex tapped his fingers idly on the smooth surface, and I started humming along. Then we both burst out laughing.

"That was one awkward silence," I giggled.

"One of the most awkward I've ever had."

I traced the marble countertop with my fingers. "I'm sorry about how the party ended when you were here last," I finally said.

"Oh, it's fine. It was interesting, actually. I watched Owen seethe from the minute we arrived, and I wondered if he'd blow his top," Alex said, shifting to face me.

"Really? I knew he was annoyed, but I never saw that blow-up coming."

"Maybe you were too close to it. I'd never met either of you, but Bonnie described the situation to me so I had a feeling he'd be annoyed that Cameron came along."

"Why *did* he come?"

I hadn't spoken with Cameron since he'd called after the party to ask if I was okay. He'd called my cell two days ago, but I didn't answer. I didn't know what to say to him.

"You know the Harpers—they do everything together. So when Ryan was invited, I think it just seemed natural for them all to come…especially since *you* were involved," he said, draining the last of the coffee from his cup.

"What do you mean?"

"They adore you! Bonnie has talked about you nonstop since you got back to town. You're one of them."

"I *was* one of them," I clarified.

"They'll always consider you one of them. Did you know Cameron keeps your wedding photo in his office?"

I nodded. "Yes, I had lunch with him there the other day."

"David told him he shouldn't have it there—that he's torturing himself with it—but he refuses to take it down."

"David told him to sell the house as well."

Alex nodded. "Before you moved back, I didn't know much about Cameron. Bonnie and I have been dating for about a year, but he's always been a mystery to me. He showed up to family dinners, smiled, and played the dutiful son and brother, but he was never really there. Over the past few weeks he's become a different person."

I pondered that for a few minutes and wondered if my presence, or lack thereof, affected Cameron in ways I hadn't considered before. Bonnie had mentioned that Cameron seemed withdrawn after I left, but hearing it from someone who wasn't as close to him was eye-opening. It reminded me of my behavior after my mother left…

Cameron's attempts to talk to me when I first got back into town had overwhelmed me. I'd felt like he was asking something of me, when in fact he'd been trying to give me something: understanding, explanations, and apologies.

I felt sympathy for Cameron and the pain he'd been in for so long. I'd found love with someone new, but Cameron had gotten stuck in his guilt and never moved past it.

Alex's hand on my shoulder brought me out of my thoughts. "He's happy you're back," he said. "They all are."

"I know. But it must hurt him to see me with Owen."

"I think he'd rather endure the pain of seeing you with someone else than not have you in his life at all."

I realized in that moment just how loved I was—by both Owen and Cameron. They both wanted the best for me, even to their own detriment. Owen had encouraged me to face my past, and he stood by my side now even as my renewed relationship with Cameron hurt him. And Cameron still wanted me in his life, even if it would never be in the capacity he truly hoped for. But both of them giving me what I wanted wasn't making me happy—let alone either of them.

"That's selfish of me, though… I have to pick one of them," I said softly, realizing this for the first time.

Why hadn't I seen it before? No matter how much I wanted to fit them both into my life, making it the perfect puzzle, that was never going to happen. The piece of my life that belonged to Cameron would never fit with the piece that belonged to Owen. It was impossible, and yet I wasn't willing to give up either part of myself.

Before this moment, I hadn't realized that any type of decision needed to be made. And now that I did, it should have been easy to choose Owen. I'd left Cameron behind five years ago. But the first time I'd walked away from him, I was hurt and angry and didn't know the details of what had happened. Now that I understood them, it didn't seem so clear.

Alex remained quiet until we made eye contact, and he gave me a soft smile. "Your heart will tell you what to do," he said, as if he'd heard my thoughts.

I quickly gulped the last of my coffee and looked down again. Alex sat quietly next to me. I was surprised at how comforting it was to have an almost-stranger there with me. I knew he didn't expect anything of me, and he didn't seem to have his own agenda or want me to pick a certain person.

The front door crashed open and footsteps stomped down the hallway.

"Stupid small town…think we're all hillbillies…" Bonnie muttered to herself as she appeared in the doorway.

Alex stood and kissed her forehead, smoothing her hair. "What's wrong, sweetheart?"

"I couldn't get *any* bridal magazines in this stupid backward town." She sighed dramatically. "I'm going to Hartford tomorrow to buy a few. Can we reschedule this planning meeting for next week?"

"Sure," I said, thankful for the reprieve. My mind was still focused on having to choose between Cameron and Owen.

"I guess we'll just get going then," Bonnie said. "Sorry." She gave me a quick hug.

"That's okay. Next week will be perfect."

I walked Bonnie and Alex out to the car and gave Alex a hug too.

"Thank you," I whispered. He squeezed me tightly in response and gave me a wink as he climbed into the car.

⊸◦❊❧✻☙❊❧◦⊷

That night, when Owen got home from work, I was still sitting on the couch thinking—in the same spot I'd been in since Bonnie and Alex left that morning. Owen smiled before sitting next to me and pulling my curled legs out from underneath me and into his lap. He began to rub the soles of my feet.

I hummed in satisfaction as I leaned on the arm of the couch and allowed him to work. Owen was always so thoughtful. When I tried to recall whether Cameron had ever done something similar, I quickly stopped myself and sat up straight, pulling my feet from Owen's grasp. It would do no good for me to start comparing them.

"Are you okay?"

"Yes," I replied, my tone harsh.

He gave me a confused look.

"Can we talk?" I asked nervously.

He sighed and twisted around on the couch to face me, then gently took my hand. This was another thing I loved about Owen — how much he loved to touch me. Just holding hands was special with him.

"Are you still upset about what happened at the party?" he asked.

"No, I'm not upset. But it did make me think."

Owen cocked his head to the side, silently prompting me to continue.

"What do you want?" I asked bluntly.

"What?"

I shook my head slightly to organize my thoughts. "I've been unfair to you since we moved here… I know you wanted me to reconnect with people and sort through my past, but now I'm not sure I want them all in the past," I said, wondering if I was making any sense. "I guess what I'm asking is, is it okay with you if I have a friendship with Cameron?"

Owen held my gaze. "I want you to be happy."

"I know." I squeezed his hand. "But what do *you* want?"

Owen dropped my hand and rubbed his over his face. "If I had my choice, no. Once you get the closure you need, you wouldn't have any contact with Cameron or anyone in his family. But I would never ask you to give up people who are important to you. I'm fine, really — and don't forget, I was the one who suggested you reconnect with him. I know I overreacted the other night, but I promise it won't happen again."

"I want you to be happy too! If me being around Cameron is going to hurt you or damage our relationship, I need you to tell me," I pushed.

"It's fine, baby. I promise," he said, kissing my lips gently.

"Are you sure?"

"As long as he keeps his hands off you," Owen growled in my ear.

"Deal."

⚜

"Where's my phone?" I yelled angrily as it rang for the second time.

"Where did you leave it?" Owen called unhelpfully from the living room where he was watching television.

I resisted the urge to yell that if knew where I'd left it, it wouldn't be lost and instead kept searching through the papers piled up on the kitchen counter. The phone stopped ringing, and I sighed.

I sat down on the barstool. Everything had gone wrong today: I'd stubbed my toe in the shower and hobbled around all morning. Then the coffeemaker broke, so I hadn't had any caffeine. Owen had spent the afternoon sulking in the living room, and I'd burned the toast when I tried to make us tuna sandwiches. Now this horrible day would not end, and I'd missed two calls because I couldn't find my stupid phone.

My ringtone sounded again, and I groaned loudly before restarting my search. I felt the bowl of fruit vibrate against my arm and pulled out two bananas, finding my phone at the bottom of the bowl.

"What the?" I yelled loudly before pulling the phone out and answering the call.

"Hello?" I said angrily, not bothering to check the caller ID in my haste.

"Is this a bad time?" a smooth voice said through the phone.

"Cameron!" I said too loudly. I heard Owen groan from the living room.

"Hey," he said, and I could tell he was smiling.

"Sorry, I couldn't find my phone."

"Yes, this is the third time I've tried to call. I thought of calling the house phone, but I didn't want to cause any trouble."

"Oh really? Desperate for me, were you?" I joked. I went silent when I realized how that likely came across to Cameron.

He cleared his throat and ignored my statement. "I actually need to talk to you — today. It's quite urgent."

"What? Is everything okay?"

"Can we meet?" he asked instead of answering my question, making me very nervous.

"Cam, what's going on?" I demanded, losing patience.

"Charlotte, please," he groaned. "Don't make this any more difficult than it has to be. I have to talk to you…it's important. Can you just trust me?"

"I don't know…" I hesitated, thinking of Owen's reaction.

"It has to be today. I *need* to talk to you today," he said.

"Can't you tell me now — on the phone?"

"This isn't a phone type of conversation, Char. *Please*. I'm throwing my pride out the window and begging you. *Please!*"

I hesitated, and I could hear a tapping through the phone. I pictured him nervously drumming his fingers as he waited for my answer.

"Okay. When?"

"Can you meet me around five?" he asked softly. "At our special place?"

That made me curious. What could he possibly have to tell me that was urgent *and* required the sentimentality of our private place?

"I'll be there," I whispered. Cameron hung up without saying goodbye.

I put the phone down, my frustration completely gone. I walked into the living room where Owen sat stiffly on the couch, watching the game with a scowl.

"What did he want?" he asked without looking away from the television.

"He wants to talk to me. He said it was urgent."

"I'm sure it is," Owen said sarcastically.

I wasn't in the mood to fight with Owen, so I just went to change into some comfortable jeans and a warm sweater before pulling on my running shoes and grabbing my coat.

I felt uneasy because I'd promised Owen I would never meet Cameron alone. I knew I was about to break that rule, but surely an emergency was worth the fight with Owen that would ensue.

"I'm going to meet Cameron. I'll be back later," I called as I headed out. I didn't wait for his answer, but he didn't try to stop me from leaving, so I'd deal with his anger when I got home.

As I drove through the center of town and out toward the highway, I tried to work out what he might need to tell me so urgently. By the time I'd pulled off the highway and parked the car, I had several ideas. The first and most worrying was that he or a member of his family was very ill, next was that something had happened to Sarah's baby, or maybe Bonnie and Alex broke up… But all of those seemed unlikely, and none of them required a trip to our special place. So I guessed he wanted to talk about us.

I walked through the trees until I came to the familiar clearing and the fallen log. As I climbed up and settled against a branch, I heard rustling and twigs cracking along the path. I looked up as Cameron appeared.

"You're early," he said.

"So are you."

He climbed up on the log next to me, and I did a quick scan. He was thin but not unhealthy, and apart from the slight bruise around his eye from where Owen had hit him, he looked fine. He didn't appear to be sick, so I relaxed a little.

"Thanks for coming."

"What's going on?" I asked nervously, picking at the dried bark on the log.

"I'm leaving," he said, watching my face.

"I—I don't understand."

"I put the house up for sale, and I contacted a friend of mine in California. He's asked me to join his clinic. I'm moving to San Diego."

His words swam in my head as I tried to find something to say.

"Why?" I asked the question, but in my heart I knew the answer.

"I got a hard jolt of reality the other day when I saw you and Owen together. When I saw…" He took a deep breath. "When I saw you and Owen kissing, it really hit me for the first time that you were with someone else. You looked so happy and comfortable, and it made me realize that I'd lost my chance with you. Then when Owen hit me, I saw just how much my presence in your life was affecting your relationship with him… And the truth is I just want you to be happy. So when I got home, I sat up all night thinking, and the next day I called the real estate agent, listed the house, and called my friend."

I nodded slowly, making sure I understood everything before I responded. "When will you go?" I bit my lip, but it was useless. I knew I was going to cry.

"I leave tomorrow. That's why I needed to talk to you today. I've been putting this conversation off all week, and I've run out of time. I wanted to tell you in person instead of just disappearing."

I cringed at his words. I hadn't given him that same courtesy when I left town, and I was grateful he was saying goodbye in person. I gripped his hand.

I hadn't seen Cameron in five years and had only been reacquainted with him for a few weeks, much of which I'd spent trying to avoid him. But having him back in my life felt like I'd regained a part of myself. I still cared about Cameron, and I hated the thought of him leaving.

"You don't have to go," I said, wiping away a tear. "I spoke to Owen, and he's okay with us being friends."

Cameron sighed and looked up at me with a half-smile.

"*I'm* not okay with it. I'm still in love with you, Charlotte. I'm always going to be in love with you, and while I honestly do want you to be happy, I can't watch it happen with someone else."

I knew he was doing the mature thing—what was best for both of us—and making the decision I'd been struggling to get myself to face. But that didn't make it hurt any less. And it didn't stop my heart from speaking words my mind knew were a mistake.

"I don't want you to go," I whispered.

Cameron lifted my chin so I looked into his sparkling eyes. "Ask me to stay, and I will," he said, gently wiping the tears from my cheeks. "Tell me you want to be with me, and I'm yours."

I wrapped my arms around my shaking body to hold myself together. Part of me wanted to jump into Cameron's arms and beg him to stay, but the part of me that loved Owen held me back. I couldn't hurt him…I wouldn't.

Reluctantly, I shook my head, knowing that in saying no, I was saying goodbye to Cameron forever. I looked at the ground so I wouldn't see the pain on his face.

When I finally looked up, I found him staring at me with a small smile and watery eyes.

"You really love him, don't you?"

I nodded.

"I really am happy for you, Charlotte. You deserve love. I'm going to miss you so much."

I threw my arms around him and pulled him close, trying to hold on to him for as long as I could. We sat for several minutes with our arms wrapped around each other, just being together.

"I love you, Cameron," I whispered softly against his neck. It wasn't a declaration or an invitation to stay. It was a fact and my way of saying goodbye.

"I love you, Charlotte." He kissed my forehead as he pulled away.

His hand cupped my face, and he ran his thumb over my cheek to wipe the tears. His eyes were wet too. Although it was five years late, we were finally giving our relationship a proper goodbye.

"I have some last-minute packing to do," Cameron said. "And you should get home to Owen."

I clung to him for another moment, but I knew he was right. This would be best for us. I would marry Owen, and he would begin a new life in San Diego and probably fall in love with a wonderful woman. The thought of him loving someone else brought more tears, though I knew they were hypocritical.

"Come on," Cameron encouraged, climbing down and grasping my hand to help me down as well.

He held my hand tightly as we walked back to our cars. I allowed him to pull me along, but with every step I knew I was closer to saying goodbye — for good.

All too soon, we stood next to my car and Cameron brushed a strand of hair away from my face before placing a gentle hand on my cheek.

"You're so beautiful." He leaned down and very gently brushed his lips against mine — just a feather-light touch that ended as quickly as it began. Cameron's eyes were closed, and he smiled as he pulled away from me.

"Have a wonderful life, Charlotte Grace Barnes," he whispered.

I wanted to tell him something profound, something encouraging, but I couldn't get anything out.

"Be happy." He squeezed my hand and took a step back.

My whole body screamed, but I held my ground. I owed Owen my loyalty, and I was not going to betray him, no matter how much I wanted to in this moment.

Cameron walked backward, keeping his eyes locked on mine until he reached his car. He fumbled in his pockets and pulled his keys free, unlocking the door before turning back to me for one last look.

I mustered all the strength I had to pull my mouth into a weak smile. It must have looked pitiful with my red, puffy eyes, but I wanted his last memory of me to be with a smile. He gave me a sad smile of his own, then got into his car and was gone.

As his taillights disappeared into the night, I allowed my grief to overwhelm me. I don't know how long I sat on the ground, but I cried until I had no tears left. Then I wiped my eyes and tried to put my thoughts in order. I'd been trying so hard to figure out how I could fit both men into my life, and in the end, the decision was made for me.

How was I supposed to go home to Owen now and pretend everything was fine? Would I be able to smile and kiss him and live with the smug look I knew I'd see on his face when I told him Cameron was gone?

I tried to convince myself I'd be fine without Cameron. I'd lived for years without him—but that was when I'd believed he cheated on me. Now that I knew the more complicated truth, it was hard to think about not having him in my life. Only Cam's announcement that he was leaving had really allowed me to see how much I wanted him around.

I longed for the comfort of a warm bed and strong arms to hold me close. But I wasn't sure whose arms I wanted. Finally, I realized I should go home. I stood up slowly and the muscles in my legs protested from being curled underneath me for so long.

I drove back to my house and sat out in the driveway for a few minutes before I went in to face Owen. The house was dark, but that didn't mean he wasn't sitting in the bedroom reading with a lamp or watching TV with the lights off, waiting for me. I closed the car door as quietly as I could.

I stepped on something as I reached the front door and looked down to find an envelope at my feet. It had my name written on the front, so I pulled it open and peeked inside. There with a folded piece of paper was something making a jingling sound. I read the three words written in Cameron's handwriting:

Goodbye, my love.

I tipped the envelope and watched as two gold rings fell out into my palm.

I stared at the loops of metal, and my mind reeled. He was really letting me go. He wasn't holding on anymore.

My bottom lip began to tremble, but I closed my eyes and held in the tears. I put the rings and the note back in the envelope and shoved it in my handbag.

I walked quietly into the dark, silent house and went upstairs. I undressed quickly before slipping into bed next to a sleeping Owen. He didn't wake up but must have sensed me next to him. He rolled over and flung his arm over me, pulling me close to his chest.

Not half an hour before I had longed for the warmth of my bed and strong arms to hold me, but now I felt no comfort in them.

Chapter Thirteen
Starting New

"Ugh, I can't eat another bite." Dad sighed, leaning back in his chair and patting his belly. "That was delicious, Char."

"I'm glad you enjoyed it," I said, clearing the Thanksgiving plates from the table.

"Has she been any better?" Dad whispered. He was trying to be subtle, but I could hear him clearly from the kitchen.

Owen sighed. "No, she's been distant ever since he left."

"Don't worry. She'll come around. She was like this after her mother left, and she came out of it eventually. Just give her some time," Dad whispered back as they moved into the living room.

I slammed the plates down on the counter. I hated that they were talking about me like I was some miserable child who disappointed them. I couldn't help how I felt. I hadn't wanted to come back to Fairfield in the first place. Cameron was thrust back into my life—without my permission—and then just as I started to make a place for him, he up and walked out. This left me a bit thrown, and I thought it was quite reasonable to feel confused.

I resented the fact that my father was comparing my behavior to how I was after Mom left. I'd been in shock then, and it was that behavior that caused me to lose Cameron in the first place. I wasn't withdrawn now. I was still spending time with Bonnie and Sarah, and I was looking into going to community college and finding a career. My sex life with Owen was healthy, and I didn't think I was neglecting him at all. What was I doing that made them think I was distant?

"Everything all right in there, Char?" Dad called.

"Yes, I'm fine," I called back, turning on the faucet.

Once the dishwasher was started, I took the cherry pie I'd prepared out of the oven and set it on the counter.

"Do I smell pie?" Dad yelled.

I walked into the living room and stood with my hands on my hips.

"Yes, but you just said you couldn't eat another thing," I pointed out.

"Charlotte, there's *always* room for pie!" he said in mock horror.

"Just so you know, I'll always have room for pie as well," Owen said. His words were jovial, but the light tone didn't show on his face.

Rolling my eyes, I went back to the kitchen and served up the pie with ice cream. We ate in virtual silence, with Dad and Owen giving each other knowing looks. The more they stayed silent, the angrier I became, and so I stayed quiet too. When I finished, I dropped off my plate in the kitchen walked down the hall to the bedroom.

I knew I was being moody, but I didn't appreciate being spoken about behind my back, and I didn't want to be fake and pretend I didn't know it was happening. I thought about confronting them, but decided to calm down and talk to Owen in the morning.

I changed into pajamas and climbed into bed, reaching over to the nightstand for my book. After about an hour of being lost in my fantasy world where aliens had taken over the earth, I heard the bedroom door open.

Owen had an empty look on his face. He wouldn't make eye contact, so I looked back down at the page and kept reading. I didn't feel like talking right now anyway.

He changed into a pair of old sweats and climbed into bed, pulling a pillow over his face and rolling away from me.

"Good night," I said softly, but he didn't reply.

❧ ❀ ❦ ❧ ☙

I slept restlessly and woke before the sunrise. Owen was sprawled out across the bed and snoring loudly, so I snuck out of the room and quickly showered before going for a walk.

The empty streets were dusted with snow, and it was still mostly dark, almost as if I was walking through a ghost town. I walked the few blocks to the twenty-four-hour diner and bought myself a coffee. I sat down to read the newspaper, enjoying that I had the whole place to myself.

I took a deep breath and inhaled the delicious scents coming from the kitchen. They were cooking bacon. After the waitress refilled my coffee cup, a few people started filing in, and I noticed it getting light outside.

I waved the waitress over and ordered a stack of pancakes with strawberries. I wasn't sure why, but I had this feeling in my stomach like I shouldn't go home. I ate my pancakes and thought about Cameron. I hadn't heard from him since he left three weeks ago — not even a message to let me know he'd landed safely in San Diego. The only reason I knew he'd made it was because I asked Bonnie.

I thought again about the rings he left on the doorstep and felt tears prick the corners of my eyes. Refusing to cry in public, I searched through my bag for a tissue and quickly wiped my eyes before leaving some money on the table and heading home. I walked slowly, watching the clouds turn from pink to white as the sun made its way higher into the sky.

As I approached my house, I felt an uneasy tension spread through my body. I didn't know where it was coming from or why it was there, but I couldn't shake it. When I let myself in I found a suitcase by the door, and I could hear banging coming from the bedroom.

I ran down the hall and found Owen pulling things from his side of the closet. I gasped, and he turned and looked at me sadly.

"Wh-what are you doing?" I asked, afraid of his answer.

Owen sighed and sat on the bed, surrounded by his belongings. "I'm going back to Boston," he said, looking at the floor.

I shook my head and my arms automatically wrapped around my body. "No, you can't." I reached for his hand but he shook me off. "Owen, *no!*"

"Charlotte," he whispered, tears welling in his eyes. "Can I ask you a question?"

I nodded, but kept my arms wrapped tightly around myself.

"Is our relationship a way for you to bide time?" he asked, looking me directly in the eye. "I have a right to know."

My mouth dropped open. "What?"

"Well, obviously you still have feelings for Cameron. Are you just with me until he proves himself good enough for you again?"

"I chose you! When Cameron left, he told me he'd stay if I asked him to. I told him to go. I picked you!"

"I just don't think you're done with him." Owen shook his head. "He's all around you, all the time. Before we moved back, I could tell there was something in your past you needed to reconcile. But since we've been here, I've felt the distance growing between us as you reconnected with your old life—with Cameron. And now that he's gone…it's like you're gone too."

"I'm done with him. He *left!*"

"And if he was here?"

I opened my mouth to speak, but I hesitated a second too long. He nodded sadly and shoved his clothes into his suitcase.

"I picked you, and I would again—even if he was here now," I said firmly, taking a few steps toward him.

"Okay, then tell me you're not in love with him," Owen said, turning around to face me again.

"Owen, what I had with Cameron is over and—"

"Tell me you don't love him," he repeated, cutting me off.

I shook my head slowly and sat down on the bed. I couldn't say I didn't love Cameron because I did, and I always would. I started to cry and covered my face with my hands.

I felt the bed sink and Owen's arm slide around me as he pulled my head to rest on his shoulder.

"Hush. Don't cry. It's understandable that you still love him. You can't help that there are feelings there."

I nodded and wiped my eyes with the back of my hand.

"I'm sorry if I pushed you into a relationship you weren't ready for," he whispered. "I could tell you hadn't moved past your previous relationship, but I was just so in love with you. I wanted to make you mine."

"I *am* yours."

"No, you're not. A part of you wants to be, but you still belong to him. I can feel it. He's in your heart."

I wanted to tell him he was wrong, but that was exactly how I felt.

"I'm the safe option for you, Charlotte. I'm the guy you can depend on, who'll never hurt you."

I nodded.

"But I don't want to be that," he explained. "I want you to feel passion for me. I need you to be consumed with me…like I am with you."

As much as I wanted to deny it all and profess my undying love for him, I couldn't. I did love him, but not the way he needed and deserved.

"I can't handle being your second choice. I can't be your rebound. I deserve more than that. I deserve someone who loves me as much as I love you."

I nodded and continued to cry, knowing this was the end. My relationship with Owen was over.

He was silent, rubbing my back soothingly while I cried. I didn't want him to leave, but he was right, he *did* deserve someone who would love him passionately — without the ex-husband baggage.

"I…I need you to know…I *want* to want you like that," I choked out.

"I know you do, sweetheart."

"You have no idea how badly I want that," I cried.

I cupped my hands to either side of his face, looking into his big blue eyes. I wrapped my arms around his shoulders just as my eyes closed and our lips touched.

The kiss started gently, our lips moving in tandem as his arms tightened around me. His tongue moved into my mouth, intensifying our kiss, and I sucked on it before gently biting his bottom lip. He moaned softly, and his hands moved into my hair, keeping me tight against his body.

We put everything we had into that kiss, knowing it would be our last. When I finally pulled my lips away, I whispered, "I love you."

He smiled sweetly at me. "Love you more," he replied.

Now I knew he was right.

I looked down at the diamond ring on my finger and sighed sadly. I held my hand out to him with my fingers outstretched. He hesitated only a moment before gently grasping my palm in one hand and sliding the engagement ring off my finger with the other.

We were over.

❧ ❦ ❧

"What do you want to do for Christmas?" Dad asked with just a few weeks to go before the holiday.

"Nothing," I said, pushing food around on my plate.

"We have to do something. It's Christmas!"

"I'm not a huge fan of Christmas."

"Please, Char?"

I sighed. "I just don't have anything to celebrate."

"What are you talking about?" Dad asked. "You are loved and wanted and a good person."

"You've always been there for me, Daddy," I said softly, taking his hand and squeezing. "Thank you. It's just…"

"I know you're feeling bad about Owen, but you told me yourself it was for the best."

"It *is* for the best. But my marriage was a failure, Cameron didn't want me, and then Owen left…it's just a lot to take."

"Cameron wanted you," Dad said, taking a long sip of his beer.

"He cheated on me," I said, exasperated. "Maybe not technically, but he chose Lucy over me."

Dad cleared his throat.

"What?"

"After you moved back in with me he came to the house a few times, but I wouldn't let him in. He begged me, saying he needed to talk to you, to explain, but I told him if you didn't answer his calls, you didn't want to talk to him. And then after you left…"

"What? What happened after I left?" I sat down next to him at the table, coaxing him to continue.

"Well, about two months after you left, he came by the house again."

I ate up his words eagerly. Having both of the men in my life walk out at nearly the same time had been a major blow to my self-esteem. Dad's story was like music to my ears.

"He asked me to tell him where'd you'd moved, and when I refused… well, I've never seen a more broken man, Char. He was destroyed. I kinda felt bad for the kid," Dad said with a chuckle.

"Will you tell me about it?"

"I didn't really want to speak with him too much. My main concern was for you… But all I know is I've never seen a man look more devastated. I heard around town that he was searching for you, but I never spoke to him to get the details."

So Cameron *had* tried to find me. I expected to find that comforting, but all it did was reinforce the fact that he'd now let me go. He'd been willing to fight for me then, but now he'd moved on.

"When I took the divorce papers around to his house for him to sign—it wasn't good. The house was dark, and he was unshaven and skinnier than I'd ever seen him—not to mention the huge bags under his eyes. Didn't look like the kid had slept in weeks. I'll never forget it," Dad said, shaking his head.

I wondered how I looked right now. I turned toward the mirror inside the china hutch. My hair hung limply around my shoulders, and my skin was sallow and pale. I had bags under my eyes and frown lines around my lips.

I looked away from my reflection and saw my dad's face—the concern and pain behind his eyes. Suddenly I felt terrible for causing him worry. I didn't want to be sad. I didn't want to cry myself to sleep every night and be unsure who I felt worse about losing. It was such a strange sensation to feel abandoned yet not know who I was craving.

That thought frightened me. I had to pull myself out of this. I'd gotten through worse before. I'd lived through losing my mother and my husband, and I was strong enough to get through losing Owen.

I thought about who I was and the person I hoped to become. I'd lived with a broken heart for more than five years, and I'd started to identify with that pain. I just assumed it would always be part of me. But I didn't want to be that person anymore. I wanted to start my life fresh—starting with reclaiming Christmas.

"Okay, Dad, we'll do dinner, but nothing big. Just you and me and a turkey. How does that sound?"

"Perfect," Dad said, smiling.

I spent the next few weeks planning the menu and shopping for the perfect gift for Dad. I also spent some time on the Internet, hoping to shore up some ideas I had about starting fresh.

⚬⟦ ❦ ⟧⚬

"You're a great cook, Char," Dad said, finishing off his Christmas turkey. "I'm so glad we did this."

"Thanks, Dad," I said just as there was a knock on the door.

"Did you invite someone?" I asked suspiciously.

"No."

As soon as I opened the door, I was wrapped in a huge hug, and I could hear Bonnie squealing.

"You're leaving town?" she yelled.

Ryan released me from his grasp, and I saw Bonnie, Sarah, and Alex gathered on the doorstep. It was snowing lightly and the air was freezing, so I quickly ushered them into the house.

"Yes, I'm moving," I told Bonnie. I wondered how she knew I was going, but Fairfield was a small town, and secrets didn't stay hidden for long.

I led the girls into the dining room and found Ryan sitting with Dad, drinking a beer.

"Just wait till after New Years! You have to spend it with us!" Bonnie begged.

"Just a few more weeks," Sarah agreed. "The baby is due in February, and I'd love for you to be here."

I laughed. "If I listen to you two, there'll always be a reason for me to stay. I'll never go."

"Exactly!" Bonnie cheered.

"I'm going. I have to figure out who Charlotte Barnes is."

"That's deep!" Ryan called from across the room, holding his beer bottle up in salute.

Sarah rolled her eyes. "Promise you'll come home when I have the baby?"

"Of course. New York City is less than two hours away."

"Humph!" Bonnie groaned, folding her arms across her chest. "I *suppose* I could place a call to my head office and see if I can get you some work in the city."

Alex smiled and angled his head toward the kitchen.

"You took my advice," he said after I'd followed him out of the room.

I thought for a moment and frowned. "Well, it didn't work very well. I listened to my heart like you said and chose to stay with Owen. Then he left me."

"Owen wasn't what your heart wanted."

I looked at him quizzically. Slowly it dawned on me that my happiness wasn't about anyone else, and I smiled. "I can't depend on anyone else to make me happy. I have to learn how to do it myself."

Alex nodded and gave me a hug. "Merry Christmas."

"Merry Christmas."

All this time, I'd thought I had to choose one of the men in my life. But it was me who wasn't fitting, not them. I'd gone from being my parents' daughter to Cameron's wife to Owen's fiancée without any time to get to know myself in between. Sure, I was single for two years between Cameron and Owen, but I was hurting so much that I didn't take the time to really look at myself. How was I supposed to know what I wanted from life when I didn't even know who I was? No wonder I was so conflicted.

I knew this wasn't going to be an easy road, but I was motivated to start the journey. This was the first Christmas in six years that I hadn't felt like I had a gaping hole in my chest. Wherever they were, I hoped Cameron and Owen were having a merry Christmas too.

<hr>

I looked at the nearly empty bookcase and smiled. It was *mine*. I'd never really had anything that was mine before. The apartment I'd rented when I first moved to Boston had come fully furnished, and other than that, I'd always shared things with Cameron or Owen. But now, this whole apartment and everything in it was mine.

I was fortunate to have found a community college that could fit me into their mid-year enrollment, and I was excited about my education classes.

I'd also managed to find a studio apartment only a few blocks from campus. It was tiny, but it was clean, and Bonnie had pulled a few strings with her boss back in Fairfield and gotten me a part-time job with the head office of her accounting firm. Being a file clerk wasn't exciting work, but they were being flexible with my hours so I could attend classes, and I needed the money. It was a fresh start, and I was in New York City: the city of possibilities.

I looked at the bookcase again and nodded in satisfaction. It held only the few textbooks I'd bought earlier in the day, but I promised myself I'd buy one book a week. By the end of the year I'd have a full bookcase.

A loud ringing made me jump, and it took me a second to realize it was my phone. I'd just had the line installed, and the only people who had my number were Dad and Bonnie. Dad had called about an hour ago to wish me Happy New Year before he headed to work.

"Hello, Bonnie," I said with a smile.

"I have a surprise for you!" she squealed into the phone.

The door buzzer sounded, echoing around the apartment. "Are you here?"

I ran over and pressed the intercom with a huge smile on my face, but felt instantly disappointed when a male voice said, "Delivery from The Golden Palace."

"Hang on a second, Bonnie. My Chinese food just arrived." I pressed the button to open the door downstairs and got my purse.

After I'd paid for the food and closed the door, I returned to the phone and sat on my new couch.

"Tell me you're not sitting home by yourself tonight," Bonnie said.

"Okay, I'm not," I said with a laugh.

"Liar."

"I have Chinese food, and I'm going to watch the ball drop on television. I'll be fine," I promised. "So what's my surprise?"

"Alex and I are coming to New York in three weeks for a concert!"

"That's great!"

I'd wondered if it would be hard for me to remain friends with Cameron's family, but it felt really natural. Bonnie and I had a silent understanding that neither of us would bring him up, and it worked. It didn't stop me from thinking about him every single day, but it helped.

"Okay, well, I just wanted to tell you, and try out your new phone number, and wish you a Happy New Year," she said, sounding a bit sad. "Oh, how is your new apartment?"

"I really love it," I said with a smile as I looked around.

"You've only been there two days! You can't *love* it already!"

"Well, I do." I couldn't explain it, but I knew my new life was going to be wonderful.

"Oh — Alex is ready to go. We're going to a party. Have a good night, and we'll see you soon. Happy New Year!" Bonnie said before hanging up.

I placed the handset on the coffee table and picked up some chopsticks. I ate a heap of honey-soy noodles and flicked through the television channels until I found the live broadcast from Times Square. It was exciting to know what I was watching on television was happening only a few dozen blocks away. I'd considered going to watch the ball drop live, but decided I really wanted to spend the night at home. I was optimistic I'd do it next year with a big group of new friends.

I ate as much food as I could and carried the leftovers to the kitchen to put away in the fridge. Even though I was alone, this was the best New Years Eve I could remember. I cheered as I watched the ball drop over Times Square and marveled at the amazing new city that was now my home.

⚜

I'd just started settling into a routine — going to class for a few weeks and finding a coffee shop I liked, even making a few new acquaintances — when I awoke one night in my new apartment, my heart pounding wildly. There was a noise coming from somewhere, and I sat bolt upright in bed, looking around for what had woken me. My phone. I stumbled out of bed to answer it as I looked at the clock on the wall. It was three in the morning.

"I hate you," I said groggily.

"You have to come home right now!" Bonnie blurted into the phone.

I was instantly wide awake. Something terrible had happened. I tucked the cordless phone against my shoulder and started running around my room, grabbing clothes to change into.

"What is it?" I asked, praying nothing had happened to my Dad or any of the Harpers.

"Sarah's been in labor for a few hours. She's at the hospital right now. Mom said not to call you until the morning, but I thought you'd want to know."

I could hear banging in the background. She was obviously rushing around as well. "Okay, I'm leaving right now. See you there."

Throwing the phone down, I pulled my jeans on and ran a comb through my hair. I ran down the stairs and out onto the busy street where my car was parked. I'd been thrilled yesterday to get a parking space on the same block as my building. I knew it wouldn't be vacant when I got back home. I pulled out and headed uptown, toward Fairfield.

Just under two hours later I drove down Fairfield's main street and straight to hospital. I smiled when I saw David's and Bonnie's cars in the parking lot. I pulled in next to them and ran inside.

"Charlotte!" Alex called when he saw me.

"Did I miss it?" I asked, breathing heavily.

"No, we're all still waiting. I'm actually going on a coffee run. Would you like to join me?"

"I should probably let everyone know I'm here."

"Okay, can I get you something?"

"Just a coffee—the strongest one they have, if you don't mind." He nodded on his way out the door.

I navigated my way through the hospital to the maternity ward and laughed when I heard Bonnie's excited voice floating down the hall. When I entered the waiting room, all the heads spun to me and smiles bloomed on their faces.

"Well, if it isn't the big city girl," David laughed, standing up to hug me.

"Hi, David," I said, hugging him back.

"It's so wonderful that you could be here," Ellen said.

"I wouldn't miss the first of the next generation of Harpers coming into the world."

The sun was just starting to come through the windows, and I was shocked that it was dawn. "How long has she been in there?"

"Just over five hours. But it could be a while yet," Bonnie said.

I sat down next to Bonnie and picked up one of the magazines on the table when someone else walked into the room, also breathing heavily. I looked up and my whole body froze. Cameron.

"Mom, Dad, is the baby here yet?" he asked frantically, looking as stressed as I'd felt a few minutes before.

"No, just have a seat," David replied. "How was your trip?"

"It felt like it took forever, but I'm here so that's all that matters," Cameron said with a smile. He turned to say hello to his sister and did a double-take when he saw me.

"Charlotte," he said.

"Hi, Cam."

"Do I get a hello?" Bonnie said.

Cameron smiled and walked over to hug her. "Hello, Bonnie Lynette Harper," he laughed.

"That's better!" Bonnie said, smiling as she sat back down.

Cameron sat over next to his mother, but we kept glancing at one another across the room.

Before long, Alex returned with the coffee, and as we woke up, we started chatting. Cameron didn't contribute much to the conversation. He just kept watching me with a smile on his face.

Mid-morning, Ellen and David went to get us all some food, and I decided to go for a walk to stretch my legs.

"Call me if the baby comes," I told Bonnie.

"Will do," she said without looking up from her magazine.

I left the waiting room and walked down the hallway, which was lined with posters of babies and breastfeeding mothers. If my marriage hadn't fallen apart, would I have had a child by now?

"How are you?" Cameron's voice came from behind me, and I turned to find him following me down the hall.

"I'm good. How are you? How's San Diego?" I folded my arms over my chest without realizing it, but I couldn't help but feel uncomfortable. The last time I saw Cameron had been extremely emotional, and I was a little embarrassed.

"San Diego is good — sunny," he said with a smile.

"How cliché." I laughed nervously. "Lucky you."

"Bonnie told me about you and Owen."

I shuffled my feet and started worrying a hangnail on my left thumb.

"I'm sorry, Charlotte. Are you okay?"

"I'd rather not talk about it."

"Oh, of course. Maybe we should get back, I'm sure Mom and Dad will be here with the food soon," he suggested.

"I was going to go for a walk. I'll be back in a little while."

"Oh, okay. Do you want some company?" he asked tentatively, rubbing his hand across the back of his neck.

"Um…"

"I'm a daddy!" Ryan yelled from the other room.

Cameron and I practically ran back to the waiting room. When we got there, Ryan was wearing an ear-splitting grin and hugging Bonnie tightly. Cameron put his arms around both of them in a Harper group hug as Alex and I stood off to the side.

"Did we miss it?" Ellen asked as she walked back into the room with a large paper bag.

"Nope, it just happened," I told her, taking the bag so she could hug her children.

All the Harpers disappeared into Sarah's room to have a look at the newest member of their family. Alex followed them and looked back over his shoulder. "Are you coming?"

"In a minute." As much as I wanted to see the baby, I didn't feel right invading their family moment. I was happy to wait until they'd all had a chance to meet and hold the tiny new Harper. I'd just sat down and opened the paper bag to see what food Ellen had brought when David came back to the waiting room.

"Why aren't you in there?" he asked, hooking his thumb over his shoulder.

"I thought I'd let you have a family moment first."

"Charlotte, you *are* part of this family. Now come on."

I smiled and followed him. Sarah sat in her hospital bed holding the baby, and everyone was cooing and gushing.

"Would you like to hold your niece?" Sarah asked as she held the baby out to me.

"Are you sure? Has everyone else held her?" I asked, looking around.

They all nodded, so I held my arms out.

"Charlotte, this is Jessica Penelope Harper. Jessie, this is your Aunty Charlotte. She's going to take you shopping on Fifth Avenue when you get older," Sarah said, handing me the baby.

She felt so small and delicate in my arms that I was terrified to look away from her for fear I'd drop her or squeeze her too hard. After a few moments, I managed to look up and saw Cameron watching me closely. Our eyes met, and I knew we were thinking the same thing—would this have been us?

"Speaking of Fifth Avenue, how are you liking New York?" David asked.

"It's great. I love my apartment, and school is going well. I love my new life."

"Me again!" Bonnie said eagerly, holding her arms out. With some relief I handed her Jessie.

Everyone sat around the room chatting and taking turns holding the baby until the evening. I had an early class the next day and a two-hour drive home, so I decided it was time to say goodbye. Cameron walked me out to my car.

"Drive safely," he said, gently kissing my forehead.

The drive home went by in a blur as I thought about what my life would have been like if Cameron and I'd had a child together. Would our marriage still have fallen apart? Our issues were trust related, I knew. Not anything a baby would've fixed.

When I got home I went straight to bed. I was asleep as soon as my head hit the pillow.

⊶❦⊱

The following morning I walked through my door and dropped my school books on the table, brushing the snow off my clothes and out of my hair. After driving back from Fairfield last night and then the early class this morning, I was utterly exhausted. I rifled though my fridge for some leftovers and sat on the couch to eat and watch television.

Just as I lifted the fork to my mouth, the door buzzed. Groaning, I stood up and went to see who was at the door.

"Yes," I asked, trying to keep the annoyance out of my voice.

"It's Cam. Can I come up?" His voice filtered through the speaker.

"Um, okay," I said, pressing the button that opened the door downstairs.

I stood still, wondering what he could want. Was his flight home to San Diego delayed out of JFK?

A soft rap on the door jolted me out of my musing, and I pulled it open. He wore a shy smile, his hair damp and his shirt spotted with wet patches.

"Hey," he said.

"Hey." I held tightly to the door. He looked so handsome I held back a groan as he walked past me into the apartment.

He pulled off his wet coat and hung it on my coat rack. He ran his hands through his hair nervously, water droplets falling to the floor.

"Oh—would you like a towel?"

"Thanks," he said. I retrieved a clean towel from the linen closet, and he ran it quickly across his hair.

"Can we sit?" he asked.

I nodded and we walked over to the couch.

"What are you doing here? Is the baby okay? Wait—how did you know where I lived?"

"Bonnie."

I nodded. Of course.

"The baby's fine," he said, taking my hand. His thumb rubbed over the base of my ring finger, and I looked down at my lap. "I'm sorry about Owen. Are you okay?"

"I'm dealing. Starting fresh. I still think about him a lot."

Cameron nodded. "He was a good guy."

"Yes, he was. But it wasn't right. We both knew it, but we fought to stay together as long as we could."

Cameron sighed and leaned back on the couch. "I'm sorry. I don't know why I came here."

"It's okay. When are you heading back to San Diego?"

Cameron gave me a weak smile. "I never moved to San Diego."

"You were in Fairfield this whole time?"

"No, I did leave, but I didn't go to San Diego. I moved here…to New York."

"Why did you lie?" I demanded.

"I didn't lie. I planned to move to San Diego, but when it came down to it, I realized I couldn't be that far from my family. So I changed my plans and asked my family not to mention it to you. I'm sorry, Charlotte. I needed a clean break."

I looked at him and slowly processed what he said. I wanted to feel deceived, but I was actually just happy to learn we lived in the same city.

"It's okay. You did what you needed to do to look after yourself. I understand that."

He smiled and cocked his head as if he'd just thought of something. "You know, we're very different people than when we were a couple."

"Yes, we are," I agreed, unsure where he was going.

"But my feelings for you haven't changed. I'm still in love with you."

Me too, my heart said, but I just offered him a shy smile.

"As I've told you, I'm a different man now, and I want you to know that's true. I've done a lot of soul searching and thinking about my priorities, and I know I'm ready to be with you now. When we were married I was too caught up in myself to see you, the real you—I thought I knew you, but all I saw was what I *wanted* to see. I thought you were this perfect angel who loved me and was a great wife—and you *were* those things. But you were also fragile, insecure, and a little stubborn."

I slapped his arm but didn't interrupt.

"Back then, I thought loving you meant ignoring those things and only seeing the good in you, but I was wrong. I know now that loving you means accepting everything about you and loving every part of you…even your stubbornness. I want to nurture the fragile part of you and reassure your insecurities. There are things we both need to work on, but I want you to know that I *have* changed. I'm ready for this. I want this with you."

Certainty burned in his eyes, and the passion in his voice was hard to fault. I could only remember one other time when he'd sounded so sure of something…

…I'd been lying on the bed, my hair splayed out all around me on the pillow as Cameron crawled toward me and knelt on all fours over my body, his hands on either side of my head.

I smiled up at him, his twinkling eyes full of love as they stared back at me.

"I love you," he whispered.

I smiled wider and opened my mouth to reply, but he leaned down and pressed his lips to mine, sucking on my bottom lip slightly.

He chuckled as I moaned into his mouth, but he abruptly tore his lips away and rolled off me. I watched in confusion as he opened the small drawer in the bedside table and started rummaging around for something. I wasn't in the mood for him to be distracted. After his declaration of love and that steamy kiss, I was in the mood for some sexy time with my man.

"Come back here," I growled seductively.

"In a minute," he chuckled. "Come sit here by me?"

He patted the edge of the bed, and I sat up and slid over to him.

"Charlotte, you make me so happy. You're my first thought every morning, and my last thought every night before I go to sleep. I love you, and I know I'll love you forever," he said, looking into my eyes.

I froze, staring at him, not wanting to jump to conclusions about what he was saying.

He slipped slowly off the bed and onto his knees in front of me, holding up a small velvet box. "Will you allow me to make you happy for the rest of your life? Will you marry me?"

I couldn't move. I was frozen in place, trying as hard as I could to make this perfect moment last forever. Slowly, I reached out and took the box from his hand. My fingers shook as I grasped it tightly and stared at the perfect diamond ring.

"Yes," I breathed, holding back my tears of joy.

A huge smile erupted on Cameron's face, and he pulling me to him to kiss me passionately. "I love you. I love you so much," he whispered into my mouth.

He pulled back and looked at me excitedly as he took the ring out of the box and slipped it on my finger…

All the emotions I'd felt for Cameron when we were first falling in love now came rushing back to me, and everything became clear. I wanted Cameron. It didn't matter what our past had been — that was all over. We'd both moved beyond it and were different people now. I was much stronger and more independent than I'd been back then, and Cameron had matured and learned from his mistakes.

"I forgive you," I blurted.

"Huh?" he asked, looking at me curiously.

I took a deep breath and felt electricity coursing through my body. "Sorry, that was a bit blunter than I meant it to be. Let me start again. We've both moved on from the past — it's behind us — and you're right, we *are* different people. We've both grown up a lot in the past few years, and I'm hoping we're mature enough now to take on a serious relationship."

Cameron looked at me with wide eyes. "Are you sure?" he asked. "I don't deserve you. I *wronged* you, Charlotte."

"You're right. But I wronged you too. We're both to blame for the problems in our relationship. I love you, Cam. I never stopped, and if you're willing, I'm here, ready to try again."

I took a deep breath and waited. I wasn't sure where my boldness came from, but I liked it. I had a whole new life, and I wanted to find out if Cameron fit into it.

He smiled as he shifted and leaned toward me. I could practically see him vibrating in his seat.

"I think we should take it slow. Go back to the very beginning. We should date and get to know each other again," he said sensibly, but I could hear the joy in his voice.

"I agree. As you said, we're both very different people than we were when we first met, and I don't think we really know each other that well now. I know you, but I need to get to know the thirty-year-old Cameron."

"I don't want to rush this, Charlotte. I don't want to ruin it again," he said, his voice shaking.

"I don't want that either. I know we're taking a chance, but don't you think the potential of what we could be together is worth a little risk?" I grasped his hand.

Cameron and I stared into each other's eyes, and I shifted toward him. My eyelids fluttered closed as I leaned in for a kiss.

"No!" Cameron said suddenly.

My eyes flew open, and I looked at him in confusion as he stood up and backed away.

"Sorry," he said, sounding calmer. "I want to take this slow."

I nodded. I was disappointed, but I knew Cameron was right. We needed time. It would take work and communication to create something new.

"I'm going to head home. I think we both need some time to think about this."

"Okay," I replied, helping him into his coat.

"I'll see you soon."

I watched in disbelief. Was he really just going to leave? I knew we'd agreed to take it slow, but I wanted him to change his mind and kiss me goodbye.

He turned back just before he was out the door and gave me a wink, and then he was gone. Excitement, joy, and a million other emotions all hit me at once and a huge smile broke over my face.

Just as I'd calmed myself down and was about to go back to watching television, there was a knock on the door. I ran to answer it and smiled when I saw Cameron standing there with a blank expression on his face.

"Hello, I'm Cameron Harper," he said seriously, holding his hand out for me to shake.

I looked at his hand and then up at his face, and he gave me another wink before returning to his neutral expression.

I took his hand and shook it. "I'm Charlotte Barnes."

"I've seen you around, and I'd like to get to know you better. I was wondering if you'd like to have dinner with me tonight."

"I don't usually go out with men I don't know." I giggled when his brow knit in confusion.

His expression became more confident as he gave me a very intense look. "You can trust me, Charlotte."

I knew he wasn't just saying it as part of this little game. I hesitated for a moment, wondering if I really could trust him—and if he could trust me. Owen had taught me how important communication was in a relationship, and I'd forever be grateful for that. Cameron knew what it was like to betray someone he loved, and I didn't think he'd take that risk again. Maybe everything I'd been through was to prepare me for this moment. Communication was still a work in progress for me, but I was getting better.

"Dinner would be nice," I finally said with a smile.

Cameron took my hand, brought it to his mouth, and kissed it softly.

"I'll be back to pick you up at seven," he whispered.

I leaned against the door frame and watched as he walked down the hall to the elevator.

"Oh, and, Charlotte," he called back over his shoulder, "you look beautiful in those sweatpants." He gave me a huge grin and one last playful wink before getting into the elevator.

"Shut up!" I called after him, laughing as the elevator doors closed.

I went back inside and fell against the closed door, excitement building inside me. In my head I started cataloging my entire wardrobe—I had a first date to get ready for.

ACKNOWLEDGMENTS

I have so many people to thank. To my mother, for encouraging me and always believing in me. To Tiffany, Shantelle, Genevieve, Chelle, and Christine, for helping me in the early stages of writing and offering their sound advice. To all of my friends and family who have listened as I have bounced ideas around, given me their opinions on plot, characters, and the ending—I appreciate you so much. To Alex, for not being afraid to tell me when I suck and being honest about what needs to be changed. To fellow author Victoria Michaels who, without even knowing it, inspired me to start writing, and the whole team at Omnific Publishing, especially Elizabeth, Lisa, and Jenny. You have all been more supportive and helpful than I could have ever dreamed. To my hard-working editor, Jennifer. THANK YOU for being patient with me and facilitating my growth as an author. The hours of work you have put into this novel are greatly appreciated—we make a great team!

And finally, to everyone who knows why "ACO" is important to this story. You are a group of people so special to me, and I thank my lucky stars for being associated with you!

© photograph by Pete Dillon

Hannah Downing was born in the United States before she moved to Australia as a child. Her love of reading developed when she was very young. Her mother would sit and read with her at night, and she also passed down some of her own childhood books for Hannah to enjoy. Hannah has always loved writing, but she began to do it seriously two years ago when she became involved with an online writing community that inspired and delighted her.

Hannah currently spends her days working as a social worker in a Mental Health Service in Cairns, Queensland, Australia, and she loves to travel, both domestically and internationally, as often as she can. Her dream is so see everything the world has to offer.